The Devil in the Dust

John E. Espy

OPEN BOOKS

Chapter 1

PAINTSVILLE WAS SWEATIN' LIKE dew fleein' from the holler under a fat woman's arms. Folks was walkin' here and there, dazed from the blazin' relentless Kentucky sun. It was late September and the soupy heat just wouldn't let go its summer hold.

Howard Music'd just gotten himself back home after being scalded by black gold when a rig he was runnin' for Dowell Oil'd blown its top over in Oklahoma. He'd been turnin' down the shaft when the blowout preventer didn't do any preventin', bit the nipple off the bell and began spewing scorchin' hot oil every which way meltin' the flesh right off of the bones of one of the Roustabouts who was doin' nothin' more than he was supposed to be doin'. A swath of that liquid fire came roarin' right over the top of that boy, who, like many Roustabouts had one name one day and one name the next, and dappled poor Howard Music with so many sizzlin' welts that he looked like he'd all of a sudden come down with a case of the Pox, but the even poorer Sammy Warwar, the name the Roustabout called himself that day, just burst into flames. He took off runnin' wild this way and that, tryin' with all the life he had left to shake off the inferno that had overtaken him, when suddenly he snapped up straight like a thick stick and then collapsed right down into himself.

There wasn't much that could be done so those that'd been watchin' let Sammy burn himself out till there weren't nothing left to burn and then shoveled him into the hole where they'd been buryin' filings spun up from the rig bit.

It was on the very day of Howard's homecoming that he'd been walkin' down the street with folks passin' by and whisperin' to each other about his pocked-marked face, sayin' how he'd been "...such a good lookin' fella, well…, before he got burned and all…" when, he suddenly grabbed his left arm, jerked it up to his chest and said to himself, "Oh no…" Then, Howard Music fell over dead, blocking the way of others who were just tryin' to get from here to there. It was by God's grace that a young man who'd just come from having finished up his residency in internal medicine, and looking for the father he'd never met, was happening to be crossing the street when hapless Howard keeled over and fell right into Jesus' waiting arms. The young doctor had saw Howard raise his arm to his chest and then collapse onto the concrete. Being across the street the doctor weaved his way between this car and that, having to slap the hood of Roger (Ratty) Ratliff's potato truck which didn't want to stop because its radiator was boiling over and Roger knew if he stopped he wouldn't be able to deliver his load. Then, that bein' the case, he'd have to be puttin' up with Dana Lynn Stamper's complainin' about his bein' late "…again" makin' her diners demanding to know *when* their "mashed taters" were in *fact* going to be hittin' the plate of their tenderloin hot shots! Ratty figured it was worth inconvenienting some feller trying to run in between this and that vehicle to steer clear of a verbal woppin' from Miss Stamper, as folks who knew her best were permitted to call her.

When the doctor finally reached the crumpled Howard Music he knelt down, rolled him onto his back, tipped his head, put his mouth over his and blew until his chest swelled up like a balloon. Then he straddled Howard's chest and began pumping it while all the time saying, "*Don't* you goddamn die on me!"

Folks were gatherin' around now, some with their heads bowed, prayin' up to Jesus to save poor Howard, addin' in a forgiveness for the doctor using the Lord's name in vain, but, if it were time for Jesus to "…harvest Howard's soul then honey just let him up and stay dead," they said.

After a couple of dozen or so compressions on Howard's chest, he went from a lookin' like a fallen peach drained of its life by that relentless sun to one danglin' off a limb, and blowin' in the breeze, full of juice, ready to up and explode with life! And, like a just rip-ened peach, and as the doctor pressed down on his chest for one last time, Howard began gaggin' and spewin' out a torrent of vomit that flowed over the curb into a waiting sewer drain. Folks who'd been watchin' stepped back from the vile bile and pressed their chins to their chests and yelled "Praise Jesus" so loud as to their being no way on God's green earth that the good Lord could not have heard their deliverance of reverence.

The doctor told Howard to lay quiet as the whirl of an approaching siren turned like a twistin' wind rounding this way and that between the buildings. In not too much time, an ambulance pulled up and two attendants lifted Howard onto a black cart, covered him with a red wool blanket and then loaded him up. In just but a few minutes Howard disappeared from the onlookers liked he'd never even been there in the first place. The doctor then looked at one of the men and said, "Can you tell me where I can find a man named Spencer Duty?"

Chapter 2

"Y'ALL JUST GO UP yonder a bit and then where Third meets Margaret Heights Road there's a house that sits up atop the hill right there at the bend in the road and that's where Spencer Duty, Jr. lives, he ain't Spencer Duty like you said though, he's Spencer Duty, Jr., as his daddy was Spencer Duty the first and likely you won't find a better man than Spencer Duty, Jr. unless you're talkin' 'bout his daddy Spencer Duty that is.

"Why when I was a youngin' I'd *never* in my life imagined that I'd *ever* be wearin' a pair of store-bought shoes and then one day Spencer Duty, that bein' Spencer Duty, Jr's daddy and Nora Duty, that bein' Spencer Duty's wife, one of the finest women God ever put on this earth, showed up at my school with shoes for *all* the youngins whose mommies and daddies didn't have a pot to piss in or a window to throw it out of, much less put shoes on their youngins' feet. I walked out of school that day, as did all the other boys and girls wrapped up in the warmest sense of pride we'd ever been privilege to know. Why... we all wore those shoes, girls too, till we'd outgrowed them and our toes were curlin' back up inside. Those of us that are still atop the ground will remember that day till they throw the last shovel full of dirt on top of us.

"Why there were a couple of boys who we caught playing mumblety-peg while wearing their new shoes, and a couple of us other boys gave them a beatin' liked they'd likely never forget, disrespectin' not only their shoes but also not knowin' how to let that new found respect of havin' shoes in the first place rise on up their legs till it reached their very souls. Those shoes were God given worked through Spencer and Nora Duty and by God those boys were goin' to

4

be respectin' that or there weren't no reason for them to have gotten blessed in the first place."

Moses Kitchen II, M.D. made his way up the road where Third curves and Margaret Heights Road starts herself. Sitting atop the hill was a big brick house with tall white pillars and a porch that'd been screened-in where one could likely sit and eat themselves a hearty breakfast in the summer without havin' to swat away the flies who'd be tryin' their darndest to take what hadn't quite made it to the mouth of the eater just yet.

Moses made his way up the driveway, then found himself standing in front of a door bordered by stained glass windows on each side. He raised his hand to knock but as quickly as his knuckles readied to rap against the oak they just as quickly uncurled and slipped themselves into his pants pocket. Here he was about to meet his father, who until just a short while ago he didn't even know existed. Moses bore him no disregard for not being there as he grew up as his daddy too had known nothing of him.

As he circled the porch one last time he pulled his hand from a pocket, furled his palm and knocked. In but a bit the door latch could be heard releasing its grip against the frame as the door opened slowly.

Through the screen door Spencer Duty, Jr. saw the gingered – haired man who now graced his porch. At that moment there was an unspeakable awkwardness. A recognition without familiarity.

Then Spencer Duty, Jr. said, "You have your mother's eyes." He looked frailer than Moses had expected. "I can't tell you how sorry I am that I didn't know I have a son. I don't know if you hate me or want to have a relationship with me—I just don't know, I don't even know what you want to call me, if anything. Is there something I can get you, have you been here long?"

Moses replied, "Why don't we just sit down and talk for a while."

"Was your mother in much pain at the end?"

"She was," Moses nodded, "I met her at the train station right when she got back from coming to Paintsville and she could barely walk. We went straight to the hospital and on the way she gave me the letter she had written telling me about you. It wasn't long after that she died."

"Do you know why she came back here?" Spencer Duty, Jr. asked.

Moses said, "All she told me was that she had to take care of something that had long been left undone. I was finishing my residency and had just come back to Butte to see her. She knew I was coming and left me a note saying that she hoped to be back in Butte before I had to leave, but she didn't tell me why she had to go so suddenly, especially with how sick she was."

A sigh escaped Spencer Duty, Jr's chest. "How much do you want to know—really know? I'm sure you have an image of your mother and I want to respect that. She came here for a very specific reason. I didn't see her when she was here and I think it was because she didn't want me to be connected to what she was going to do. I only found out about her being here and what she'd done in the letter where she told me about you."

Moses looking confused said he wanted to know. Then Spencer Duty, Jr. began, "Eleanor came here to kill a man. Around these parts he was called the boy Boyd. He killed a young girl and then set it up to look like a retarded man had done it. Your mother defended the man the boy Boyd framed. His name was Robert Lewis, he was a Negro who'd come up this way from Mississippi with his momma and daddy. The *only* thing Robert Lewis ever did wrong was to steal onions from folks' fields or take ones that the grocers threw out because they'd gone bad. He ate onions like other folks eat apples.

"The young girl was killed and raped back up around Greasy Crick, the boy Boyd was the one who'd done it and he along with a crooked prosecutor and sheriff set Robert Lewis up to be blamed for it. There wasn't a shred of evidence against Robert Lewis, *nothing*. It was quite the spectacle. No one would defend him, he was a Negro and retarded, so not one other attorney would come within a hundred yards of taking his case—plus everyone *knew* he was guilty of killing and raping the girl.

"Then the boy Boyd killed a Constable who'd gotten onto him and Robert Lewis got blamed for that murder too. Try as she might your mother did her best to defend the poor man, whose momma and daddy even offered Eleanor their little spot of land and milk cow for her services. Needless to say, she wouldn't take anything. The thing was though, there was a man on the jury, I think his name was Chaffin. He was the only decent one of the bunch, who saw what was going on and hung the jury. Well that was it, the jury was hung, we were, at least for a few minutes, just flabbergasted and then the judge, who was as crooked as the rest of them, overruled the jury and declared Robert Lewis guilty of murder and sentenced him to death. A few months later Robert Lewis was strapped into the electric chair at Eddyville and right before the executioner was ready to throw the switch he had a heart attack and died.

"Well, at least that was the official story. But there was an *Urshu*, you probably don't know what that is…"

Moses nodded, having no idea…

"Sarafina showed up around these parts from what folks'd said for more than a hundred years or so. She was an Urshu, a *watcher*, an ancient one who helps mind humanity. Robert Lewis' mommy and daddy told Eleanor that one night Sarafina showed up right before he was set to die and told them that she'd been sent to correct the wrong that'd been done and called to deliver up Robert Lewis right into the arms of the Lord. I know not coming from here and all, it sounds plumb flicted. It just depends on what you believe, but I can tell you this much, Sarafina showed up in the death chamber, just out of nowhere that day, and right after Robert Lewis slumped over she just as quick disappeared.

"It was also Sarafina who long ago took my momma and daddy's hands in hers and passed them onto the Archangel Gabriel right as they took their last breath," Spencer Duty, Jr. said. "I'm sorry son, my mind just got to wandering a bit.

"Well, before Eleanor left Paintsville she said someday she'd make right what'd been done to Robert Lewis and I figure once the cancer came looking for her that she decided the time to settle scores was getting short so she came back and shot the boy Boyd with your grandpa's shotgun. Your mother wasn't one to let wrongs not go righted if she could."

"I still have that shotgun," Moses said.

"If you don't already know, you will learn that sometimes you have to do what is right, especially if the law can't be counted on to do what it's supposed to do."

"Eleanor said in her letter I'd find that you're a good man, in fact she told me you were the best man she'd ever known. In just this short time I can see that too." He continued, "I'd been thinking, that if things went well between us about setting up a practice here in Paintsville, us getting to know each other, figuring out this part of my life. But, if you'd rather, I'll move on," Moses said.

Spencer Duty, Jr. looked at Moses and said, "This is a big house and in a Kentucky storm it sounds like it's asking to be turned inside out the way it creaks and moans, there's a lot of empty rooms, choose whatever one you want until you decide to get a place of your own. What do you want to call me?"

"Let's start with *Spencer*," Moses said extending his hand.

"Can I introduce you as my son?" Spencer Duty, Jr. asked.

"Introducing me as your son would be paying me a great honor."

Chapter 3

OLD LADY MCCREADY'S RHEUMATISM and gout were flarin' up again. She was about as tenacious in her dedication to soaking her achin' joints in epsom salts as anyone who'd ever been a sufferer. Dr. Kitchen'd said she needed though to get out of her homeplace and to be movin' those stiff joints this way and that to help loosin' them up and start doin' more cohortin' and less sufferin'.

Well, Old Lady McCready didn't think much of Dr. Kitchen's doctorin' with him failin' to realize the depth of her distress. But even though she was approachin' her thirtieth year of sufferin' the bedevilment of rheumatism, Old Lady McCready agreed that after she salted herself every mornin' she'd do her righteous best to take a walk up the road, no matter how much pain in her joints she had to endure and how she'd likely have to cut out the toes of her shoes because of her gout swollen' toes, *just* to make Dr. Kitchen happy. Especially with him bein' new and all.

Dr. Kitchen patted Old Lady McCready on the back as she hobbled out of the examination room, saying in a week or so she needed to come back so he could see how she was doing. What he didn't know though was that she'd come from a *long* line of sufferers, her momma and her momma before her havin' endured hardships from before the dust bowl times. And now, Old Lady McCready wasn't about to forget the responsibility of the endurin' that'd been passed onto her. But nonetheless she said, as the door closed behind her, she'd "... sure enough try her best..."

Buster Spradlin, about fifty-five or thereabouts, was sittin' in the other examination room waitin' for Doc Kitchen. His wheezin' sounded like a blight of locust comin' for a crop of wheat. When

Doc Kitchen walked into the room he looked right at poor Buster and said, "Goddamn, how long have you been like this?" Pulling his stethoscope up to his ears, Doc Kitchen began listening to the guttural sounds comin' outta Buster's lungs. "Christ Mr. Spradlin, you need to be on oxygen." And on that, Doc Kitchen opened the door and told a nurse to get an oxygen tank and "...put a mask on Buster." In just a few minutes he was breathin' better, although Doc Kitchen knew from listenin' to his lungs that he'd never be breathin' anywhere near completely right. Buster like his daddy before him as well as all his brothers were miners, putting in the likes of fifty or sixty hours a week diggin' coal.

Doc Kitchen had Buster wheeled into the x-ray room so he could see what his lungs looked like from the inside out.

Looking at the films, he shook his head in dismay.

When Doc Kitchen was in medical school, they had studied black lung disease but he'd never seen a case up until now. Buster's lungs were so filled with coal dust that even the x-ray couldn't even see through it, so just a silhouette of his lungs showed up. *But* x-rays didn't even begin to show half the suffering that he was goin' through, slowly suffocatin' to death day in and day out. It was like he had a rope around his neck that just kept tighten' and tighten' until one day he wouldn't be able to get his breath at all. Then the terror'd start as he realized he'd sucked the last thimble full of air into his lungs that would ever be. And in that moment when he'd come face-to-face with the demon of death, he'd start twistin' and jerkin' like he was hangin' from a gallows till he turned blue and by God's graces finally died.

Now, even with the help of an oxygen mask, Buster was hackin' up thick scraps of coal crusted tissue that were now startin' to sluff off from the insides of his lungs like skin sluffs off a man whose been burned real bad. The problem for Doc Kitchen was that there wasn't really nothing to do besides giving Buster oxygen. He'd give him some Meticorten for the lot good it would do, Buster's breathin' bein' about as far gone as a man's breathin' can be and all.

Doc Kitchen remembered when he first went on clinical rotation. Before that it'd all been studying anatomy, microbiology and biochemistry. This part connects to that part and does this. "To see the *tubercle bacillus* colonies under a microscope use a *Ziehl–Neelsen* stain and if you are so inclined to remember the *PCO2 equation* then you will understand from a *physiologic perspective* one of the most common of all clinical observations: a patient's respiratory rate and breathing effort." But, it wasn't until Doc Kitchen was just a few days into his first clinical rotation when he walked into an exam room to take a patient's history that what he had been *studying* became manifest into flesh and bone.

For some reason or other, he remembered it was a Tuesday that he opened the door to the exam room and saw a young mother sitting against the wall with her hands folded in her lap. Standing with her back to Doc Kitchen was a young girl. Her scrawny legs and knobby little knees looked barely able to hold her aloft. And then, the young girl turned around.

From behind she was a child, a little girl, maybe he thought, she had the croup, maybe her mother brought her to the clinic because she thought she had been exposed to the mumps at school, maybe even she was getting winded when she was playing and had asthma. But, not this day.

When she turned around Doc Kitchen saw the little girl transform into an old woman, wrinkled and gaunt, her eyes sunk deep into her skull, the wafer-thin skin of her face barely clinging to the bones underneath, her tiny mouth drawn against her misshapen teeth—Doc Kitchen at that moment, encountered the only case of Progeria he would ever encounter. He also encountered an overwhelming sense of helplessness.

The little girl, "Lilla" she said her name was, looked seventy even though her mother said she was only eight. She was wheezing and stricken with shortness of breath that was getting worse. When Doc Kitchen asked Lilla what was bothering her, she said "I can't breathe too good." Her fragile ankles were swelled up like balloons and she teetered from side to side as she walked to and fro.

Doc Kitchen called the chief resident who examined Lilla. "Of course you know she has Progeria, and it looks like she is going into congestive heart failure, likely from hardening of the arteries," the chief resident dispassionately said. "We can put her on medication to thin her blood to get it to flow through the constricted veins feeding the heart, but her heart has aged like the rest of her body and has likely just about run its course."

It wasn't too long after that her heart couldn't take being starved anymore and right as she was making her way to breakfast one morning little Lilla fell over dead.

Chapter 4

IT DIDN'T TAKE LONG before Doc Kitchen was coming face-to-face with the black lung one way or another day in and day out. It seemed like every man he saw had the black lung lurkin' somewhere in his chest. And even though boys about the age of fourteen or so weren't supposed to be working the mines, there were a few who'd been brought in by their mommas who'd been doing coal since they were about nine or so and whose breathin' was startin' to sound like their daddies a wheezin'. Doc Kitchen knew by the time those boys'd be breachin' their twentieth year they'd be just about as broken down as their old man in their fortieth year. It was a goddamn shame he'd say to himself over and over again, wearin' him thin.

He was settin' up to leave for the day to do his final rounds at the Paintsville Hospital, when Annamae Blakely came rushin' in to see someone about Brileigh, her ten-year-old daughter by Avery Blakely who'd died a few years back at the Hurricane Crick mine disaster right there in Hyden, ninety miles or so just south of Paintsville. Thirty-eight miners perished that day, after havin' "...crawled 2,400 feet straight down to dig coal, in a three-foot-tall mine," the Leslie County newspaper said, "Blown to bits they were." The only way anyone could identify those poor souls was to look at their social security numbers penciled on the back of their belts. It was a cryin' shame.

Hyden Judge Georgie Wooten it so happened was down at the mine that day when it blew. He'd been on the goddamn Finley brothers who owned the mine to get off their pitiful hind ends and "...make the mine safe for minin'" but they weren't about to spend a plug nickel that someone wasn't forcin' them to spend on a damn thing if they figured they could get by with it.

The blast was so furious that that fireball was like some kind of livin' thing when it came roarin' up out of that hole. Judge Wooten at that very moment had been giving hell to a Finley brother when the shaft exploded. And, right after the shaft became a scorching hell, so did Judge Wooten, grabbing Finley by the nape of his collar and damn near beatin' him to death.

As he held Finley down on the ground beating him with his fist, Judge Wooten figured with each blow that he'd be sharin' a prison cell with one of the many boys he'd sent away to the Castle on the Cumberland. It took four men to pull Judge Wooten's ragefulness off that Finley sonofabitch. And those four men, when asked what had happened, havin' witnessed the goings on, *swore* on a stack of Bibles, each had said, that Finley had been hit by flying debris when the mine blew its stack. A couple of those men later on in their life came before Judge Wooten on something "not amounting to not much of anything" and from the bench the good judge promptly said, "...case dismissed."

Well, Brileigh was huffin' and puffin' like she'd herself'd been a smoker all her little life. That poor suffern' child stood there in the waiting room, spittin' up black phlegm into a hanky that Annamae later apologized to Dr. Kitchen for not bein' as white as she liked to keep her and Brileigh's hankies. *Never* had Doc Kitchen seen so many folks struggling to get air down into their lungs. When he questioned Annamae about how long Brileigh'd been havin' trouble breathin' she said that "before Avery died and all at Hurricane Crick, when I'd be washin' his clothes from the mine, the coal dust'd just be a flyin' and Brileigh'd be standin' there, tryin' her darndest to help me, handin' me this and that and bein' so small and all, like youngins are, when the coal dust shook loose off those clothes, it'd get all over her.

"Sometimes then, she'd run out yonder and go up to her daddy and smile at him with her big white teeth showin' through her coal dirtied face and say, 'look at me, Daddy, don't I look like a little colored girl?' Well, Avery'd get to laughin' so hard and he'd scoop her up and swing her over his shoulder and be huggin' on her. Then he'd put her back down and she'd come a runnin' to help me get back to washin'.

"There was just so much of that coal dust everywhere, it was light as a feather blowin' this away and that." Even Annamae was havin' shortness of breath as she was relatin' her misfortunes.

When Doc Kitchen listened to Brileigh's lungs they sounded like the little girl with Progeria looked. Just about as soon as he placed the mask over her face, Doc Kitchen cupped his palms around the edges so oxygen wouldn't be leaking out the sides. In but a minute or two Brileigh started breathin' easier. Annamae, forever grateful, said she'd be sure bringin' by a fresh apple pie for Doc Kitchen.

Problem was that Brileigh's lungs, like all the other sufferin' folks, they weren't going to get any better. Even if she weren't around another speck of coal dust ever again that grit'd still be silently rustling around in her lungs, scaring them up like windblown sand pitting glass.

That night Doc Kitchen talked with Spencer Duty, Jr. about what he was seeing more times than he could count each and every day. He said the helplessness that haunted the hallways of the hospital was as pervasive as the men dying from one room to the next consumed by the black lung. Doc Kitchen even started calling it the *miners' plague*. The moat, like the moat of old, were economic, those who ran the mines verses those who mined them. Those who made money off those whose bodies would be ravaged by every conceivable danger lurking in the depths of the darkness.

Spencer Duty, Jr., listening, shook his head and said, "That's all about as bad as it can get but these men also have to be careful not to upset the Tommyknockers." Doc Kitchen certainly had heard miners make an inkling sometimes when they'd be talking about being down in the hole but the idea of angry gnomes raising hell or causing mayhem…

"When you're here for a while longer you'll get to use to things not being one way or the other like where you came from. In these parts what you might think of as lore lives right side-by-side everything else. If someone comes to see you for a wart and you treat them with medicine, they're going to go home, cut a potato in half and rub it on the wart, *just* to make sure. It may not make sense to you but it sure does to them. The miners in these parts and over in West Virginia have always been nothing more than throwaways for the mine bosses. There's not much else for men folk to do here except mining, so once their daddies have passed their age of usefulness their boys up and take their place in the hole. And, you can be sure that most of those miners' wives one day or another will bake their man a small saffron cake to leave for the Tommyknockers, to keep the miners safe. Mostly, they'll just talk about it amongst themselves, but they're just about as afraid of displeasing the Tommyknockers as they are the mine bosses. One set of fear lives above the hole and the other down in the hole, but both are as real as can be."

Chapter 5

IT WASN'T LONG AFTER Doc Kitchen had a talk with his daddy that he'd decided to set up a clinic that would at the very least diagnose the miners' plague without them getting the rigmarole from the mine doctors.

He also wanted to see his namesake's cabin. Before she died Eleanor left Moses a drawing of how to find his granddaddy's shack, tucked away up in the sugar maple grove. The reason he told Spencer Duty, Jr. was for inspiration but truth be known it was as much for fortitude as anything else, knowing what he'd be taking on if he did what he said he was going to do.

Moses followed the map to what was left of a rain gutted logging road just about halfway between Paintsville and West Van Lear. It wound up this way and that way, trees down here and there rooted in the thick muck from an uphill run off. On the map there was an arrow that said go this way, up an embankment and then down over its backside. When Moses crossed over top he saw the etching of what was left of the shack. He peeled back the brush that had reclaimed most of the hut which was smudged by limbs, leaves and liter—the outline blending with the shadows arcing with the light of the sun. When Moses pried open the tin door he, like Eleanor before him, saw what little that was left of the cabin. A few old pots here and there, even a few spent shotgun shells revealed themselves when he kicked the debris littered floor. Moses wondered what his grandfather thought about as he and his brother sat and talked during those cold Kentucky nights. Imagining the hardships that he had never known and the tenacity to go from here to where Moses' life had ended. He remembered Eleanor saying to him that "…remembering doesn't mean a goddam thing if it doesn't move you to do something worth doing. It's easy to get lost in nostalgia but that can become an excuse for not doing a goddamn thing. Do something with your life that's worth doing!"

The shack smelled of wood smoke even after all these years with coal dust lofting in the air as Moses shuffled from here to there. A cross was etched into the wall, likely carved by the pocket knife that his granddaddy carried wherever he went. A man couldn't survive in these parts without one. And now, Moses carried the same whittler which had been passed down to Eleanor and now to him. He always had a hesitation about losing the folder but a knife that had spent its life bein' dulled up by hard work wanted to be smoothed with honing oil and brought back to an edge on a wet stone, not lie fallow in a drawer and rust away from uselessness. Whatever trepidation Moses had would be ground away over time.

Chapter 6

HANGING FROM ABOVE, A bulb socket swung on a frayed wire like a flailing spider. Doc Kitchen sat at Murzie Meade's bedside, him being about as debilitated as a man can be disabiliatated. Old Murzie, try as he might now, couldn't even get out of bed to go and relieve himself, so Wannie May Meade, his wife now of thirty years or thereabouts, was havin' to carry the thunder mug back and forth, emptying the slop out back, humiliating poor Murzie just about to death. They, Murzie and Wannie May, had been given away at fourteen and had been together for evermore. But now, they hadn't been able to have relations for what Wannie May embarrassingly said was a 'month of Sundays.' Wannie May said she was more than willin' havin' enjoyed their bodily times, but "…when you can't get your breath to get you to the toilet, you can't get your breath to be movin' much in other ways either."

Murzie with each breath tried as he might to suck air down deeper into his lungs, but the air would only go so far before running up against specks of coal dust that'd clumped together and took up the space like a bunch of goddam squatters settlin' in to take over what wasn't rightfully theirs in the first place. With each ebb and flow, the depth of Murzie's breath became the receding tide of his life.

Sitting with a man whose lungs gurgle with each bolus of air going in and each bolus coming out, a man whose lips are blue and whose mind is turnin' to rust, brought Doc Kitchen to an agony of his own. It's wasn't just his helplessness, but being faced with what he considered an epidemic. He hadn't even been in Paintsville for very long and now if he began rabblerousing it wouldn't take much time before he was rode out of town on a rail. He also knew that once he began to do what needed to be done that he'd never be able to stop, it would consume his life.

It was just a few short weeks after Doc Kitchen had sat with Murzie Meade that Wannie May called saying that he'd done passed on. "It was a good thing," she said, not meaning a word of it beyond just being thankful that Murzie wasn't sufferin' anymore. But, Wannie May would miss him terribly, not for sure how she'd even go on, much less pay for buryin' Murzie. Jones-Preston Funeral Home wanted upwards of $700.00 to put poor Murzie in the ground.

It was a bit later that day that Mr. Charles E. Preston, the head undertaker, called Wannie May saying that Murzie's expenses had been taken care of. "He'll have a nice sendoff," Mr. Preston said. Confused, Wannie May asked who'd do something like that and all. Mr. Preston said he wasn't obliged to reveal her benefactor but rest assured Murzie would be laid out proper and for her to get on with her grieving without cluttering it up with worry about how she was going to pay for sending Murzie on his way up to the Lord. "He'll even have a nice new suit on when he meets St. Peter," Mr. Preston said assuredly.

Chapter 7

PAUL B. HALL, M.D. HAD been the medical director of the Paintsville Hospital for ever and a day, startin' around 1934 or thereabouts. Being a forward-thinking man, he kept insistin' that the hospital have the best newfangled x-ray machine that could be had. Each and every time he found one that showed the innards of a person better than the innards of the last one, then well, he said, to do his job proper the hospital needed to fork over the money and give him what he wanted. The hospital board figured each time they saw him arriving for a meeting wearing his ever-present black Kentucky Colonel string tie that he'd be wanting more money than they'd say they had.

The board would use up all its breath arguing this and that with him, until finally they all ended up blue in the face with his contentiousness, and being knuckled-under by Dr. Hall's fervor for practicing good medicine. "I just always want what is best for the folks who entrust their lives to me and this hospital," he would say. "How the hell do you argue with that?" the board would then end up sayin' and give him what he wanted.

Dr. Hall hadn't seen much evidence on the x-rays of men with breathing problems so he wasn't saying so much that they had black lungs. And, when Doc Kitchen began x-raying more and more miners, he too didn't see what he thought he should have seen in men who could barely catch a breath and many who'd fall into death in just a few short days. Dr. Hall said, "Some x-rays show up a set of lungs that look like their filled with dirt and others just don't happen to show much of anything, how can I up and say a man has black lungs when the x-rays don't always say so? It's just a conundrum that I just can't figure on…"

The mine bosses and president of the United Mine Workers, 'Tough Tony' Boyle, *demanded* that doctors be "100% certain" before they said that *any* miner had black lungs. And, "that *100%* had damn well better be backed up by goddamn x-rays and if it ain't then those miners are pulling a fast one and *by God* these struggling coal companies, who go out of their way to take care of these men and their families, had better have some recourse to go after these swindlers other than just kicking their ass out of a job, goddamnit!"

Tough Tony would make the rounds to just about all the mining towns, especially in Kentucky and West Virginia, those people down there he'd say were so "…goddamn stupid, you could tell them anything and they'd believe you, I mean Jesus Christ, they still shit in piss pots they keep under their beds."

"I've walked into that hospital in Paintsville and some goddamn miner's laying there, taking his last few breaths and I look him right in the eye and say, 'It's men like you that's made this country great.' Then you pat that sonofabitch on the shoulder, stand there for a few minutes shaking your head up and down, acting like you understand what the hell he's saying through his goddamn wheezing, tell him how sorry you are for his troubles… But… you have to make sure that other folks standing around take notice of your *compassion*, your *concern*, how that miner means *so much* to *you*, and you *personally*. Then you turn around and get the hell outta there. If these miners had their way hell, they'd bleed every goddamn cent they could out of the coal companies, then where the hell would this country be, I mean Jesus Christ. They've been going on about having black lung for as long as I can remember. Hell, John L. got so sick and tired of listening to them that he just stopped coming around and sent his lackeys to bear the brunt of their complaining. Most of them only have a fourth or fifth grade education, what the hell else are they going to do, there's only so much you can do with people like that and they need to know their place, let them do what they can do, then when they can't do it anymore you go onto the next one whose waiting in line and there's *always* someone else waiting in line, Jesus Christ, we ain't going to be running out of these ignorant bastards anytime soon."

It was just before Doc Kitchen went home from doing his rounds when he saw Dr. Hall writing up a couple of orders. That's when

Dr. Hall said he wanted Doc Kitchen to meet Tough Tony, who'd just happened to be coming through Paintsville on his way up to Wheeling. He said he wanted to stop in and see if there were any of *his* men in the hospital and if there was anything he could do for them.

Chapter 8

PRETTY MUCH RIGHT OFF Doc Kitchen didn't think much of Tough Tony, remembering for some reason or another Eleanor saying to him, "Never trust a short man with a square head."

To this day he had no remembrance why she said that or even when, but as soon as Doc Kitchen laid eyes on Tough Tony's square head, talcum white face, cold eyes and short stature he took to him an immediate disliking, and perhaps more importantly distrust. Dr. Hall said for Doc Kitchen to take Tough Tony from ward to ward, introducing him to any miners who were suffering and whose wives would be sittin' weeping and wringing their hands beside their men.

All the while Tough Tony kept slapping Doc Kitchen on the back, telling the suffering miners and their wives how he had confidence that "the Doc here..." was "gonna be making y'all well enough to get back to mining and feeding your family, just like you've always done." But most of the men couldn't even wheeze out anything that made any sense, not just because of their black lungs but because what little oxygen that was going to their brains had made them mostly lose their minds.

Lighting up a cigarette, Tough Tony looked at Doc Kitchen with undo agreement and said, shaking his head, "If these men hadn't smoked so goddamn much, they wouldn't be suffering like they are. Poor bastards."

"What these men are suffering from," Doc Kitchen retorted, "isn't caused by smoking, it certainly doesn't help, but these men have black lung disease."

In but an instant Tough Tony stepped forward and shoved his finger into Doc Kitchen's chest, "Show me the goddamn proof, *show it to me!*" he demanded. Not waiting for an answer, Tough Tony turned and stormed down the hallway. Looking back, he screamed at Doc Kitchen, "*When ye be an anvil, lay ye very still. But when ye be a hammer, strike with all thy will. Don't* make me your goddamn *anvil* doctor." Then he drove on up to Wheeling, fuming all the way.

Dr. Hall told Doc Kitchen, who was thunderstruck by Tough Tony, that he reckoned he ought not to of brought up the black lung to Tough Tony. "Why," Dr. Hall said, "Tough Tony's spent most of his life saying how there's nothing to black lung, he *swears* up and down it's caused by cigarette smoking and you know x-rays will show some rock in the lungs but most of the time it doesn't show much else. So, the way I see it, Doctor Kitchen, if you're going to go making a fuss and upsetting Tough Tony, then you'd better reckon some way to back it up." Doc Kitchen said he didn't understand what the hell Tough Tony expected to see when he went from a hospital ward filled with *miners.*

"He comes round ever so often to make sure that everyone in earshot hears him say there is *no such thing* as black lung. He makes it look like he gives a hoot about the miners but truth be told, he doesn't give two hoots. *But* you need to figure that he'd do just about *anything* to stay the president of the UMW so you need to be minding your p's and q's."

It was right then that Doc Kitchen came to realize that his destiny had been spoken for.

Chapter 9

"I HATE TO ASK you Wannie May, I know you have just lost Murzie, but I want to try and help make things right for men like Murzie. The mining companies have denied benefits for years for miners, and hell, they deny that black lung even exists. One way to start going up against them is with samples of these men's lungs. I want to take a piece of Murzie's lungs before he is buried. Will you let me do that?"

Doc Kitchen knew that he needed to be methodical. To lay out proof that the mining companies couldn't continue to deny. He also knew that it was going to pit him up against Tough Tony. Eventually he'd have to convince Dr. Hall that he needed a spirometer, but before that he had to convince the dying miners' wives that he needed to cut their men open before they put them in the ground.

Wannie May's foreboding decision to let Doc Kitchen open up her poor Murzie weighed on her as awful as awful could be, she'd say to her youngins right up until the day that she passed on to join Murzie in Heaven. "But, if it helps those other poor souls then Murzie'd wanted that. I'll be knowin' soon enough if he's a standin' there with his hand out waitin' for me when I pass on or if he just ain't there at all… well then, I'll know that too."

Doc Kitchen showed up right about the time that Charles Preston was getting ready to embalm Murzie and push a trocar into his right carotid artery to get him ready for being laid out so folks could come and show their respect and say their sorrows at his passin' to Wannie May.

"This is quite irregular, Doc, I just don't know what you have in mind," the undertaker said.

Doc Kitchen went on to retort that he was gathering up some

samples of miners who'd died and likely'd had the black lung. *But* that he was going to have to open up Murzie's chest to take a few pieces of tissue. Charles Preston, having never heard the likes of such a thing, being right before he filled Murzie up with formaldehyde, was just beside himself with disconsternation.

Doc Kitchen said he would most certainly be obliged if Charles Preston could be of service to him *and* medical science, not only now but also with other men who came the way of Murzie, having suffered something terrible in the final years of their lives. "I'll be willing to be of service," Charles Preston up and said, "but it's going to be upsetting to folks as they most certainly don't take much favor with their men being cut open after they're *already* dead. They *know* what killed them, they couldn't breathe for two cents and so they up and died, and that's that," Charles Preston reiterated.

"Well, what we know for sure is that they are *dead*," Doc Kitchen replied, "*But*, if we can show for certain, without any shadow of a doubt, why they *are* dead, then maybe we can do something about them being dead in the first goddamn place."

Charles Preston stroked his cheek with the palm of his hand like he was massagin' back his disconcertin' contemplation into some kind of complacency. And, when his hand moved from his cheek to his pocket, he let out a sigh and said that his daddy had been a miner and had likely died of the black lung. "I don't want to get so high falutin' that I forget where I came from. So, if you'd like, I've spent a lot of my years of being alive talkin' to folks about being dead, and if I do say so myself, I've gotten pretty good at it, so when a miner comes my way who I hear has died from the black lungs, I'll let you know. You're not from these parts so it'd be better if I talked to the widaws, it'll bode well for you that your Spencer Duty, Jr's boy though."

On that, Doc Kitchen picked up a scalpel, pulled the sheet from over Murzie's body and began a cut from the top of his groin to just above his sternum, slicing several times to get through what little fat layer there was. It looked to Doc Kitchen that in addition to having the black lung Murzie had also spent much of life hungry. There was some yellow fat that showed itself when the blade began making Murzie's chest into twos but not enough to keep a man warm on a cold morning. As Murzie's chest muscles became more exposed, Doc Kitchen pulled back on either side, cutting them like a butcher dehides a cow. When the Pectoralis muscles were cut, Murzie's chest was splayed open like a wild turkey fanning its tail feathers. Then Doc Kitchen found the landmark tips of the clavicle and the sternum and used chest cutters to cut the cartilage until the breast plate was free, exposing his heart and lungs. "Jesus Christ," Doc Kitchen said, having only seen x-rays and the *results* of the disease. He'd never laid his eyes on these poor bastard's lungs. In the chest cavity of this man were lungs that were hardened, how they could even begin to inflate was unimaginable. They were scarred, shriveled and *black*. *Thousands* of peppered colored specks tainted Murzie's mostly grayish lung tissue. There was evidence that the intercostal muscles were atrophying because they simply weren't being used and poor Murzie's heart was broken. The damn fibrosis in his lungs increased the blood pressure in his pulmonary artery and caused the right side of his heart to fail and fail and fail until it couldn't fail anymore and it just stopped.

In all he had seen Doc Kitchen came to a realization in that moment that men with the miners' plague are for all practical purposes hung by the mining companies, the UMW and the government. They suffocate to death. The only difference between a lynching and black lung was the time it took to die. At least on a gallows when the trap door snaps opens, you drop and your neck breaks. With black lung, the trap door opens sliver by sliver, agonizingly slow, so the rope slowly tightens around the neck, until it is so tight that so little air gets in that they can't even get enough contraction in the gall bladder to vomit. And, once the noose begins to tighten, there is nothing that can be done. It is a condition that guarantees a destiny of death. "Jesus Christ," Doc Kitchen said again.

Looking into the innards of a man brings many things to bear as you are standing there, on this occasion, Doc Kitchen again remembered Eleanor saying, "Do something with your life that is worth doing!"

In that moment he silently answered, "I will, Mother."

Chapter 10

Dr. Hall was brokenhearted that afternoon when Dr. Kitchen's knuckles rapped on his office door. It'd been just a few short hours since long sufferin' Mrs. Emily Pickles Pelphrey of Paintsville had succumbed to the suddenness of a stroke brought about by the horridness of her sudden witnessing an act of illicit fornication between her long menacing husband and first cousin, Mr. Ernie Pickles Pelphrey, also being of Paintsville.

Dr. Hall had been called that early morning by the thirteenth of her thirteen children who said that her momma had gone out to the barn and witnessed an act of unspeakableness, then she stumbled back into the homeplace, began babbling nonsense, screamed that she was blinded by the Lord for what she had just been forced to witness, likely by Satan himself and then the thirteenth child said her poor mother's face contorted all up on one side and then she up and died.

By the time Dr. Hall got there Mrs. Emily was so stiff that he couldn't even begin to straighten her without snappin' her body that'd been riddled by giving birth to one child after another and then finally a set of triplets, the first set of triplets in all of Johnson County that'd lived. She lay there in the farm muck, looking tragically, Dr. Hall thought, like a poor great mule of a woman with what'd been the last elements of grace kicked right out of her.

Ernie, who'd been known to be a drunkard and one who folks'd say was "odd" when he came to realize that Miss Emily had witnessed his unholy act, was so vexed with abasement that he slung the milk cow's halter over a barn beam and strung himself up, begging the good Lord for His forgiveness right before he leapt off the hay stack.

Dr. Hall didn't even know that Ernie had done what he'd done until he saw the thirteenth fall down in grief as she came out of the barn with a look on her face like he'd only seen in other soldiers during the Great War. By the time he got back to the hospital Dr. Hall was feeling a suffering of sorts himself, having tried as he might to redeliver both Emily and Ernie back to this earth but clearly the good Lord was having none of it and decided to keep them for His own. Now he had to do some figurin' about what Dr. Kitchen was going to be pestering him with.

"Dr. Kitchen, now what do you want with a spirometer?" To which, Dr. Kitchen said that as Dr. Hall knew, x-rays weren't showing what they needed to show with these men who were suffering with the black lung and that with the breathing problems these men were having, well, something had to be done. So Dr. Kitchen said he wanted a spirometer to measure lung function. He was also going to be taking samples of deceased miners' lungs to back up his findings on the spirometer regardless of whether or not the x-ray showed black lung or not.

Dr. Hall, being the pragmatic man he was, but over these many years having also seen the suffering himself, said he'd talk to the board about getting it approved.

Chapter 11

Spencer Duty, Jr. hadn't fitted a foot now for a good long time. As a matter of fact his knuckles were gnarly and his knees certainly weren't as bendy. Not to mention that folks didn't take kindly to seeing crumpled up fingers buckling up their youngins' shoes. Spencer Duty, Jr. figured it was time for younger fingers to pick up the task at hand. Boys and girls, all over Kentucky, still loved to go to the only shoe stores with peddle pony carousels that sat right in the middle of each and every Dooties Booties. Those youngin'd come runnin' right through the half-pint size door that was there just for them and first thing head right for a pony. Then their mommas'd let ride 'round and 'round for a bit, talkin' amongst themselves while waitin' for the next shoe dog to come over and ask them how they could be helped.

Never had buying shoes been known to be fun until Dooties Booties came along. Spencer Duty, Jr. had trained a lot of young men and women looking for a good profession that'd last them throughout their years. "Folks always need shoes," he'd say. Each and every year Spencer Duty, Jr. would visit all the stores throughout Kentucky and spend time talkin' with what were now men and women who'd been boys and girls at one time or another and whose feet had been cared for by the great Spencer and Nora Duty themselves or Spencer Duty, Jr. And, even though he knew it sounded commonplace to say, Spencer Duty, Jr. would almost always shake a hand here or there and say, "Where have all the years gone…"

It was the same night that Moses had talked with Dr. Hall about the spirometer and let him know what he was up to that Spencer Duty, Jr. told him that he planned on leaving everything he had to him. He'd been figuring on it for a while now, unsure before when he had no kin but now that he had a son, it was "well, only right." A conglomerate had been dogging him for years to let go of his stores but, "No, I'm not going to be doing that" he said.

Now he could leave his money to Moses without him being saddled with the burden of having to sell this or that and make the work he was doing easier on him. When Moses told his daddy what he was planning to do Spencer Duty, Jr. sat him down and told him the story of how his daddy, being barely into his manhood, had related the story of the great Van Lear mine disaster in the '20s. "Your granddaddy went around the junction gathering up the widows on the back of his apple truck right after the blast. It was on that very apple truck that I carried my momma and daddy up to Cumbo mountain, a pile of scrap is all that is left of it now, shrouded by the pall of tall tops of wrap around Poplars. Sometime, I'll take you up top Cumbo and you can see your grandparents' graves for yourself.

"I'm proud of what you're doing son, I want you to know that. No matter how much proof you get trying to prove the suffering of these men, well the mine bosses aren't going to take it laying down."

Moses then related that Dr. Hall was looking into getting a spirometer for him to be able to see how well the miners' lungs work by measuring how much air gets taken in, how much you breathe out *and* how quickly you can blow it out. If you have black lung disease, "all of that will only be a small percentage of what it should be *if* your lungs were working the way their supposed to. But, spirometers are expensive so whether the board will approve the request or not, I'll have to see."

Spencer Duty, Jr. spoke up and added, "I've known those men on the hospital board and there's a lot of coal money sitting around that well-hewed table."

Chapter 12

ALBA RADO AUXIER, WHO, when introduced'd say, "Folks just call me Ox," had married Alka now about twenty-five years ago or so. And try as they might, the good Lord had not seen to bless them with offspring. But just about every night, even though Alka was well past her breeding years, Alba Rado *insisted* that perhaps Jesus would see fit and release one more opportunity for procreational divination.

Alka herself was a beast of a woman, full of breast, stumpy of height with hair as dry as a robin's nest. But, Ox loved her just the same, he'd been known to say. He'd also been known to tell whoever'd lend an ear that miners were just about the biggest assemblage of ingrates that God had ever put on this earth.

Ox, who, when he was a lad, had come over with his momma and daddy from Kansas during the dirty thirties right about when the black blizzards blinded youngins and gritted up just about anything that most folks were lucky enough to have to put in their mouths. He'd *known* for forever and a day what ruinous damnation was. His daddy, he'd say, "Use to wear cardboard in his shoes to keep the rocks from pebblin' his toes and his momma, I overheard her say, that when she got her womanly ways she'd trim up a rabbit pelt to catch her monthly release."

Ox knew with his remembrances what real suffering was and one was least not to forget it in his presence. Because of this he wasn't particularly bottomless in his understanding of anyone else's suffering.

Alka's beastliness, she'd once said, had not always been so, in fact when she met Ox boys would say that her gams were the bee's knees. And, back then even Ox'd tell her how pretty she was, bring her flowers and parade her here and there like an ornament adornin' his arm.

He'd never so much as raised a disrespectful hand to Alka until their wedding night when he laid the back of his hand across her face for her backtalkin' ways, which he said he'd grown awful tired of and it needed to be brought to a "stoppin' too right here and now." So poor Alka figured that it'd be best to fortify herself to endure the time after times when Ox'd grow tired of this and that. And in the dedication of her fortification Alka would droll on that she'd never met a bowl of mashed potatoes and gravy that she didn't think the best of.

When Dr. Hall brought something to Ox's attention as the chairman of the hospital board, he was always about as affable as a man could be in what was his way of usually disagreeing. Most especially when it came for doing anything exceptional for anything having to do with treating the ills of miners. Of which there were many. Ox'd been the president of Middle States Coal Company for just about as long as anyone could remember. Seeing them through thick and thin with this and that complaints by goddamn regulators.

He'd also sat on the hospital board for just about as long too. "Now don't go gettin' your bowels in an uproar," he'd say, whenever Dr. Hall came wanting this or that. Well, the board'd give in on x-raying but Ox wasn't about to offer up much else to help those that were already being given more than he figured they deserved. "They *dig* coal and that's *all* they do! They're like goddamn voles in a hole and we drown *those* sonsabitches when they become a nuisance." Ox would say to Alka, who would always nod her head in agreement for fear of upsettin' Ox, whose vexed temperament at his homeplace was disresembling of his Janus-faced temperament when his size fourteen feet weren't dapplin' the air with their own dust.

Alka'd been known to show up at Dr. Hall's office here and there with this and that bone twisted hither and yon. No matter what Dr. Hall'd say though, Alka'd say back that she'd fallen down the stairs or their four-legger, Boone, had run past her chasing a squirrel and knocked her on her noggin' in the process.

Dr. Hall, just not bein' sure what to do, would always nod, saying that she needed to be more careful and then he would add that if she perhaps ever wanted to take the late bus out of Paintsville, the one that comes through just about midnight or thereabouts, to head on back to Kansas to spend some time with her family, who Dr. Hall said he figured, were getting on in years and likely would welcome some visitin'. He even said, that since he and Mrs. Hall's homeplace was closer than Alka's to the bus station, that she could drop off her suitcase a day or two before, whenever was convenient, and then just stop by and pick it up on her way to catch the bus. She would always give her thanks for Dr. Hall makin' such a generous of spirit offer, but, she said, Ox'd never permit her to do such a thing. "Well," Dr. Hall'd say, "if you ever do go changing you mind, just drop your belongings right on the front porch and Mrs. Hall will tuck them away until you arrive to retrieve them."

It wasn't long after one of Alka's visits to Dr. Hall when Ox showed up just missin' seeing her go out the side door that Dr. Hall used as his private entrance. Ox had just got off the phone talkin' with Tough Tony about the doctor who'd been stirin' things up and now Ox'd just seen that Dr. Hall'd gone and asked the board to up and buy a spirometer for something or other having to do with the goddamn miners. "Well, you know that I sympathize with these folks' adversities, but we can't go spending good money on folks who make their asthma about as bad as it can get because they won't stop their bad habiting. The UMW has been about as generous as generous can be with their donations to this hospital and they ain't going to want to see their generosity going where it don't need to be going, so let's be rethinking our priorities."

Dr. Hall had been figuring that Ox would be the wall that'd stand in the way of getting Dr. Kitchen what he needed. So nodding in agreement not that different than Alka did, Dr. Hall made a call and said that having discussed what was needed with Ox and having been turned down flat that he would in fact be much obliged if the money that had been promised could be forthcoming. Spencer Duty, Jr. said on the other end of the line that it would be an honor for Dooties Booties to donate such a valuable piece of medical equipment to the hospital, but with an underlying stipulation that "Dr. Moses Kitchen and his assigns be given free and unencumbered use of said equipment." In but a short while Dr. Hall had contacted the Warren E. Collins Co., who'd been at 555 Huntington Avenue, in Boston, since 1920. And, in not too long after that, a Collins Double Bronchospirometer showed up one afternoon at the hospital much to the serous disconsternation of Ox, who was flummoxed how such a thing could have happened under the tutelage of his watchful eyes. Now, not only did he have to answer to Tough Tony but also to the folks at Middle States, who'd been paying him to do *whatever* needed to be done and to make sure things kept goin' on the way they'd been goin'. As he stomped away from seeing the crate being unloaded at the delivery dock of the hospital, he fell right off the side of the ramp. When his portly head came face-to-face with a snapped off piece of pipe it took his right eye right out of its socket.

Dr. Hall and Dr. Kitchen worked well into the night, side by side to undo the damage that Ox's disconsternated state had done. He'd be wearing an eyepatch now but, and as Ox would forever say, by the "grace of God," the pipe hadn't broken through his skull to his brain.

Now he had to turn his head sideways to see someone on his right with his left eye. Looking awkward as hell he was always cocking his head this way and that. Around the hospital when he walked by the nurses they would whisper under their breath, there goes "Oxslipital."

Chapter 13

Doc Kitchen began to line up men whose breathing sounded like a raspy saw being bowed by a man with a tremblin' arm. Silas Pistols Profitt, who'd married Sissy Patience Profitt, his third cousin, after havin' illicit relations and her being with child, and therefore it being necessary to make Sissy an honest woman in the eyes of the Lord, looked pitiful sittin' with his spine held at attention hopin' for an easin' of his breathin'. When Doc Kitchen called him in, Sissy helped Silas to stand and waited for him to take a breath that'd hopefully get him enough air to walk the few steps he'd have to take to where he'd be able to sit again.

Once Silas got to where he was goin' Doc Kitchen sat him down in front of a buffed up, stainless steel contraption with two pillar-like canisters that rose up like the tin columns of a still. Comin' off the back was a tube that Doc Kitchen told Silas to breathe into just as hard as he could muster and then blow out with the same mustering. Well, Silas, sat back and with the determination of a bull in heat put the hose into his mouth and began to suck with all his might. In just a few short seconds, poor Silas began wheezin' and coughin' to the point where Doc Kitchen said for him to stop, fearin' that he was going pass out right then and there. Giving him a while to rest, Doc Kitchen then told Silas to breathe in again, this time though he said just do the best he could, but more like he was siphoning gas out of his daddy's car, just nice and steady. Silas'd certainly siphoned some gas in his day so he knew exactly what Doc Kitchen was sayin' for him to do. And, as he pulled what air he could into his lungs, a chart that sat right in the middle of the two stainless pillars showed exactly how much air he *was* taking in and how much he *should* have been.

Thing was, that the line that showed how much air a healthy man should be breathin' in and what Silas was able to call forth was like a river that'd split in two and would never meet up again.

"Hold it for just a second," Doc Kitchen said. Silas, with Sissy rubbing his back, held on for as long as he could and then Doc Kitchen said, "...blow... blow... blow hard." Giving it his all, Silas blew until he couldn't blow no more and the chart showed not only that he could barely do himself proud with his blowing but that there was little that'd got into his lungs in the first place to come roarin' back out. In all of her born days, Sissy Patience Profitt never had given it a second thought that she'd be facing a widaw's sympathy as a young woman. But, sure enough, now that Silas was disabled and without any means of supporting his family that was sure enough what was overtaking her mind with consideration.

With Sissy on one side and Doc Kitchen on the other, arm in arm they helped Silas stand up, hobbling to the door and out to their truck, him breathing and wheezing all the way, puckering up his lips like a fish that'd all of a sudden found itself in a dried-up stream.

Silas was the first miner that Doc Kitchen had done any measures with on the spirometer. In a few days, he had said he would come back and let Doc Kitchen x-ray his lungs too. Sissy wasn't so sure seeing what it had taken out of poor Silas, but being of strong-willed stock, Silas would have none of Sissy's concern interfering with him deciding to do what he could to not only help his family in whatever way he had left, but to also help the other miners who were suffern' right along with him.

Chapter 14

THE OX WASN'T PLEASED with what was transpiring. Miners, but mostly their wives, were startin' to talk amongst each other, and so other folks could hear and weren't whispering like they'd done before, about Doc Kitchen and him bein' able to get a better idea about provin' what the black lung was doing to their men. They'd always known but nobody'd ever listened and the mine doctors were still going on and on about smoking and asthma, this and that. They'd been saying that kind of bullshit now for upwards of fifty years or more and they weren't about to let up.

One of the wives'd told another that the Doc had said that the x-rays of her man's lungs looked like the creases in the sole of a boot that'd been stippled with gravel and that no matter what it'd never be coming out. That gravel'd just taken over that boot so it wouldn't be doin' much walkin' from here to there, "that's for sure," he would say. It wasn't any different with the lungs that had been encrusted with coal dust, they weren't going to be doing any more breathing than those boots were going to be doing any more walking.

Ox was getting call after call from Tough Tony, indicating that he'd even had a talking to with Alka and that if Ox wanted to continue enjoying the life of comfort he'd been enjoying now over these many years then this goddamn seditiousness with whoever this doctor was, who was stirring the pot, needed to stop. Tough Tony'd found that word *seditious* now a while ago and anybody who disagreed with what Tough Tony said was "seditious," and like a dog that couldn't be learned, needed to be put down.

That was very upsetting to Ox, having now known the many pleasures of having what he wanted when he wanted it. Alka, for all of her complaining about whatever just about she could find to complain about, said in no uncertain terms that Ox needed to do what needed to be done. She'd become accustomed to being accustomed to, no matter how many times she'd went to see Dr. Hall, and having her desires met when her desires needed meeting.

Chapter 15

IN WHAT WAS NOT a very long time at all, Doc Kitchen had a waiting room full of wheezing miners readying up to go in and breath into the breathing machine. Then, right after that, he'd send them onto the backroom to get a chest x-ray. That night and each and every night, Doc Kitchen'd take the recordings of the spirometer and compare it to the chest x-rays. And, for the first time since around 1920 or thereabouts, it couldn't no longer be said that miners were of their own making responsible for their own ruination.

It wasn't long before Doc Kitchen was getting calls from as far away as Marion County, West Virginia. Folks there were saying that the mine bosses weren't listening to anything they had to say and that the rest homes were filled up with miners who were long on breath and short on wind. They were wondering if Doc Kitchen could maybe come over and see what he could do. "It's the asthma and smoking," was what they'd been told.

Everywhere though, it didn't matter if it was in Kentucky, West Virginia or hell Pennsylvania for that matter, was the problem that once the miners'd lost their ability to mine, they weren't no use to nobody. And being of no use meant what little they made mining dried up faster than a poorly fed coal seam. Then to add insult to injury, when they'd go to say they needed benefits because of they'd come down with the black lung, they were told in no uncertain terms that if they hadn't had so many bad habits then they wouldn't be in the shape they were in and so there just wasn't anything that could be done. Then they were sent on home, with the "sympathy" of the coal companies, mind you.

In those areas where a coal company owned the junction, miners coming in to replace those who'd become infirmed because of their "bad habits" needed a place to be put up and so the afflicted were told it was time to be on their way.

Lots of folks just ended up hither to yon, drifting from town to town, begging for food, *mostly* for their youngins and a bit for gas to get them to the next town. But, folks in those towns'd get tired of hungry boys and girls sittin' atop the hoods of cars, makin' those folks who *were* workin' feelin' like they'd up and done something wrong just because they *weren't* hungry. Things were just gettin' real bad.

Right in-between just about everything else Doc Kitchen got called over to the hospital to help Dr. Hall. It seemed as though now that Doc Kitchen'd come to town that whenever there was an emergency he got called. Formerly, as would be related, it'd been only Dr. Hall but now folks'd come to depend on Doc Kitchen too, even though some were swaddled in skepticism because of his lacking of gray hair, they were coming to understand that even though he could be irascible he knew what he was talking about. But, nodding their chins to their chests, and in certain cases it'd be said, "…well he did his best." It was on that very afternoon, right when Doc Kitchen was beginning to compare spirometer recordings with the chest x-rays of twenty men, that the hospital called and said for him to get on over there.

After Doc Kitchen had graduated University of Utah School of Medicine, he headed on over to Rochester, Minnesota, to do his residency at the Mayo Clinic in internal medicine and general surgery. He did a lot of rotating through the emergency room, so he got to see a lot of different things that a lot of docs would never get to set their minds to figuring. But, since his time in Paintsville, the emergencies he'd seen had certainly rivaled just about anything else he'd gotten to see.

When he got there, a lot of fury was being stirred up in the ER. Bodies it seemed like were just about everywhere, and they were all dead except one. There they were, lined up against the wall, one right after the other.

It seemed like the farmer Felix Flannery was doing his planting like he'd done every year since he'd first began farming helpin' his daddy out, now a while ago, right there around Buriek Branch. Right about as he was beginning to trowel the head of the furrower blade under the soil, he learned that Chief Osborn'd come and fatally wounded his uncle Hi Ho Bradley while attempting to arrest him a week or so before. Really his name was just Hi but ever since he'd been a youngin folks just automatically added on the Ho whenever they saw him. Well, when Felix'd found out the news about uncle Hi Ho and like the seeds he'd been ready to sow, his fury set its tentacles just about everywhere throughout Felix's personhood, until his hands couldn't help but do what his wits was comin' to demand.

Felix grabbed his shotgun, loaded himself into his potato truck and went huntin' for Chief Osborn. A bit later Felix eyeballed Chief Osborn walking up to his homeplace from his patrol car. With his fury pushin' at his back, Felix jumped from the potato truck, leveled his shotgun at Chief Osborn and without taking the time to do any figurin' pulled both triggers, which caused whatever breath Chief Osborn still had in him to come roaring out the holes in his buckshot filled chest.

Chief Osborn'd always been known to carry his Police .38 in the waistband of his trousers and when the shotgun blast sent him backwards, his revolver dislodged itself from his britches and like it itself was looking to revenge the murder of its keeper fell right at the feet of Joe Eddy, Chief Osborn's boy, who'd come bursting through the screen door when he'd heard the goings on. Joe Eddy tripped and fell plumb at the spot where that pistol was resting, waiting to be picked up and used for retribution to right the wrong that'd just been perpetrated.

Joe Eddy's fingers encircled the grip of the .38, leveled the sight right at the chest of Felix and pulled the trigger three times, severing Felix's spine just as many times. But, Felix having not come unprepared, reached under his shirt as he was falling to the ground, pulled a .45 and shot poor Joe Eddy right through the top of the head.

The Mullins boys, Mills and Miles, came runnin' from down the road, coming upon Chief Osborn, Felix, who was doing his best to crawl like a twisted cricket to just about anywhere, and Joe Eddy, who like his daddy, was dead. Well, as Mills and Miles was standing overtop those deceased and one not, Wes Hall, Chief Osborn's friend since they'd long ago been youngins together, became convinced in that awful moment that Mills and Miles'd gone ahead and done the dastardly deed that now beset upon Wes.

Wes Hall, just about everyone knew, even when he went to visit the outhouse, carried with him a German Luger that he'd liberated from the dead hands of a kraut he'd killed during WWII. The only thing that Wes hated more than a Nazi were rattlers, so he never took a step without his Luger and seeing Mills and Miles looking about as guilty as a couple of men can look, Wes toggled the Luger and portioned most of the clip between the two. For some reason or other, it hit Wes right about then that he may not have done the proper thing. So, in his reconnoitering of what had just come to pass, Wes came to figure on the grievousness of what he'd done and in so doing so put the barrel of the Luger in his mouth, havin' saved the last round for himself. Folks later on would say that the disposition of the Nazi that Wes had taken the Luger from had never left its grip and in the end had *his* way with Wes.

Chapter 16

"JESUS CHRIST, IT LOOKS like a slaughter house," Doc Kitchen said, when he walked into the ER. Layin' side by side was Wes, Mills and Miles, Joe Eddy, Chief Osborn and Felix, who was the only one still doin' any movin', bein' the only one with much blood left in him, the top half of him in so much pain he was shaking the walls with his screamin' and well, the bottom half not feelin' one thing at all. Dr. Hall was pronouncing each of the dead with an official time and saying that they'd do a post on the deceased after they did some figuring over their bodies and all.

Doc Kitchen and Dr. Hall then stood over Felix, looking down at a man who, wounded the way he was, was going to be trailing just a short while behind the others who lay dead right next to him. Being though that he was still alive, Doc Kitchen ordered IVP Morphine, Ringers Lactate and D5W, figuring it would provide some comfort for a man with not too many breaths left to breathe. In examining him, Doc Kitchen said that Felix's spine was transected at about T6. And, if that weren't bad enough, the other two bullets had torn apart his intestines and bladder, then bounced around destroying his pelvis and instead of lodging somewhere, those goddamn bullets decided to abscond with what little dignity poor Felix had left and blow off most of his testicles and penis as they ended up leaving through one of the many holes they'd made.

Felix, figuring he was dying, and figuring right for that matter, in about as panicked a state of mind as a man can panic in, said, "Is there *nothin'* that y'all can do?" and in a moment not sure of where it came from, Doc Kitchen, said, "We can cut you in half."

Dr. Hall, figuring it'd be pointless startin' up an argument, most especially figuring that there wasn't too much to lose, nodded in agreement and said, "We'll do our best." But Doc Kitchen, who was having none of Dr. Hall's doctory sugar-coatin', looked at Felix and said, "It's likely that we'll kill you, though. There's not much left of you to work with. It's the only chance you have and there isn't much of that."

Felix, in a state of bewilderment, looked up at Doc Kitchen and said, "Are you gonna leave my Johnny?"

Doc Kitchen said squarely, "Everything below your waist will be gone… *everything*. You'll have a bag for your urine and your feces and be in some kind of wheeled contraption for the rest of your life. Or we can let you die. The decision is up to you."

Felix, figurin' he'd better be figurin' about as fast as he'd ever figured, nodded his head up and down.

Waitin' right outside the curtain that was pulled around Felix and listenin' with just as much impatience as he was waitin' was Detective Oscar Oppenheimer, though folks in Paintsville called him Detective Oppenhammer for his lack of any good naturedness and lifelong irascibleness. He was known to carry the same snub nose .38 that John Dillinger dropped while escaping from FBI Agent Melvin Purvis at Little Bohemia Lodge up Wisconsin way.

Detective Oppenhammer was always pulling that revolver out, showing it around, spinning the cylinder, and pointing to the four notches on the left grip that he said Dillinger had etched in for the four lawmen he'd cowardly gunned down. Now, Detective Oppenhammer wanted to pull back that curtain and take care of Felix the way he deserved to be taken care of. He'd listened to enough of the bullshit about saving his life and all. There wasn't one goddamn judge within a hundred miles that'd fault him for doing what needed to be done, and right as his fingers encircled the grip of JDs snub nose, being aged himself now, he felt a sharp pang in his chest and before anyone could do anything he fell over dead as a doornail, grabbing onto the privacy curtain and tearing it right off its polished up chrome rod.

Felix as part of his figurin' figured he'd end up dead no matter what, especially when he heard that Detective Oppenhammer was standing outside the curtain. Now he saw Detective Oppenhammer dropping dead as a sign of redemption and be that he'd no longer have his bottom half at least he'd have his top half and urged Doc

Kitchen to get on with doing what needed to be done to make his redemption complete. There was just one more thing that Felix needed to do some figuring on as the nurses were preparing him to be halved. Given the mayhem he'd brought about he'd likely be given the electric chair for his deed. But, with only half of him being left there wouldn't even be any way to electrocute him. Hell, he figured, they may just up and let him be, just not knowing what to do with him.

Chapter 17

ONCE THE WORD GOT out what Doc Kitchen was going to do to Felix, other docs started showing up from anywhere where they thought they could get there in time to observe the surgery. There'd only been a few hemicorporectomies done anywhere in the world and most of those were done from battlefield or crush injuries and most of those souls had either not survived the surgery itself or died shortly after.

The first thing Doc Kitchen did was to make new conduits for Felix's urinary and fecal output. That was about as difficult as difficult could be but all in all was the part that would take the less time. But in about four hours Felix had two tubes that would empty into bags once the amputation of his pelvis and lower extremities were complete. As Doc Kitchen was making the circular anterior and posterior incisions Felix was turned like a pig on a spit. Carefully, cuts were made through the spine, transecting the aorta and inferior vena cava and then Doc Kitchen heard what he swore was a '*pop*' and Felix separated into two parts. Now the thick flaps of skin that Doc Kitchen had left would be folded over this way and that and then trussed up, not all that different than preparin' the Thanksgiving turkey to make sure the stuffin' stayed right where it was supposed to.

One of the observing doctors asked what Felix's odds of survival were.

"Well," Doc Kitchen said, "there were no surprises during surgery, everything is positioned where it's supposed to be and his heart rhythms are stable. We have to see if what's left of his colon activates or if he begins losing electrolytes and dozens of other things could crash him, but for now he is stable. I anticipate he will be in the hospital for about eight months and then *maybe* we can discharge him, at least medically to a nursing home. Who knows how the court will proceed but I can't imagine any prison would have the kind of medical care he will require for the remainder of whatever time he has left. Obviously he will require a wheelchair and constant attendance."

The operation had taken about eighteen hours or thereabouts. Doc Kitchen was expressing his appreciation to Dr. Hall and thanking the rest of the folks for assisting when, right as he was rolling his surgical gown into a ball and tossing it into the clothes bin, she walked in.

Janice E. McGarrity, M.D. had just completed her residency in internal medicine at Pennsylvania Hospital, after having graduated top in her class from Hahnemann Medical College. She'd been look-ing for a place to open an office when she happened on a magazine article talking about the need for more doctors in Eastern Kentucky. In not too long of a time, Janice had packed what little she'd let herself have and made her way to Paintsville. Dr. McGarrity set up an office just down the road from the hospital and had privileges before just about anyone'd realized that a woman doctor had hung out her shingle. When Doc Kitchen saw Doc McGarrity walk into the room, he said, "Jesus," and then thinking quickly, he thought, *she has hair the color of spun honey.*

"*Who* in *God's name* cut this man in half?" she said, demanding an answer. Raising his head from adding a suture to one of Felix's suppurating wounds, Doc Kitchen said he most certainly was the one and what business was it of hers, *if* he might ask. Her response was terse and without apology, saying that anyone in their right mind would have let the poor man die. "Jesus Christ," she said with even more indignity. "If he lives through the next few weeks, not to mention the next few days, he will need a lifetime of care."

This is a hell of a way to meet someone, Doc Kitchen thought. "For the benefit of the doubt, I don't know who the hell you are, who you think you are or where you're from but wherever that is, and it has taken me some time to figure this out too, things are done differently down here. It's just not the way things are done up north. And, given that you don't have an accent, I know sure as hell you're not from around these parts. Die or lose half of himself, he chose to let one half of himself die and half of himself live."

Doc McGarrity walked over to poor Felix and began looking him over, bending down about as close as she could get, examining the way the flaps were tucked and sewed and how the drains were placed and draining the way drains were supposed to drain.

Doc McGarrity looked up at Doc Kitchen. "You did beautiful work. This procedure has only been done a few times, most patients don't even make it off the table, remarkable… I'm Janice McGarrity."

"I'm Moses Kitchen."

And so, what would become a lifetime of doing the *remarkable* together had just begun.

Chapter 18

Ox was disconcernated. He'd just gotten himself a beatin' from Tough Tony's tongue, that'd said that he'd heard this Doc Kitchen'd just did some kind of surgery that'd hardly ever been done before and now folks'd be looking at him like he was a somebody. And, *nobodies* who become *somebodies* can cause a lot of ruckus, when they have no business doing so. Tough Tony in no uncertain terms told Ox that it was his job to make sure that Doc Kitchen didn't get too big for his britches. He'd been draggin' miners in to use that goddamn breathing machine and now with all this notoriety he might be taken more seriously. Ox stupidly couldn't stop himself from correcting Tough Tony and up and saying, "Well, it wouldn't be *notoriety* because that'd mean that Doc Kitchen'd was *notorious* like Jesse James or the like."

Well, bein' corrected that way didn't sit well with Tough Tony, who uncurled his tongue about to the point where it leapt out of his accusin' mouth. Telling Ox that if he *ever* so much as questioned him again, much less engage in any correcting of him, then "I'll smash you like a goddamn pumpkin on Hell night."

Poor Ox thinkin' that he'd just been conversing hadn't done one bit of figurin' on what words may have come from his mouth, he was just jawn' or so he thought, not meanin' to get on the wrong side of Tough Tony. But from that point on, Ox took that admonishin' as a lesson and began figuring on each and every word before speakin', especially any words at all to Tough Tony, figurin' that you could likely sharpin' an ax on top of his head. It weren't likely that if Tough Tony got something stuck in his craw it sure wasn't going to be dislodged anytime soon. So, it'd be best Ox figured again that he mind his Ps & Qs.

Chapter 19

It DIDN'T TAKE LONG before Doc McGarrity and Doc Kitchen were doin' this and that together, most especially enjoying picnickin' right over around Jenny Wily State Park. Doc Kitchen had grown up climbing Haystack Mountain in the Boulder Range near Butte while Doc McGarrity was used to taking long hikes in the back hills of Fairmont Park, there in Philadelphia.

It was just a few days after Doc Kitchen and Doc McGarrity began wooing each other that they were driving right in front of Jones-Preston Funeral Parlor which sat right next to the First United Methodist Church there on Main Street. As they passed the establishments Janice began yellin' for Moses to pull over right then and right there. With equal enthusiasm she said, or Moses thought he heard her say, "*Look* paperweights, paperweights!" Not knowin' Janice too awful well Moses figured that everyone had proclivities for this and that and it seemed that one of Janice's was paperweights. Maybe she collected them, he thought. Then when Moses pulled over, Janice leapt from the car and dashed right into Patty Peter's Pretty Petunia Flower Shop, which was right after the ally way beside the Methodist Church. Moses sauntered into the flower shop behind Janice, looking this way and that for paperweights with none being anywhere to be seen. He walked over to Janice, who was looking at some bulbs in a bag sittin' on a table top.

"Where are the paperweights?" he asked.

"What did you *say*?" Janice asked back.

"Paperweights, I don't see any paperweights and I figured you must like paperweights to be taken over by such excitement."

Janice started laughing about as hard as anyone had ever had a laugh in their whole life. "You're going to make me wet my pants."

Moses' eyes caught a glimpse of one of the bagged bulbs sitting right behind Janice. *PAPERWHITES*, it read. And in that moment, Janice's laughter stopped, they looked into each other's eyes and their lips for the first time tenderly met.

They soon became inseparable, backing each other up on call with Janice now joining Moses in his research on black lung disease.

It also wasn't long until Doc Kitchen and Doc McGarrity showed up at the mine, watching the miners climb onto the rubber conveyor belt, belly first while the boss man tossed his lunch pail onto his back as he was hauled into the dark depths of the hole. Miner after miner, lunch pail after lunch pail, their jaws chewin' chaw because there's no smokin' in the mines, "not unless you want to kill us all, you stupid sonofabitch…" the boss man'd say sometimes to the boys going underground for the first time. Some of the boss men would slip a slice or two of Ready Rubbed Ripe Old Kentucky Plug into the young men's hands to get them by till their shifts were done. Most of the boys began smoking somewhere around eleven or thereabouts, so their need for a smoke, by the first time they went down into the earth's bowels, could be a mighty one.

When Doc Kitchen and Doc McGarrity had seen the men going down they were about as clean as a man could ever get himself to be after minin' coal. But when the miners came back up and the first gust of warm air hit them as they emerged from the hole, whirlwinds of black freckled slag bestrewed off the miners like dust devils being spawned in a freshly harvested potato field. Doc Kitchen right then looked at Doc McGarrity and said, "The Devil's in the dust."

Chapter 20

IT WASN'T LONG AFTER Doc Kitchen and Doc McGarrity had come back from watching the miners at the mine when Doc McGarrity got a call to come to the emergency room. It seemed as though Cornelius Slaughter, a pig farmer, had been getting ready to butcher up a hog, having straddled its back, and gotten ready to shove his stickin' knife into the sow's neck, when that damn pig reared up like it was a horse that'd just been ankle bit by a snake, throwin' old Cornelius right into the side of the barn. Well, it weren't the pigs neck that'd gotten stuck but somehow or other that Stickin' knife, not even bein' all that sharp and all, had twisted in Cornelius' hand and come down right where his thumb met up with his forefinger, leaving them both dangling by what was left of his hands innards. And as bad luck may have it, that sow went runnin' up into the hills never to be seen again. Cornelius' wife, Trudy, havin' been raised by a family of drinkers and had married Cornelius when she was just turning twelve or thereabouts to get away from their heathenism, had been knocked on her bottom side by the pig when it made its escape from being destined for the scalding pot. Figurin' that wasn't right and all she went lookin' for Cornelius and sure enough found him wrappin' his hand in his neckerchief, stretching it as tight as could be to get the bleedin' stopped. Trudy went and got the flatbed and took Cornelius on over to the hospital, where it was figured that likely Doc Kitchen or Doc McGarrity might be the only ones who might not have to amputate and take away Cornelius' lively hood.

When Doc McGarrity showed up she began unwrapping Cornelius' hand. Old Cornelius being the way he was and all started getting persnickety and said he didn't want no damn nurse doing what a doctor should be doin'. Doc McGarrity said she was a doctor and all and if he didn't behave himself he'd likely lose his damn fingers and get blood poisoning to boot. There was likely hog blood on the stickin' knife and the bacteria had already gotten into his blood stream. So, he should shut up and "hopefully" live or keep on making a ruckus and for sure die. Figurin' what'd be best, Cornelius went on and figured for the better to do as he was told and kept quiet.

Doc McGarrity worked long into the night until she was sure that she had reattached as best she could this tendon and that nerve, but said hand surgery is something that requires a special skill so she'd done the best she could. She figured it'd be best to give Cornelius a shot more of Lidocaine to help with the pain that he'd be sure to be feeling once the last shot had worn off.

Doc McGarrity bent over to position the needle just where she wanted it in Cornelius' hand. As she was about to give the injection, she tucked her rear end outside the curtain, when at that very moment Ox was strolling by. And being the imperturbable soul that Ox was and consumed with self-possession, he smacked Doc McGarrity's bottom side. In but an instant Doc McGarrity spun around like she'd been sittin' atop a top. The curtain flung wide and Ox thinking that he'd been affirmed in his affections reached out to take hold of whatever he could take hold of and in his eagerness he misfigured that Doc McGarrity was having none of his shenanigans. When Ox's hand came forward toward her breast she grabbed his wrist and injected 100mg of Lidocaine directly into his arm. "If you *ever* touch me or any of the nurses here again, I'll cut your hand off. Oh, and, your arm will be useless for a couple of hours…"

He stood stunned and looked cockeyed at Doc McGarrity, feeling his right arm rapidly going numb. The nurses who saw what had happened were snickering at the humiliated Ox, whispering among themselves. It'd be all over the hospital soon. Poor Ox had to use his right arm to rub along the walls as a way of making up for the loss of his right eye, and *now* he had to turn his head hard to one side so he could see right with his left eye. Never sayin' so much as one word, Ox made his way out the emergency room door, got as best he could in his car and sat there until his arm came back to life, rubbin' what had grown to be an awful kink in his neck.

Cornelius would be in the hospital for a while but, thanks to

Doc McGarrity, he wouldn't lose his hand. But later on he would discover that the stickin' knife never felt as sure in his grip as before. So, figurin' on that, Cornelius decided that it'd be best if he went about just farming and keeping Trudy as happy as he could, bein' now that he saw himself as a cripple and all. He thought to himself that he looked like he had a claw instead of a hand and he wasn't sure how a pretty young thing like Trudy'd be wantin' much to do with him in the marital bed as she had before. *Well, time will do the tellin'*, he thought.

Chapter 21

Doc Kitchen and Doc McGarrity joined their practices and unless something came along that required their attention other than the black lung, they pretty much did most of their figuring on that. "It's a dirty sonofabitch" Doc Kitchen said, "and there's not a damn thing we can do to help these men except put them in an oxygen tent."

"Hell, even the goddamn UMW kisses the mine bosses' asses," Doc McGarrity furthered.

Miner after miner came in, sat down in front of the spirometer and blew as best he could and miner after miner left barely able to get himself enough air to walk out the door.

A few of the men would wince when they had to move this way or that. Always the older ones, 'ancient,' they would say when they talked about themselves. One miner, Delbert Delbart, who was, he said, "Eighty something or there about, but I figure that's close enough for any man," walked bent either to the left or to the right but never straight up and down. Even when he shifted from east to west or west to east havin' crossed over north, his face'd all curl up like he'd just took himself a gulp of spoiled milk.

Doc Kitchen saw his consternation and asked him did he have a case of the rheumatism? "Na, it ain't nothin' I ain't been livin' with mostly now for oh seventy some odd years, guess it be." Then Delbert Delbart undid his shirt. The finger-thick welts on his back looked like leeches that had boroughed and died under his skin. Some of the welts hitched up while others lived alone. Every time he moved, they sprawled out like they had a pulse of their own and were tryin' to kick the other off his back. "Bein' a breaker boy when I was a youngin' an all, the boss man used to whip us something awful. You miss a hard lump here or there and they'd beat you within an inch of your life. Daddy, he worked down the hole, I, like most of the youngins, was too young to do minin' but we needed the scrip. They got machines to break the coal up now so boys don't get the beatins like we used to."

It was right about that time that Doc McGarrity walked into the room and saw the mess that was Delbert Delbart's back. "*Jesus Christ*," she said.

It was relentless, each and every miner who came to see Docs Kitchen and McGarrity showed the same thing. Even boys they'd see brought in'd be complaining of not having the breath they should have had for playin' or helpin' their momma and daddy out with chores and all.

Doc Kitchen talked to Dr. Hall, sayin' that for the most part, other than accidents, cancer and heart disease, black lungs were all he and Doc McGarrity were seeing. And even the cancers and heart disease were likely caused by being exposed to coal and coal dust. Dr. Hall was sympathetic as always but said that until the mine bosses got behind them and stopped saying that black lung was a figment of the imagination, "Well, there really isn't much that can be done, except to keep doing what we've been doing now going on fifty years or more, which isn't much.

"Hell, even the study done by Dr. Meriwether back in 1928 or thereabouts was *never* published. The Bureau of Mines buried it. I got it because my wife's cousin was married to the second cousin of Dr. Meriwether's wife and she mentioned at Easter dinner having a copy of the study and gave it to me when I was an intern.

"I heard tell that Ox's been told by Tough Tony that you all'd better be minding your p's and q's. I don't like Tough Tony and wish Ox would have never tied the hospital to him by taking his money. You know Tough Tony was born out there where you hail from, Montana, long before you though."

Doc Kitchen asked what the title of the study was.

Dr. Hall answered, "Silicosis and Tuberculosis Among Miners of the Tri-State District of Oklahoma, Kansas and Missouri. There have been other studies, as you well know, but this was the first *organized* study and because its findings didn't fit what they wanted it to say, and the miners who were part of the study were for the most part

Negros, so the Bureau of Mines just put it in a drawer and it never saw the light of day. Perhaps there is something in there that will help you and Dr. McGarrity, even if the information is outdated it may still provide you all with a path forward."

Before too long Dr. Hall had given Doc Kitchen the study. He and Doc McGarrity read it together and were not surprised by the findings. The miners all had black lung or what they called silicosis. It was the medical term and it sounded better than the black lung. Miners didn't care about the medical name, they only cared that they couldn't breathe.

Chapter 22

TOUGH TONY WAS GETTIN' more outraged by the day. He'd talked till he was blue in the face to Ox and it just wasn't sinkin' into his thick skull. It was like he had rocks in his head, not understandin' *who* Tough Tony was and all.

Tough Tony was a son of a bitch and anyone who knew anything at all knew that. He'd been born in the old Bald Butte mining camp somewhere around the turn of the century and'd grown up about as rough as rough can be. As soon as he was able to swing a pick axe, he picked one up, hauled his self, right behind his daddy, into the gold mine and began swingin'. It was said that there wasn't one man who didn't carry as much fear of Tough Tony as they ever lugged gold up from the hole. He'd get his bowels in an uproar and hit you right up the side of the head with a shovel or plant the tip of that ax right between your shoulder blades. Tough Tony'd rant and rave about this and that, but no matter what, he wouldn't get you from the front, he'd always come up behind you when you weren't lookin'. But one thing was for certain, he'd *always* get you if he thought you'd done him wrong.

He worked himself up in the UMW. After the much-loved president, Tommy Kennedy, passed on, Tough Tony took it over, lock, stock and barrel. He was hated by just about every miner that'd ever swung a mattock. But none dared challenge much of anything he said or did, until Joey Yablonski came along. Tough Tony figured it had to be made known that challenging him weren't something he'd up and tolerate, so he hired a couple of dumb ass thugs and they shot Joey, his wife and youngin' right in their own beds. Cowards that they were, killed them that night turnin' their dreams into nightmares.

The only thing Tough Tony wanted was to kiss the asses of the mine bosses and owners, who saw to it that he was handsomely rewarded with just about anything a man could want, except *respect* that is. And now, it was lookin' like Ox had gotten on the bad side of Tough Tony and sure as could be that wasn't likely to have an outcome that anyone could call good.

There was to be an understanding that if Tough Tony told Ox to jump, well, like it is said, he would say, "How high?"

Chapter 23

IT WASN'T LONG BEFORE Doc Kitchen had brought Doc McGarrity home for Spencer Duty, Jr. to meet and in an odd way give his blessings. It certainly wasn't an expectation but growing up without his daddy, it was something that Doc Kitchen wanted. Doc McGarrity was charming and tearful when she said that her momma and daddy had been killed in a car crash, both at the same time when she was just a youngin', then havin' been reared up in a place called Shawn Acres. There'd been a plaque on the wall that said that *Shawn* meant 'God *is* Gracious,' but there certainly was nothing gracious about that damn place, she'd say. And the only acreage was taken up by building after building of cold, dank, broken-down domiciles. Each one was kept to order by a house mother who Doc McGarrity, right before she ran away, replaced her secreted box of chocolates with laxatives. As she made her way up to the road from the orphanage, she imagined the old bitch eating one laxative right after the other and then shitting herself as she tried her best to make it to the only toilet in the dormy that had any heat.

Doc McGarrity figured that if she ever got caught, they'd beat her within an inch of her life, so at sixteen, she lied about her name until she became of legal age. She stayed put at the edge of Newton, about a hundred miles or so from the home for lost girls, in an abandoned farm house that sat right on a fork of Neshaminy Creek. That way she could get water and keep herself cleaned up. Most of the time she had her only meal at Council Rock High School where she had registered, saying that her mother was so infirmed she couldn't come with her to sign the admitting papers, but she'd be sure and take them home to her. She brought them back the next day. None was the wiser.

Doc McGarrity graduated top in her class. It wasn't long after that she took her birth certificate, that she'd taken with her from Shawn Acres, and had her real name put on her diploma. Then she went onto Bucks County Community College, Hahnemann University and then finally was accepted into Hahnemann Medical School. It had been a long journey but one she was proud of and felt none the worse for wear.

It wasn't until Doc McGarrity began talking with Spencer Duty, Jr. that Doc Kitchen learned where she'd come from and what she'd had to endure. If there was ever a woman that Spencer Duty, Jr. would have picked for Moses, then it was Janice.

Chapter 24

EACH AND EVERY DAY the Ox was gettin' a call from Tough Tony demanding to know if he'd taken care of the problem yet. And each day he'd say it was more likely there'd be repercussions if he didn't get something done sooner rather than later. Doc Kitchen and Doc McGarrity were going around now giving talks to miners and takin' black lungs from the dead around with them to hold up and prove their point. Why Doc McGarrity'd even had the gall to take a piece of dried-up lung that looked like toast that was supposed to be brown but was in fact as black as black can be, and crush it between her fingers, making it look like her hand was spuing coal dust. Hell, sometimes she'd even blow on it. Tough Tony'd say that the goddamn miners'd just sit there with their goddamn mouths hangin' open, lookin' about as stupid as they were in the first place. But, "goddamn it, it just weren't goin' to be tolerated anymore," he say.

It was long about nine o'clock or so when the knocking at the front door was gettin' more insistent with each rappin'. Seemed it went from soundin' like the man peddlin' brushes to a man who had lost his patience about something or other.

When Spencer Duty, Jr. answered the door he saw Ox standing on the porch with what wasn't a very happy look on his face. He said he wanted to come in and have a few words. Doc Kitchen and Doc McGarrity were at the hospital and likely would be all night, fixen' up Houston S. Elmore's broken bones. Seems he got to whippin' his lame brood mare who, on that particular occasion'd had just about enough. When Houston went around behind her, readying one more lash with the leather strap, Oakey, even though her sight was slighted by the fly mask, decided it was time to do some dishen' out of her own and kicked Houston just about damn near to death. When Willadean, Houston's wife, found him, she said she saw Archangel Michael standin' over him waitin' for him to take his last breath.

It was well known that Houston used to beat Willadean with just about the same ferocity as he beat Oakey, so when she saw him there, breathin' more shallow than a creek flows in winter, she stroked Oakey's withers and waited right along with the Archangel Michael. She waited and she waited but Houston's goddamn breaths wouldn't stop coming, short as they were. Figuring the Christian thing to do was to call for an ambulance, so she did. When he got to the hospital, they called on Doc Kitchen and Doc McGarrity to set this bone and that but first to unwrap Houston's ribs from squeezing his heart so tight that his breathin' sounded like a wheezin' mule.

After Ox had gone on and on about Houston and said that he prayed up to the good Lord for his savin' graces, he told Spencer Duty, Jr. that he'd *better* be doing something about Doc Kitchen and Doc McGarrity or else word was that they'd be lookin' for someone to fix *them* up.

The only thing that Spencer Duty, Jr. asked was who might bring the havoc that Ox spoke of down on those that he loved more than life itself. Ox was not a brave man, big yes, brave no. So, in that moment where he had to figure on Spencer Duty, Jr.'s question, he puffed up his chest and said that likely he'd be the one who'd call forth the thunder to bring harm to Doc Kitchen and Doc McGarrity.

Spencer Duty, Jr. nodded and motioned for Ox to follow him into the kitchen. He pulled the percolator out and began fixing up some coffee. Ox sat down at the table, resting his jowls in the smooth palms of his thick hands, waiting for Spencer Duty, Jr. to express his distress at Ox's threat and serve on up the coffee that he no doubt saw himself as deservin'. Just that afternoon Spencer Duty, Jr. had been planting roses in his back garden. Standing in the corner was his shovel.

The last thing that Ox remembered before feeling the back of the peat covered blade of the shovel crack his skull was Alka, just that mornin' tellin' him that her daddy'd always said that he'd amount to nothin'. Spencer Duty, Jr. hadn't spent a lot of time figurin' about killing Ox with the shovel. But he did know that if a man comes callin' and threaten' that there are only two ways for it to end. Whoever he is doin' the threatenin' is either goin' to do what he'd said he come to do or he wasn't going to get the chance and Ox's fate was hindmost from what he'd been set on doin'.

The old Princess Elkhorn Coal Company had closed up mining operations around Van Lear, not far from Paintsville about 1937 or thereabouts. Spencer Duty, Jr. used to play up around one of the old closed down mine portals that'd been sittin' now forever and a day. He rolled Ox out the back kitchen door, pushed him over the concrete wall and right into the back of his truck, for sure makin' the springs groan when Ox bounced onto the bed. He covered him with a canvas tarp, took him on up to the mine portal, backed up and shoved him through the hole. There'd been some debris build up since he was a boy so he had to take a pry bar to get Ox movin' on down the shaft.

When he freed him from the fallen lumber and rocks, Ox went tumblin' down more than 200 feet until Spencer Duty, Jr. heard him splash into the water that had flooded in from this way and that, mixin' with the arsenic and acid saturated coal dust. Even with his fat and all, it wouldn't be long before Ox was dissolved down to nothin', bones and all.

Chapter 25

Doc Kitchen and Doc McGarrity announced with the help of Dr. Hall that they were going to have a miners' meeting about the black lung. The only problem was where to have it that would likely hold all those folks who'd show up. The school said "no," they couldn't use the gymnasium, saying it wasn't that they didn't want to be cooperatin' but someone might fall off the bleachers and get hurt and all. The hospital had a meeting room but the board thought it wasn't such a good idea to be looking like it was buttressin' Doc Kitchen and Doc McGarrity's black lung rabble rousin' especially with so many of the mining companies boss men sitting on the hospital board and not one church stepped forward to offer up their sanctuary, mostly saying that it was reserved for preaching and receiving the Word of God. With each letter of refusal Doc McGarrity sent a printed up '*Thank you*' note for their consideration. In each note she wrote,

> *Dear Pastor _____, Thank you for your consideration of allowing Doctor Kitchen and myself to use your Holy conse-crated sanctuary for presenting and discussing the debilitating and life-threatening effects of Black Lung disease, also known as the miners' curse. In our pursuit of a place to present real medical information to those afflicted with this horrible disease we have been privileged to encounter these Words of Jesus from Matthew, 14:27:31.*
>
> *But straightway Jesus spake unto them, saying, Be of good cheer; it is I; be not afraid. And Peter answered him and said, Lord, if it be thou, bid me come unto thee on the water.*
>
> *And he said, Come. And when Peter was come down out of the*

*ship, he walked on the water, to go to Jesus. But when he saw the
wind boisterous, he was afraid; and beginning to sink, he cried,
saying, Lord, save me. And immediately Jesus stretched forth his
hand, and caught him, and said unto him, O thou of little faith,
wherefore didst thou doubt?*

Thank you again for your consideration,
Janice McGarrity, M.D.

It was but a few days after Doc McGarrity sent off her thank you's
that Rev. J.H. Burton of the First United Methodist Church, right
there on Main Street, sittin' next to Jones and Preston's funeral home,
came looking for her at the hospital.

It seemed as though he hadn't got her original request and he found
her 'thank you' confusin'. He also said he was the District Director
of Social Concerns for the church. Well, when Doc McGarrity told
him of her and Doc Kitchen's plight and the Black Lung blight that
had been befalling miners for countless years, Rev. Burton said he
couldn't agree more and that following the Word of God was *his*
calling and *not* following the word of the mine bosses. Whatever way
he could help they could for sure count him in.

It didn't take too long until Doc Kitchen and Doc McGarrity had
set up a come to meetin' for the miners and their families. They were
even goin' to be bringin' along a spirometer, and a treadmill figurin'
it'd be easier on the miners if they came to them. Doc McGarrity was
goin' to bring along a box of black lungs too that she'd taken from
the corpses of miners. She had to be careful, bein' sure to pack them
in cotton because they were so brittle.

Rev. J. H. Burton would open the First United Methodist Church
gatherin' hall right up and have the ladies of the church even prepare
a Sunday-go-meetin' supper, taking the cost right out of the church's
general fund. Some of the parishioners weren't so happy about that
but the good Reverend figured again that he was answerin' his call
and if the church decided to move him on along to another church,
well… he figured Jesus had to go from here to there too so he'd be
keepin' in good company. Why the Reverend had even asked the
old maid, Aunt Luna Dimples, to fix the fried chicken, if she'd be
so kind to take a likin' to the idea, of course. In all but the time that
it took a mosquito to nip the neck of a youngin' readyin' to jump

into a creek, Aunt Dimples said she'd be *proud* to do the preparin' of her prize-winnin' fried chicken. Long as no one asked for her secret recipe, mind you, which was known only to her and God, she said, then she sniggered and said, "Well, of course to the chickens too, but they don't do much talkin'."

It was goin' to be quite a day, Rev. Burton said, and praise be to God.

Even though he was the District Director of Social Concerns he so many times felt that it was a title that he was not just deservin'. 'Do this' and 'some of that' but none of it spoke very much to the thises and the thats. But now he felt that he had been called as part of his callin' to help Doc Kitchen and Doc McGarrity. Jesus had carried his ministry to the folks of Galilee and Judea. Even though his preachin' brought forth the Word, he also brought forth food, healin' and love. Reverend Burton had felt for a long time that pastors isolated themselves behind the pulpit and were more afraid of the church board than of the Devil himself.

Rev. Burton announced the meeting in his service the Sunday before and said that he'd be about as appreciative as one could be if folks came out and had *about* as good of a chicken dinner as they'd likely ever had, and when he said just that Aunt Dimples rose from her place in the pew and said "There ain't no *abouts* about it, y'all know it *will be* the *best* fried chicken dinner that God ever let the life of a chicken be taken for. So don't be goin' on about no *abouts*."

Well, Rev. Burton, feelin' humbled, apologized right there from the pulpit and said he meant no disrespectin' whatsoever and he had had Aunt Dimples fried chicken and indeed it *was* the *best* and there was no *abouts* about it, the best fried chicken that'd ever been dipped and fried. Aunt Dimples, satisfied that her reputation had been restored, nodded her head and sat back down.

As he shook the hands of those who had been congregating, Rev. Burton put a handbill in each parishioner's hand and said they needed to post it wherever folks' eyes would read it. And post them they did. There were folks arguin' over who'd seen this or that telephone pole or tree first and pesterin' businesses to put the flyers up in their windows.

It wasn't long until everyone in Paintsville was talkin' about the come-to-meetin'. They all said too that in addition to Aunt Dimples fried chicken there was plannin' to be field peas, collard greens, Dana Lynn Stamper's mash taters and corn bread.

Chapter 26

THAT MORNIN', REV. BURTON asked the Lord what to do, for when he looked out the parsonage window, he saw folks lined up from here to there. Some of those poor men who could barely breathe were bein' held up by their women folk and youngins, weazin' something awful puttin' one foot, barely able to make it, in front of the other. Some that likely wouldn't be alive much longer'd come out for one last meal and socializin', figurin' that at least it'd take a bit off the cookin' and talkin' burden of their wives.

He'd figured that they'd fill the meeting hall but the number of folks that he saw lined up that mornin' *alone* would make it bust at the seams. And, upon his askin' the Lord for guidance, a knock came at his door. When Rev. Burton answered he couldn't believe his eyes. There standin' in front of him was none other than Hazel Dickens and Carl Nelson themselves! *How could this be?* Miss Dickens said she'd heard about the meetin' and her and Carl just happened to be over in Lexington and wanted to come on over and see if they could lend up some music. Well… in that moment Rev. Burton knew that Jesus had tapped him on the shoulder and blessed the comin' of the upcomin' come-to-meetin'. Beyond any doubters who'd done any doubtin', he'd say.

And likely, he thought, the good Lord'd be sittin' Himself, takin' in what'd be some of the best mountain music to ever grace those parts. It was a beautiful sunny day and so he'd have the woman folk bring the eats into the meeting hall and have Doc Kitchen and Doc McGarrity stand up to say what they was going to say and do their tests back in the back right beside the kitchen door.

When he called Doc Kitchen to tell him what God-given graces had befallen, Rev. Burton said he didn't know where all the folks were going to sit. "There on the ground?" he pondered. Doc Kitchen remembered that Spencer Duty, Jr. had a barn full of chairs that he set up when he had company picnics for Dooties Booties. Rev. Burton called Spencer Duty, Jr, who said it would be his honor, and he called Ol Dickens, him bein' no blood to Miss Dickens, mind you.

Folks didn't know to address Ol Dickens as anything else, but it was said when he was a youngin', bein' always as big as a boy could be, he used to slip up behind his daddy and scare the Dickins out of him. Well, the name just stuck and after a while folks just forgot what his God-given name had been, likely he himself too. Ol Dickens'd drove a truck since he'd been able to reach his foot to the pedal, so he used to haul just about everything for folks around Paintsville. It wasn't long before he had those folders stacked up on the back of his flatbed, delivered to the church and opened up for folks to rest their weary rears.

As the day went on, kin and unkin alike were comin' from every which way, north, south, east and west and in between. Aunt Dimples had set up her fryer and was bonin', breadin' and fryin' faster than she'd ever had to bone, bread and fry and folks were comin' back for *sure* for more than one helpin'.

After folks had been fed and were relaxin', they could be heard repeatin' amongst themselves, "That fried chicken sure hit the spot." While another'd pipe up and add, "Those greens and mashed taters sure enough did too."

Rev. Burton said than he wanted to introduce Doc McGarrity, who'd come to talk about the plague of the black lung. Doc McGarrity stood up in front of everyone and said, "Doctor Kitchen and I are here to talk to you about what many of you men are suffering with, day in and day out. We want to ask you to breathe into a tube and walk for a bit on a treadmill for us, because we want to see how your lung function is. Then we're going to take everything that we learn today and put it all together so we have a good idea of cause and effect, and most *importantly*, something we can *prove* and that the mine bosses cannot *disprove*. That is that black lung *exists*. We also want to use what we learn to help you get the benefits that you deserve. If you can help us out, we would surely appreciate it. Doctor Kitchen is set up in the back of the meeting hall. It won't take very long, and while we're doing that Aunt Dimples will be frying up some more chicken."

Back in the kitchen none other than Hazel Dickens herself was cutting up chicken after chicken and helpin' Aunt Dimples with the frying. She was also helping herself to samplin' the *best* fried chicken she'd ever had, noting she'd had "some pretty darn good fried chicken in my time."

Miner after miner lined up and breathed into the spirometer and walked as much as they could on a treadmill. Never before had there been such a sample size of so many miners, who some with what seemed like their last breath gave so freely to not only help themselves, but to also help every other brother miner and their families too.

After the last miner had blowed as much as he could blow, Doc Kitchen and Doc McGarrity went outside and thanked everyone. Then Doc McGarrity took the dried-up lungs out of the box she brought and said, "Folks, this is what Doctor Kitchen and I are trying to prevent," and she took the dried-up lung tissue and crumbled it between her fingers, particles blowing yonder here and yonder there, like coal dust to the wind.

"I want you to know, I didn't do *anything* to that piece of lung tissue except cut it from some poor soul's chest who suffocated from the black lung. Some of you men are so far along with the disease that this is how your lungs look. We're not going to lie to you, there is not much hope. *But* we want to do our part to stop this horrible suffering from happening to those of you who *aren't* that far along. We thank you from the bottom of our hearts. Here is Rev. Burton."

"Folks, just this mornin' I looked out the window and saw y'all linin' up and I said, dear Jesus, help me to know what to do, where am I goin' to put y'all?

"Then, there was a knock at my door and *who* should be standin' there but Miss. Hazel Dickens and Mr. Carl Nelson themselves, sayin' they heard about the upcomin' goins' on and wanted to offer y'all up some music. Lord Jesus, I said, no matter how much I was raised up in my baptism, I will *never* cease to be amazed at how Jesus hears our prayers and delivers us in our times of need."

Miss Dickens then stepped up, bowed her head and said, "Lord God, we're here to offer up our hearts to you sweet Jesus, for carryin' us through these hard times and meetin' You when we feel Your hand touchin' our shoulders callin' us homeward. In Jesus' name we always pray. Amen."

As if the Lord's voice had entered the souls of each and every one sittin', restin' their digestin, a resounding, "AMEN" could be heard echoin' out of the mountain canyons like it was God Himself callin' back to the folks.

A sound like a new wida's grief drew from the draw of Mr. Nelson's bow as Miss Dickens looked out and began…

Black Lung, Black Lung
Don't matter how strong
Black Lung, Black Lung
don't matter how strong

Don't matter at all
It's gonna fill up your lungs

The Black Lung, Black Lung
my brothers in arms
No matter at all
we ain't got too long

The Black Lung, Black Lung
is waitin for me
No matter at all
it's gonna bring me to my knees

The Black Lung, Black Lung
you sonofabitch
You steal our breath in
that goddamn dirty ditch

The Black Lung, Black Lung
You don't give a damn
bout the mouths we feed
much less we can't breathe

Black Lung, Black Lung
Don't matter how strong
Black Lung, Black Lung
don't matter how strong…

And on she sang and sang and sang till the sun had long gone down with the night and her throat was dry as burnt toast.

There was no applause. When Miss Dickens could go on no more, and the rosin had worn too thin to make the strings of the fiddle sing, folks rose up one by one, miners limpin' from the kneecap mange and most gaspin' with the black lung, to walk past Miss Dickens and Mr. Nelson, cuppin' their hands in theirs, thankin' them, offerin' them a bed for the night and the *best damn biscuits and gravy* they'd ever eat for breakfast, "As God is my judge," they'd say. After the last hands had been shaken and the thank yous been said, Miss Dickens and Mr. Hall turned and heard hundreds of folks on their feet clappin' so hard till their hands looked like dried-up dead possum paws. In all of their days of performin' they had never heard anything like it. It went on so long that Miss Dickens stood up and said, "We sure are appreciatin' of y'all puttin' their hands together the way you are and all, but don't wear the skin off y'all's palms showin' your appreciatin'".

Doc Kitchen and Doc McGarrity were about as humbled as humbled could be from witnessin' such a spectacle and Rev. Burton said more "Thank you, Jesus'" than he'd ever said at any one time in all his preachin' days. Looking out on folks, he saw one afflicted miner after another, leanin' against their women and youngins like frail lake reeds strugglin' to stay upright against a fierce wind.

Rev. Burton then prayfully said to himself, "*God grant them rest...*" He wasn't sure if he was askin' God to grant them a reprieve from their agony or to mercifully put them down like a sufferin' dog.

In the back of the meeting hall sat the spirometer, the treadmill and the particulars about each miner's lung, some of whom most likely wouldn't live through the next week.

Chapter 27

TOUGH TONY HAD DRIVEN all the way from Pennsylvania to Paintsville looking for Ox. He'd been watching the goings on with Miss Dickens and Mr. Nelson and was about as fit to be tied as a man could be. He'd told Ox to take care of this before it got out of hand and sure enough he witnessed firsthand how out of hand it could get, not to mention where it'd be goin' from here.

Tough Tony'd always been of the mind that if you want something done right you've gotta do it yourself. And now goddamn Ox, accordin' to the folks Tough Tony'd been in touch with, had just up and disappeared. One day here and the next day not. He'd even gone over and talked to Alka who said Ox'd went out one night and just never came back. Folks'd been talkin' for a month of Sundays about how little Norma Yarborough was. They called her little because she was a midget but came from a good Christian family who was of normal height and all. It was bein' said she and Ox were meetin' up by one of the old mine shafts and having untoward relations but nobody could say for sure.

So, Alka said to Tough Tony, likely was Ox just up and left with Norma, who by coincidence hadn't been seen around for a while now either.

Unbeknownst to Alka though, Norma had been called back to Marrowbone to take care of her daddy, whose mind, which he had been taking leave of, had surely now all but gone. When Tough Tony left Alka he threw open the storm door so hard that it tore it right off its hinges, lettin' a swarm of flies loose in the house. Alka *hated* flies, swattin' them whenever she saw one, but now the whole damn house was filled with them and Alka's life was turned into a living hell. Runnin' from lamp shade to lamp shade, just about wearin' her arms out with all the swattin', she had to do.

Tough Tony, after screamin' at Alka, turned around his car and headed right back to Pennsylvania, cursin' up one side and down the other, slappin' the steering wheel somethin' awful and almost hittin' a cow mindin' his own business, walkin' down the road, that'd come through a downed fence. Rantin' and ravin', "These goddamn ridge runners." He didn't know the difference between a hillbilly and a ridge runner.

Coal company profits had been up 170 or more percent since he'd been president of the UMW. He'd been good to them and they'd been good to him back. There wasn't a woman he was wantin' of and couldn't have, "One way or another," he'd snigger and say. Now these two down in Paintsville were causing him a problem, a problem he thought he'd had taken care of. There were problems seemin' on all sides now. This whole Jock Yablonski thing was heatin' up, goddamn 20,000 fucking West Virginia miners had wildcatted not that long ago, sayin' they thought Tough Tony was the one responsible for Yablonski and his family's murder. He tried his damnedest to convince them otherwise, but they didn't seem to be havin' any of it.

Now with these two doctors down in Paintsville collecting medical evidence about the black lung, Tough Tony's life was in fact getting tough. He'd given Al Pass, who was on the UMW Executive Council, $20,000 he'd embezzled from the pension fund to hire some men to kill Yablonski and his kin. Pass hired Paul Gilly, Aubran Martin and Claude Vealey to break into Yablonski's house, one man for each person and then shoot them all. And that they did.

Tough Tony swore over and over again that he didn't have nothing to do with the killings. Hell, he'd say, he wasn't nowhere near the goddamn murders. But, he sure wasn't sorry that Yablonski was dead. Now the goddamn feds were investigating.

The last thing he needed was to be bothered with this shit going on down in Paintsville.

Chapter 28

SEVERAL OF THE MEN that had given what Doc Kitchen said was their last breath passed away a week or so later after havin' bein' blessed by Miss Dicken's singin' and Mr. Nelson's fiddlin', not to mention Aunt Dimple's fried chicken. One afternoon three died within an hour of each other. Pretty much weezed themselves to death.

Try as they might, they'd suck and suck and suck, sometimes even callin' up what little gumption they could to rise up a bit to see if their chests were blowin' up the way they were supposed to. When they'd see that their breathin' was as plumb as a Totty Tillies flat-chested daughter, well, those poor breathless bastards'd realize that their striven' for respirin' was no more than a labor in vein.

Their women and youngins were right there with them, holdin' their hands wonderin' what Jesus' plan was for makin' their men folk suffer the way they did. Odell Jenkin's little daughter Trula looked at her daddy right before he went on his way and asked if they had mines in Heaven. Her anguish about her daddy goin' away to be with Jesus was one and the same with her frettin' about how her daddy was going to make enough scrip to buy a pig for slaughterin' in the promise land. As he closed his eyes for the last time, Odell heard Trula say, "But Momma, Daddy can't be goin' hungry."

No one complained as their men died off, mind you. They prayed heart and soul that Jesus'd meet each one of them once their last breath was done breathed and if He could find the time, they knew He'd be mighty busy with all the goins' on and all, lead them hand in hand to Heaven, announcin' them upon their arrival. It was best not to upset the Lord with complainin' right before someone's passin', they'd whisper amongst themselves.

One thing the ready to be deceased *insisted* on before they deceased was that they be laid out in their best Sunday-go-to-meetin' clothes. They *for sure* didn't want to meet up with the Lord not properly attired and all. It was important to make sure they'd be properly bathed and shaved after their demise.

Their kin were *always* disconsernated something awful when their beards kept growin' and their fingernails kept gettin' longer after the dead'd been dead for a while. It was not long after he came to Paintsville that Doc Kitchen came by the Dinwiddie's offering his condolence. Dicie Dinwiddie's man, Fish, so called because aside from eatin' Dicie's dumplins, he loved nothin' more in this world than fishin', well, Dicie sat beside the late Fish, lookin' more cleaned up than he'd looked in a month of Sunday's mind you, trimin' his fingernails and frettin' something awful over the fact that she'd just cut them the night *before*. Doc Kitchen told Dicie that Fish's fingernail weren't growin', but that he was gettin' dehydrated, being laid out and all, so his fingertips were drawin' back under his nails, makin' it look like they'd been growin'.

As Doc Kitchen made his way to the door, a few folks nodded their heads. Lookin' back he saw Dicie holdin' Fish's head up and tryin' with all her might to pour a cup of water down his gullet. Figurin' that it'd be best if he didn't say anything, Doc Kitchen went on out the door.

Rarely did the families have enough money saved back to pay for a funeral, although Jones and Preston Funeral home, havin' been servin' Paintsville for so long, gave the miners a little off and let them pay on time.

Mostly though folks just stretched out their men on a layin' out board, which most of the time was an old door that no longer had any hinges lookin' for a door frame to be hung on. Usually, it'd been passed on from one set of kin to the next and leaned against the side of the homeplace until it was needed again, which as the days counted onward it always was. Those whose time had not yet come would spend as much time as needed offering a blessing or two over those whose time had. Sometimes without a proper embalming the jaw'd kept wantin' to open up like the deceased was gettin' ready to up and say something. When it happened the left behind youngins'd go yellin', "Daddy done come back, Momma. Daddy done come back," upsettin' just about everybody within the shot of an ear. So best it was to tie a handkerchief under the chin and over the head to keep the jaw of the departed where it otta be—closed. If it was a sultry Kentucky day, they'd always put a wet towel over the face to keep it lookin' like it should until they could get on with the burial. Of course, they'd take off the handkerchief and wet towel when folks were comin' to walk by, nod and pay their respects. Some families were so damn poor they didn't even have a couple of scrip coins to put on the deceased eyelids to keep them from opening at night, so they had to borrow them from one of the respecters who'd come by, *always* assurin' them they'd get them back just as soon as they lifted whoever it may be into their coffin and nailed down the lid. They also figured that once the pine box was sealed the deceased weren't goin' to know if their eyes were open or not.

If the youngins weren't of the mind to mind that day and left the door standin' open, the smell of the dead'd always bring in whatever stray cat that might be roamin' around. If there wasn't someone payin' attention to the poor stiff, that feline'd jump up and try its best to scratch the eyes right out of the head of the dead.

Chapter 29

THE GATHERING HAD PRODUCED the largest group of facts and figures that had been gathered up about the black lung. Doc Kitchen and Doc McGarrity compiled the findings from over a hundred miners that day, drew up charts that were easy to understand and began going to union halls, churches and schools, just about anywhere that would have them.

"Jesus", Tough Tony'd say, when he heard about the hell they were raisin'. Not to mention the fact that 'Poor Tony' (that's how he like to think of himself) was still havin' to concoct whatever he could about the Goddamn Farmington Mine explosion over in West Virginia. Ninety-nine miners were minin' that day and seventy-eight of them were blown to smithereens. "Jesus!" he'd say whenever it came to mind or he had to figure on a way to work with CONSOL so they didn't have to pay these glorified ditch diggers one goddamn red cent. Likely the best way was to run it through the courts, till the time ran out and then there weren't nothing that could be done. It'd been done before, so he figured it'd best be done again. "Shit!" he'd go on, "They ain't *ever* going to figure out what caused a blast that big, hell, it shook the ground twelve goddamn miles away." And, "If you *can't* figure it, you *ain't* gotta pay for it."

After looking at everything, Doc Kitchen and Doc McGarrity saw that the blood gasses that they'd done that day too showed that there was significant impairment of oxygen transfer and utilization by the muscles because of impaired lung function. Plus, the coal dust made the lungs less elastic, so they couldn't fill up with air, and especially during *anything* physical, most *especially* mining.

It started with a cough, shortness of breath and spitting up black phlegm. Hell, you'd see that in the youngins and sometimes even in the miners' women folk, who'd do their warsh. Then the aches and pains'd get worse along with the tightness in their chests *and* the agony in their bones from swingin' a pick axe all day long. You could always tell when a man was gettin' to the end, when he couldn't talk to you without takin' a breath in between each word he was tryin' his best to say. Wantin' like hell to say something and then not bein' able to finish what he was sayin' because he didn't have the air for the words to take wing on.

With the blood gasses, the treadmill, the spirometer and the x-rays, Doc Kitchen and Doc McGarrity were going to go to the first black lung medical meeting up in Chicago and present what they'd found. Hell, the goddamn government, after all these years, *still* denied benefits for these men and wouldn't hold the coal companies liable for anything. It was about a damn shameful as anything shameful could be.

Chapter 30

EVER SINCE SPUD SPURLING could remember, folks called him Potato Face. He'd been a breaker boy, a mule driver and a miner for about as long as anyone else could remember. Hell, sometimes, he'd been known to just break out in song and wheeze out what he used to be able to sing to those damn mules, as he led them into the hole.

"My sweetheart's the mule in the mines,
I drive her without reins or lines,
On the bumper I sit,
I chew and I spit,
All over my sweetheart's behind…"

He was an *ugly* boy. Potato Face had never grown any whiskers except a sprout of a stubble here and there and had hair that was dry as toast. He was always itchin' and scratchin' so bad that folks'd wondered if he had the mange. But, be all that as it may, he'd been a good boy and an even better man. He'd give you the shirt off his back, folks would say. Potato Face wasn't the kind of man who went around preaching about Jesus *this* and Jesus *that*, but he lived by the Word.

The wet soundin' croakin began early on and just kept gettin' worse and worse until one day when he was down in the hole, just about to tamp a fuse to blow a seam of coal, he took to a coughin' fit. His lungs sounded like the Red Sea was partin' right inside his chest. One of the other miners caught his arm right before the tampin' hammer came down too hard on the back end of the fuse. He was coughin' so bad that his whole body was twistin' this way and that, like he was possessed of the Devil. By the time they got him topside, he'd done died. It wasn't long before he was brought to the hospital for

Doc McGarrity to look inside him. When she cut his chest open, poor Potato Face's lungs were so deflated that they looked like he'd been run over and then, just for good measure, whoever'd run over him came back and ran over him again. "Jesus Christ," she said as she peered inside. "He was so young." That night, she said to Doc Kitchen that no matter how many times she saw the insides of these poor men or tended to them as they passed away, she'd never get used to it. *Never* had she envisioned this kind of life for herself. But now, there was *nothing* that would tear her away.

"They're going to get sick of us, you know," Doc Kitchen said. "We'll be saying the same thing over and over again, and the truth is we will fight this till the day we die and the likelihood is that once we go someone else will have to pick up where we leave off."

Chapter 31

HELEN STRINGFIELD WAS KNOWN just about as far as you could go in any direction for her buttermilk biscuits. They were so light and flakey that it was said that her secret to keeping them from floatin' away when they came right out of the oven was the prayer she said over each batch.

She was about as good a woman as God ever gave a rib to, raisin' her four youngins after her man, Stuart, who was known to be a stutterer and always said, "Statata…urt," when asked his name, was drowned when he jumped into the Big Sandy to save a youngin who he'd never end up knowin'.

Stuart, Helen and their three youngins with one on the way were picknickin' right along the bank of the Big Sandy. Helen had just said to her youngins, "Don't get too close to the edge their girls, it's a been rainin' and the bank is mighty soft." Well, just about that time Stuart saw another man's youngin slip down the muddy bank and fall right in. Without thinkin' a thought, Stuart jumped in, drifted with the current to the middle of the rushin' river and by the grace of God grabbed the little one by the hem of her pretty dress as she flailed by. He swam against the current to get close enough to the bank, where, being a strong man, threw her through the air, landin' her just about in her momma's frettin' arms. And then, poor Stuart was sucked under and taken to his heavenly reward.

Helen figured that there must be a gateway to Heaven somewheres deep in the Big Sandy and that right after Stuart saved the little girl, Jesus tapped him on the shoulder and said it was time to be on his way. She also figured that given as good of a man as Stuart was he'd, unbenounced to him, been set forth on a path to do this one final thing all his life.

It wasn't known until a long time later that that little girl had walked right into the Big Sandy because she was lookin' up to the sky. She'd always had her head up in the stars, her momma and daddy'd say whenever they were asked, why their youngin always was lookin' up toward Heaven. Well, it was a lot later when her little life became a big life bein' that she was one of the scientists who'd build the first telescope that'd fly off into distance galaxies, sending back pictures of God's creation never before seen. *But*, she would sometimes say, that she was still afraid of the water.

Well, when Spencer Duty, Jr., now havin' taken over Dooties Booties from his daddy and momma, heard about Helen's bad fortune and most especially with her havin' one on the way, he said that at least all your youngins won't have to go without shoes in their lives. And from that day forward those girls always had warm shoes on their feet. And when they'd outgrow one size, they'd come right into Dooties Booties and get a bigger pair. But never in the entire time that Dooties Booties was fittin' Helen's youngins' feet with warm shoes were they ever made to feel like they were bein' singled out for charity. They'd come in, get their shoes and the clerk'd put them in a bag and say that he'd put it on their account. That's what Spencer Duty, Jr. had instructed them to say. There wasn't any account, but that way they wouldn't have to be embarrassed around other folks who had enough money to pay.

Helen, figurin' that she had to figure on some way to make ends meet, started sellin' her biscuits. The reknownedness of her biscuits caught on and it wasn't long before folks who'd made their own all their lives just couldn't seem to make biscuits as fluffy and light as Helen's. And so, she was able to provide for her and her youngins, makin' the ends meet right up against each other. She also made sure that each and every Friday there was a warm basket of biscuits on Spencer Duty, Jr's doorstep which, like this morning, he would use to make the best damn biscuits and gravy that ever a man was known to eat.

When he carried the biscuits into the kitchen, he was greeted by a cluckin' sound that said in its own sweet way, "Good morning"

It'd been a snowy February day when Spencer Duty, Jr.'d gone out to the chicken coop to collect the eggs. On his way back to the house he heard behind him a cluckin' that was too close by to be from the coop. When he looked down there was a Rhode Island Red followin' him and just cacklin' away. He bent down, picked the hen up and carried her back to the coop. The next day he went out and found her limpin' this way and that, tryin' her best to get away from the other chickens who were tryin' their best to peck her to death. Her one leg had turned black with frostbite from the snow and was barely hangin' on. He picked her up and carried her back into the house, figurin' that he'd have to put her out of her misery. Instead, in figurin' some more, Spencer Duty, Jr. snipped off her leg thinkin' he might whittle her a wooden stump. He sat her in a box and went onto figurin' how in the world to carve what he'd figured. The next mornin' he looked into the box and saw what he thought was the leg that he'd cut off and had set on the window sill sittin' right there beside her. When he got to lookin' closer, he saw that she'd done lost her other leg.

For sure now he figured her sufferin' was great and it was time to take her head. But the red feathered girl sat right up and clucked away like she still had two good feet, lookin' right eye to eye with Spencer Duty, Jr. So, he went out, got some hay, found a good size box and sat her in it. She pecked around here and there and pretty soon she'd made that box her nest.

Little by little, where she'd lost her feet, thick white nubs grew. And, little by little, Rhoda, what he came to call her, became just about the happiest chicken that'd ever been. Each and every mornin' now for seven years on, Rhoda greeted Spencer Duty, Jr. with the sweetest chortle that'd ever been sung. When the weather warmed he'd take her out to the garden where she'd dash here and there on her nubs, peckin' bugs and occasionally even layin' an egg. She stayed in a box right in the kitchen and loved just about more than anything to get the trimins' of whatever Spencer Duty, Jr. happen to be fixin' up.

That mornin' Spencer Duty, Jr. cut one of the biscuits in two, leaned down and gave half to Rhoda. It was hard to say who loved Helen's biscuits more, but for sure it couldn't be denied that Rhoda smelled the wafting aroma and let it be known she was sure ready for her mornin' treat. As he began to stand up, Spencer Duty, Jr. felt like a hod of bricks had fallen on his chest and his left arm weighed so much right then that he couldn't even lift it up. He looked at Rhoda, who for some reason or other had stopped enjoyin' her biscuit and become as quiet as could be, not uttering a cluck. Then, much to the momentary dismay of Spencer Duty, Jr., he realized what was happening. He reached out to Rhoda one last time, gently touched her comb and collapsed onto the floor. Rhoda left her box, curled herself up against Spencer Duty, Jr., and began softly pecking him, tryin' to get him to wake up. But as he had done for her now many years ago, she, try as she might, couldn't give Spencer Duty, Jr. back his life.

It was later that afternoon when Doc Kitchen and Doc McGarrity arrived and found Spencer Duty, Jr's body. Rhoda was still sitting against him and began clucking when she heard the kitchen door open. There was no reason to try and bring him back, he'd simply been dead too long.

Moses sat down beside him and placed his head against his father's and began crying. He had been fortunate to have discovered his father and cherished the time they had had together. But, always he would say, it was not long enough. Janice sat beside Moses, gently caressed his back and wept.

She too had come to know Spencer Duty, Jr. as a father, one she had never had. A generous, kind man, who had welcomed her like a daughter. They also knew he would do whatever it took to protect those he cared for. Janice had moved in with Moses not long after he discovered what paper whites were. They shared for the most part the top floor of the big house that Spencer Duty, Jr. offered to Moses when he came to Paintsville.

Folks talked. "They're shackin' up," they'd say. That kind of thing sure wasn't too well accepted in Paintsville, and for a while it was more the subject of conversation at the barber shop and at the ladies' mornin' coffee rumorin' than Doc Kitchen and Doc McGarrity's doctorin'. But, as the days passed and other folks' troubles and the peculiarity of their lives made for a disclaimin' of their own, Doc Kitchen and Doc McGarrity's livin' arrangements faded away like a direful cloud that the cleansin' breath of the Lord'd blown to the wind.

Word spread far and wide about Spencer Duty, Jr's passin'. Johnny Chandler, the mayor of Paintsville, even proclaimed the day of his death as Spencer Duty, Jr. day.

It'd been just a few weeks before that Spencer Duty, Jr. had told Doc Kitchen and Doc McGarrity that when his time came that there was a shoebox at the back of his closet that they should open. Doc

McGarrity wondered if he'd had a premonition about his coming passing. After his body had been taken to Jones and Preston's Funeral Home and after a few hours had passed in the disparate quietude of the house, Doc Kitchen and Doc McGarrity went to Spencer Duty, Jr's bedroom and found the shoebox. Folded on top was a letter addressed to Moses.

> *Dear Son,*
>
> *The most important thing for me to say is that you could have decided to never come looking for me and to be angry because I wasn't a part of your life. I am most thankful that you didn't do that and that you bear no grudge for Eleanor not telling you about me. And, I too do not bear any grudge for her not telling me about you. She did what she thought was best for the three of us and for that I have nothing but respect and admiration. Your mother was the most extraordinary woman I ever knew. She was tough and yet knew how to carry herself in a way that her toughness didn't take over her life. And, she was brilliant and beautiful. I deeply regret that you and I did not know each other in your growing up years, but I am blessed that we have had this time to get to know each other and in our own way, become father and son. I also want you Janice to know that if I ever had a daughter, it would be you. The joy of seeing you and Moses together day after day opened a new chapter in my life, one that I never imagined. My hope for the two of you is that you choose to marry. I know that you do not hold to any particular faith and are skeptical of the Lord's love but I remember my daddy and momma telling me that one Christmas Eve, not long before they became husband and wife, going out to the barn at midnight. There the pigs and the cows were leaning down with their heads bowed giving thanks, right before the stroke of midnight. My daddy and momma weren't ones to make up such things so I figured there must be something to what they said and I gave the Lord a place in my life. I have never regretted that I did. For some reason I thought I'd pass along that story and maybe it will have the same effect on y'all that it did me. Moses, I know that your mother left you some money and that as a doctor your future is sound. I am leaving the house and all of my belongings to you. Janice, I know that medical school is*

expensive and know that you must still be dogged by debt, therefore, whatever your debts are from medical school will be taken care of and money set aside for you to have a good financial foundation for your future. If you and Moses combine things you will never have to want for anything.

DOOTIES BOOTIES has made me a wealthy man. Most of the employees have been with the company for many years. Mrs. Applewhite is still fitting shoes on youngins and is so old that her bones creak and crack each time she bends down to do a measuring. She began working for Daddy and Momma and stayed on through thick and thin. Many of the folks have been that way. I know that you do not want to be running a shoe business so what I want to do is for Dooties Booties to become employee owned, in essence leave the business to them. The oldest employee getting the most and the newest the least, but everyone getting some part. If they decide to sell the business outright then that is their decision and they can split things up however they decide. But those folks could all have a good future should they decide to keep things going as they are and even expand in the future. The folks at Porter, Banks, Baldwin & Shaw have my will.

I have already spoken to Dr. Hall, and there has been money set aside for a new wing to be built at the hospital, specifically to research black lung disease. It will be the first of its kind that is part of a rural hospital. It is to be called "_The Moses Kitchen and Janice McGarrity Research Center for Black Lung Disease._" You and Janice will be the directors and there will be money dedicated to whatever you need to run the center. I have learned a great deal being in business all of these years and now is the time to put it to the best use that I can think of. It will be hard to say that black lung doesn't exist if it has its own research center. The last thing is that when your mother wrote me and told me about you, she also sent a lock of her hair. It is at the bottom of the shoe box. Moses, above all else, put her lock of hair in the pocket of my shirt when you bury me. I don't want to go into the afterlife, whatever that may be, without a part of Eleanor being with me. I can only pray that once the last breath has left my body that I will feel her hand reaching out to take mine.

I don't think there is much you will have to do. The lawyers *know how to set everything up. Yet, there is but one final thing. Should you not agree with any part of my plans you have one week to tell the lawyers and everything will go to you and you can decide to do whatever you see fit with what I have left behind.*

My dear Moses and Janice, farewell. Know that my love for you is endless and everlasting.

All my love, Dad

Chapter 32

MOSES AND JANICE SAT on the edge of the bed, squeezed by the grief of Spencer Duty, Jr's death on one side and what he had written on the other. Dr. Hall had just told them that morning that Tough Tony had been indicted for embezzling from the UMW and that likely folks doing work on black lung would be able to get on with their work without having to be worryin' about him and his goons. Funny, Dr. Hall also said, "Alka, try as she might, just can't explain where Ox went off to. She first thought he'd run off with little Norma Yarborough, but found out later that she'd up and gone to tend to her daddy, who'd lost his mind. She figured, I guess, that she'd try and help him find it. But that poor woman just can't explain how Ox just up and disappeared on her. Well, truth be known though, folks are sayin' she's better off without him."

A funeral is something that mostly folks go to, say and nod their good byes and then are on their way. The daily dead get remembered for a bit of a while but the sad fact is the remembrances don't last long. There was one fellow though, Manford Bunyard, who'd been known to be just about the biggest collector of license plates ever known anywhere. It was said that the family of Frederick Tudor, who everyone knows was issued the first U.S. license plate, "1" in 1903, gave Manford that plate for his collection after Frederick's demise.

When he went to license plate conventions, Manford would proudly bring it along for others to see, and truth be known, covet. Not being one to care well for himself, Manford succumbed to the sugar after losing his teeth and both feet, pretty much givin' up what little will he had left. Sayin' there was only so much a man could take and only so many mashed taters a man could eat, he passed away the very night he was to be given the Best Plate Plaque for acquiring a 1921 Alaska, with just a touch of rust, that he'd found nailed to a barn wall. Well, he didn't have no specifications for his burial, but his wife, Essie Bunyard, figured the best way to honor his accomplishments was to have Manford's brother, Tobe, build a pine box covered top to bottom in license plates. Mourners came from far and wide to pay their respects and to walk around Manford's coffin, bowin' their heads and takin' in the pageantry of the plates. Even though Manford passed on now many a year ago, when folks drive by the Old Town Cemetery they acknowledge a remembrance of Manford and his license-plate-covered coffin.

Spencer Duty, Jr. was laid out in a simple knotty pine casket, a grey suit and a tuff of red hair tucked away in his shirt pocket. When Moses touched his mother's cutting, he remembered the last time, moments before she died, that he brushed her hair off her forehead, her breathing becoming more shallow with each breath, her eyes fluttering, until she gasped, took in one more breath and then her chest collapsed, never to rise again. The cancer had been brutal. Her doctor had told her the best thing she could do was to die with dignity. Eleanor told him to go to hell, saying *"No one, no one* dies with dignity. That's for the oglers, not wanting the doomed to make them uncomfortable for what awaits them."

Not one of the folks from Dooties Booties failed to come and show their respect. They didn't even know of their good fortune yet. Then there was the parade of shoes. Men, women, boys and girls all showed up in spit and polished shoes that they'd got from Dooties Booties. Thelma Mahen, who was in her eighties now or upwards thereabouts, got her very first pair of shoes from the original Dooties Booties Trust that Spencer Duty, Jr's daddy and momma had set up after Spencer Duty had snatched up the ruby clutch that Mr. LaViers', the CONSOL enforcer from way back when, haughty wife had been clutching when Doc Kitchen's granddaddy, Moses Kitchen the first, and Spencer Duty had burned down his big white house by the river and ran him and the rest of his kind out of town. There'd been so many rubies on that clutch that it made sure every boy and girl in Van Lear had gotten shoes, when many of them had never had none.

Well, Thelma Mahen had just come into her teen years and had only ever had burlap wrap for her feet, up until then. And on that day back when all the children were fitted, she walked out of school feelin' so tall she had to duck her head so as not to bump into a cloud. The least she could do, she figured, was to pay her respects wearing the same pair of shoes that she credited with changin' the course of her life.

Thelma had kept them for that long sittin' on her kitchen window sill as a reminder that she was going to make something of herself. "By God," she'd say, "that's what I did," going into the army, getting trained as a nurse, serving at the front in the war, patching up soldiers as best she could and then coming back to Paintsville and working at the hospital. The morning of Spencer Duty, Jr's service, Thelma had wrangled her feet into those dried out shoes and hobbled as best she could right on into Jones and Preston's Funeral Home. Thelma was well known around those parts and when visitors saw her comin' up the walk way, shamblin' along on her hickory stick, they stepped aside to let her pass by. Moses and Janice shook her hand and helped her to Spencer Duty, Jr's casket. Thelma then, as best she could, clicked her heels together, stood at the best attention that her rheumatism ridden bones would let her and saluted.

In not too long of a time, the Reverend Burton asked folks to sit down and then began the service. "We have come together today to bid farewell to a good man. Not someone who was flashy or tried to draw attention to himself, but someone whose words matched who the man was inside. I have served as pastor in Paintsville from when I had hair on my head. And in that time, I have stood before many folks at the finality of someone's life sayin' what a wonderful person the deceased was. Sometimes those words were hard to come by and my words were short. Now I am in a different position as I have more words than I have time to say about indeed what a good man Spencer Duty, Jr. was. I could say this and that about his accomplishments but those you can read in the paper. I would rather talk about the man."

"When I first came to town I met Spencer Duty, Jr. at a church supper. He'd ask Miss Helen Stringfield to bake up enough of her famous biscuits so no one would be deprived. I was pushing my little daughter Dixie in her wheelchair. She was needin' braces for her legs from being run over by a drunkard when I was in Bible school. Money was real tight and we were savin' up for Dixie to get her braces so she could get back to walkin' on her own."

"When Spencer Duty, Jr. walked up to us and introduced himself, he bent down on his knee, put out his hand and shook hands with Dixie. He didn't look down on her. Then he asked what had happened to Dixie, when I told him, he said he was sorry for her troubles and walked away. A few days later, I received a call from the Cincinnati Children's Hospital sayin' they wanted to get an appointment set up for my little girl to get special made braces for her legs. I thanked them for their call but said I didn't call and that my wife and I certainly couldn't afford such a thing. The woman I talked to said all of the expenses would be taken care of, all we had to do was to schedule a time to come on up. They were even going to put us up at a hotel close to the hospital. It was never spoken about, but there is only one person who could have done such a thing. And, I now know that there are many stories from people sitting out there grieving. Sometimes, people do things for others with the intent of others knowing the good they'd done, but Spencer Duty, Jr., when he did something for someone, did it quietly. Later on, he told me one afternoon that any "little bit of good" he may have done would be between him and the Lord. Well, my guess is that he showed up in Heaven with Jesus a brand new pair of shoes to replaces those worn out sandals, sat them right beside the Pearly Gates, never sayin' a word where they came from. That, ladies and gentleman, is the the Spencer Duty, Jr. I am proud to say I knew!"

Folks lined up far and wide, up and down the street and formed a cavalcade of cars, carts and carriages to accompany Spencer Duty, Jr. on his journey to the top of Cumbo Mountain, where he was laid to rest beside his momma and daddy.

It was just a few days after Spencer Duty, Jr.'d been put in the ground when Peter Peyton, who'd been known for just about as long as anyone could be known for to regularly drink himself into an awful state, came into the emergency room at Paintsville hospital, shaken up so bad that his bones were rattlin'. He was stammerin' so bad that Nurse Harmony said he needed to bring some calmin' upon himself because he wasn't makin' not a lick of sense. Well, in a few minutes, Peter Payton spoke up and said he'd been partakin' of illicit shine up atop of Cumbo, leanin' back against Ida Mae Selvage's headstone, which he said, the cool slate took some of the bite out of the moonshine with each sup he'd partake of. Well, then he said,

"I looked up and there walkin' hand in hand were Spencer Duty, Jr. and some woman with red hair, dressed all up in a white dress with a yellow bow in the back, seemin' to make their way right over the back of Cumbo. I ran to see where they'd went and once they started down the backside they just up and disappeared."

Nurse Harmony said for sure the liquor was talkin'. But she figured it'd be best if she called Doc Kitchen, who was still at the hospital finishin' up his rounds.

When Doc Kitchen pulled back the curtain and saw Peter Payton, he thought he looked like a man who'd been just about frightened to death. The pallor of his skin looked like all the blood had been siphoned out of his body. Nurse Harmony hadn't said why she wanted Doc Kitchen to see Peter Payton, just sayin' that he was real upset and that she thought it'd be best if Doc Kitchen came and took a look at him. When he related the cause of his fright Doc Kitchen felt faint. Never in his life had he heard such a thing *and* Eleanor had been buried in a white dress that had a yellow bow in the back. Even laid out in her casket you couldn't see the yellow ribbon. Doc Kitchen gave him a tranquilizer and said it would help. He didn't bother to talk to Nurse Harmony and just left the hospital and went home to Doc McGarrity. For the first time in his life, as he related the story to her, he thought, perhaps, death as we know it may not be what we know of as the end.

Chapter 33

SHORTLY AFTER THE FUNERAL, Moses contacted Porter, Banks, Baldwin & Shaw and said there was to be one change to the will. The research center would be known as The Spencer Duty, Jr. Research Center for Black Lung Disease. Doc Kitchen and Doc McGarrity had agreed immediately that they should only be the primary physicians but the name of the research center should bear Spencer Duty, Jr's name.

The black lung meeting in Chicago was coming up fast. Doc Kitchen and Doc McGarrity were becoming known as the top researchers of black lung disease in the country. During the meeting the establishment of the SDRC for Black Lung Disease, as it would become known, would be announced as would the analysis of the results from what was now just called the miners' meeting where all of the test data had been collected. Doc's Kitchen and McGarrity would present that the standard tests conducted on miners to identify lung disease pretty much came back normal with no damage showing up to their lungs hardly at all. But when they exerted themselves during the test's they quickly became breathless and just about collapsed on the treadmill. At first it hadn't made any sense, then they drew blood while they were exercising and sure enough what they had suspected was borne out. The blood tests showed that the alveoli in the lungs were damaged to the point where they weren't able to transfer enough oxygen to their blood. If that happens then plain and simple, you can't breathe. And, it will eventually kill you.

Chapter 34

Now that tough Tony was going to be headed to prison and no longer exerting his influence, miners were rejoicing. Arnie Miller had just been elected the president of the UMW. He'd been a miner and had the black lung, so it was figured far and wide that he'd be the kind of man who'd finally get them not only what they deserved but also what they needed.

CONSOL and the Pittsburg Coal Company though had just about had it with the constant naggin' by the goddamn miners about "… havin' the black lung," and "I can't breathe." That was all they heard and every goddamn letter and application for disability was claimin' the black lung. They gave these men and their families work and all they asked was that they do their job and keep their goddamn mouths shut about havin' this and that, but mostly the black lung. And now they had this clinic right in the heart of coal country, with folks who were collecting enough medical evidence, as they called it, to where it was going to make it hard to deny the miners' claims. It just seemed like they went from one thing to another.

Doctor's Gaylord and Rafferty De La Croix had just finished up their residency when they went right on into the Army and worked in a field hospital in Vietnam. The Doctors De La Croix were twins, "We are *identical*," as they would say. Not that anyone had to ask. No one could tell them apart, hell they were both even the same rank. Most twins, identical at that, had some differences that folks could use to tell the differences, but the De La Croix twins seemed to have carefully cultivated their sameness. It was unusual for one of the twins to finish a sentence without the other picking up, sometimes right in the middle of a word, saying what the other was getting ready to espouse. When they were in their medical training, the other docs found them *insufferable*. Their colleagues said they thought they were royalty. They were good technical surgeons, but they also had an opinion on *everything* and there was only *one* opinion that mattered and that was *theirs*. "Medicine *is* this and medicine *is* that," and if it wasn't then it should be because they said so. It was also best that you didn't disagree with them about what they said medicine was.

Their diagnoses were inflexible, if they thought it was one thing and the others doctors thought it was something else then they would rely on their other as *the* expert and say that science was on *their* side and that they sure wouldn't mind being remembered for that once they were gone.

When they got out of the Army, they went on and trained mostly as radiologists specializing in diagnosing diseases of the lungs. The Doctors De La Croix then heard about a new Diseases of the Lung Center that was going to be starting up at the Inner Harbor Diagnostic Institute. They immediately applied for a respective position. Distinguishing them apart was simply impossible. They informed their colleagues that they were to be addressed as Dr. Gaylord or Dr. Rafferty. If they were being addressed together then they were to be called the Doctors De La Croix. Their reports were "crisp" and "to the point..." Never giving an inch in what they said they saw in an x-ray and what they didn't, just like it'd been in Vietnam. And too, just like Vietnam, it was best not to disagree with them. It didn't take long until they were the top radiologists at the Institute as it had come to be known.

When CONSOL heard about the Inner Harbor Diagnostic Institute, it bein' one of the world's best hospitals and all, starting up their Diseases of the Lung Center they began investigating the Doctors De La Croix, talking to just about anyone and everyone who'd ever known them. They even talked to the other docs they'd served with in Vietnam. It wasn't long before the boardroom talk at CONSOL centered around how best to convince the good Doctors to be *who* they were *meant* to be and to get paid what they *rightfully* deserved. The board also decided to have none other than B. T. "Bobby" Tucker himself talk to Doctors Gaylord and Rafferty. Bobby'd been consulting with CONSOL and the Bituminous Coal Operators Association now for a while and was seen as just about the slickest negotiator and champion for coal that anyone could remember. Folks called him the *'Titan of the industry.'*

When Bobby called Dr. Gaylord, he didn't know he had got Dr. Rafferty, it didn't take much of his well-known arm twistin' negotiatin' to convince the two doctors to work with them. But… it had to be *understood*, they had to take a hard line, as a matter of fact, about as hard of a line as a doctor can take when it came to diagnosing the black lung. Bobby said they wanted to do what was fair, but they weren't going to be giving away the farm. Plus, it would be understood that since the doctors would be savin' the coal companies money by doing what was right, they would be handsomely rewarded for each case that they *didn't* diagnose as the black lung.

After not too much figurin' Doctor Gaylord and Rafferty decided that it would be best for their career if they went ahead and worked with just about any coal company that approached them, not just CONSOL. Being two who thought like one, they could also help with all of the claims for disability that were coming from the miners and their families. "Can you imagine," they'd say, "what would happen if all of these claims against the coal companies were proved to be medically legitimate? These miners down there live like animals, no education, no morals, drinking and smoking… And then they want someone else to take care of them the rest of their lives."

Chapter 35

Chicago was brisk in October, the relentless wind coming in from Lake Michigan with waves rolling in so fast as to challenge any ocean. The way they were howling it seemed like the gales of November were setting up early. There were those who said that 25,000 ships had been lost in the Great Lakes and at least 30,000 souls had been taken by these mighty unforgiving beasts. They weren't talked about that way, but the Great Lakes may as well been landlocked oceans.

Doc Kitchen and Doc McGarrity arrived at the Palmer House on East Monroe Street a few days before the conference was set to take place. The hotel was opulent, most especially given where they had come from and what they had become accustomed to. Doc Kitchen had spent some time as the Chief of Chest Diseases, at the *Brooke General Hospital* in San Antonio and Doc McGarrity had spent time in Philadelphia but it had been a while now that they had been in a city that never went to sleep.

There was one thing they were both longing for, Italian food. Fried chicken and biscuits and gravy, they figured, would be the death of them. So, on that first night they walked west from the hotel and spent hours at The Village, Chicago's oldest Italian restaurant. There was a picture of Al Capone hanging on the wall, with a strand of spaghetti hanging out his mouth, mugging for the camera. The rumor was that he didn't like the picture and had the photographer beaten to death for not giving him the respect he deserved.

When they got back to the Palmer House, they went to the registration desk. They listed their names on the sign-in card separately. The polished up looking clerk asked them, "I see that you have separate names. Are you married? Because we do not permit couples who are not married to cohabitate in the same room. If you are not married you will have to get separate rooms." At that point Doc Kitchen looked at the clerk and said, "How *dare* you insult me and my wife. I demand to speak to the manager at this moment." The buffed clerk, now stuttering, immediately apologized for what he assumed was a mistake on his part. They never answered his question, and were sure to list their M.D.s after each of their names. At that point the clerk slapped the brass bell sitting on the counter, calling for the bellhop to take their luggage to their room. Once the valet cart was unloaded, the tip palmed and the door securely shut, they both laughed at the gullibility of the counter clerk. But each of them knew the questions would continue as would the looks and assertions of indiscretions. It was also at that very moment that Doc Kitchen decided that he would, before the week was out, ask Doc McGarrity to marry him.

It was shortly after the door latch clicked that Janice tossed her dress aside, surprising Moses that she was wearing nothing underneath. A few hours went by before they emerged at the cocktail gathering preceding the conference. Their research on black lung was about to change the way doctors thought about the disease and most importantly how they diagnosed it. There had never been a larger sample of miners at the same time and administered the exact same diagnostic protocol. Docs Kitchen and McGarrity hadn't even started out thinking that way when they first got the idea, but as the men kept coming the black lung came right into the light. Physicians from all over kept coming up to them and saying how their work was going not just to impact diagnosing black lung but also other diseases of the lungs. My God, even James D. Hardy, MD came up from University of Mississippi Medical Center to shake their hands. Docs Kitchen and McGarrity could barely believe it when he presented himself, saying what an honor it was to meet them both. And how proud he was to see such young physicians doing work that would have implications for years to come. It was impossible not to be humbled by shaking the very hands of the man who had done the first lung transplant in 1963.

It wasn't long before two short, stocky men, also young, approached them, but not offering their respective hands. They stood back, cocked their heads in opposite directions and looked at Doc Kitchen and McGarrity with disdain. Doctor Gaylord De La Croix said, "I don't understand why you two are commanding so much attention, neither of you are experts in radiology or even diseases of the lung for that matter." Then Doctor Rafferty added, "I am going to have to see your work before *we* can even begin to evaluate its efficacy…" Doctors De La Croix then turned and walked away. There are some people who present themselves as inviting interaction with warmth and conviviality, but Doctors De La Croix had within a few seconds presented themselves as two very odd and instantly dislikable strangers.

After several more introductions, walk arounds and dips in the fondue, Moses and Janice decided to excuse themselves and go to their room. It wasn't long before they were making love. As Janice was atop of Moses, he gently took her face into his hands and said, "Will you marry me?" Her answer was a "My God, Yes!"

It was about 2:00 A.M. when Rev. Burton's phone rang. The good Lord always seemed to want to call souls to Heaven in the middle of the night, he thought, as he answered the phone. On the other end he heard Janice McGarrity say, "Rev. Burton, I know it's late, but when Moses and I return from Chicago will you marry us?"

"Praise be to God," he said.

"Okay, we will see you when we get back."

And on that Janice replaced the phone on the cradle. Having not bothered to get off Moses, she put her head on his chest and went to sleep.

Chapter 36

DOCTOR KITCHEN AND DOCTOR McGARRITY were the first presentation the following day. They presented overheads of the x-rays taken combined with the spirometer readings and the arterial blood gas results. The evidence was clear, their findings showed that the most definitive way to diagnose black lung disease was by combining the results of the three tests and then comparing one against the other. Dr. Hardy spoke up and said, "Ladies and gentleman, I think that what we are hearing today is the advent of a new way of understanding diseases of the lung. Not just black lung, and I use this term deliberately, rather than the formal medical name *pneumoconiosis*. My reason for doing this is because black lung describes in no uncertain terms the devastating effects this disease has on the men it effects. Whereas pneumoconiosis is most certainly more formal. We must not become complacent or arrogant in our understanding of diseases and how they can destroy entire communities. My congratulations to Doctors McGarrity and Kitchen for their outstanding research."

Other attendees also lauded praise on what Doc Kitchen and McGarrity presented, at least until the very end. Then Dr. Gaylord De La Croix stood up. "Neither of you, as I mentioned when we spoke to you briefly, are radiologists or for that matter pulmonary specialists." To which Dr. Rafferty said, "I don't know how you can come here and present what you refer to as a *proper* way of diagnosing what is *euphemistically* referred to as *black lung*. As radiologists we have seen thousands of chest x-rays and have yet to see *one* case of diagnosable pneumoconiosis." Dr. Gaylord added, "Ladies and gentlemen, after all we are physicians, so let us use the *proper* medical terminology when describing what *may* or in fact *may not* be a *condition at all*."

Dr. Rafferty, speaking in the same voice, and with his head so close to Dr. Gaylord's that it looked like one or the other had two heads, then said, "How many of these individuals come to physicians complaining of not being able to breathe, but we watch them come right up to our doors, and they are not huffing and puffing, in fact they seem fine, yet they complain that they can't get their breath. Obviously, you will retort that this is the very thing that you presented on, but doctors, I continue to be skeptical and I have seen or heard nothing today that has convinced me otherwise." And on that note, Doctors De La Croix promptly stood up, humphing and walked out.

The doctors De La Croix were the final comments of the day. They had made their point with not only disregarding comments but also in their dramatic exit.

On the drive back to Paintsville, Moses and Janice talked about having children. It wasn't something that either of them wanted right away but certainly, they both said, it was something they wanted in their future. Janice also laughed at how she'd responded to folks at the conference with, "…Y'all."

Once they arrived back in Paintsville, they stopped at Castle's Jewelry and bought simple gold wedding bands. Then they went to what had been Spencer Duty, Jr's, home for so many years, but now had been handed down to Moses. They didn't bother to unload the car, they simply went inside, and upon undressing, fell asleep.

The next day Moses went to the bank and had Janice's name put on his bank account. After that he walked over to the title company and redid the deed to the house. He made sure that Janice's name was on it too. When he got to the hospital he told Janice what he had done. She was surprised. Pleased, but surprised. "Why?" she asked. Moses said, "One thing I've learned being a physician is how tenuous life is. We can be here one minute and dead the next. I don't want in any way to leave you struggling or wondering. It sounds somewhat trivial to say, but whatever I have is as much yours as it is mine. No matter how much time we have together, it is never enough…"

Janice remembered being at the orphanage. Each and every day survival was defined by keeping what was little was yours, guarding it, knowing that no one was going to give you anything. Meeting Moses had turned that upside down. Even in the beginning he seemed so generous with his time, money. And when she first met Spencer

Duty, Jr. he was the same way. At times, it was like she was around someone speaking a foreign language which she didn't understand, but suspicious of. But, over time, she just realized, that had gone away.

In a short while after their work was done at the hospital, Moses and Janice knocked on the door of Rev. Burton. They had in hand their marriage license. Rev. Burton didn't even bother to put on his robe and stole. In a short while the "I do's" were exchanged with the Rev. Burton finishing things off with, "You may kiss the bride." He knew neither Moses nor Janice were believers and yet knowing them had made him amend his amens. Sunday after Sunday he saw members of his flock praise the Lord with verse and song yet some wouldn't share so much as a potato with their hungry neighbors. Moses and Janice were as about as devout in their disbelief as Rev. Burton was in devotion to the Word. And yet they lived day by day by everything the Word stood for.

Chapter 37

Doc Kitchen and Doc McGarrity figured out early on that if it weren't for each other, then they couldn't do the work they were doing. They saw other doctoring situations in their office and at the hospital yet the majority of what they saw was the suffering that being destitute brings. The mines, like they always had, paid the men next to nothing and the black lung drew them closer to death. One night while lying in bed Janice told Moses that it was like death followed each miner around with a scythe, hacking a little bit off of them at a time, until there was nothing left. She'd never seen anything like it. Paintsville didn't attract too many new folks. It, like so many other mining towns, bred the same type of agony year after year. Moses said, "No one likes a story that doesn't have a happy ending, people want stories to nullify the misery which we are so often surrounded by. Jesus, there's no such thing as a pretty death."

The next afternoon they both pulled time in the ER. It had been a quiet day until about six o'clock or so. That's when Little Jimmy Yarborough came in demandin' to be seen just as soon as the doctors could see their way to treaten' "…the goddamn pain in my head." Jimmy was called, "Little Jimmy" because he was about six feet, five inches, or thereabouts, folks said his height had never been fully measured because no one could reach up that high. Little Jimmy also weighed somewhere between 350 and 400 pounds depending if he'd had a mess of fixins' the night before.

He was also known to drink hard liquor until there weren't any left, but he'd always been one to keep standin' no matter what. He was married to Prudance, whose momma and daddy'd spelled her name with an 'a' instead of an 'e'. Likely, Little Jimmy had said when he first met her at thirteen or so, was because they was hopin' that she'd become good at dancin', which he never let her forget she hadn't. Well, Little Jimmy was it seemed always throwin' fits about not gettin' his way about this or that. And on this particular day he'd gotten really upset with Prudance because she no matter what wouldn't give him any babies, so he picked up an old chromed Rohm, .22 short pistol he'd found up in the rafters of an old barn where he'd been workin' hay, and shot himself in the head. When he walked into the ER, his hairy sweaty potbelly looked like it had absorbed his overall straps. He was screaming, "…my god, my god, my heads on fire…" Doc McGarrity took him back to an exam room, pulled the curtain and began to look at where poor Little Jimmy had shot himself. There was a small raised red bump right above his left eye and a small dried blood splotch right above his right temple. Still moanin' Little Jimmy hadn't said what he'd done. When Doc McGarrity began to question him, she found out that he'd taken the revolver, placed the tip of the barrel against his skull and pulled the trigger. But Little Jimmy had tipped the barrel just enough so that the anemic bullet had crawled its way under the skin and didn't penetrate his skull, being as pig headed as he was. Now the cartridge rested between the bone of his skull and the skin of his forehead, burning as he said, "…like a sonofabitch." Even though he was in pain and there was little doubt that Little Jimmy was suffering, Doc McGarrity couldn't help but find some bit of irony in his predicament. Doc McGarrity injected a cc of Lidocaine under the skin, waited a few minutes then took a scalpel, made a small four-prong incision, folded the flaps of the skin back and lifted the small deformed cartridge out of it burrow. She looked at Little Jimmy and said, "Do you want it as a reminder not to do it again?" In a matter of seconds, Little Jimmy was thankin' Doc McGarrity up one side and down the other, praising her to high heaven. "If you ever need *any-thing* Doc I am a man who is at your service." Then he took the small round and slipped it into his watch pocket. Once Doc McGarrity had stitched up Little Jimmy she pulled back the curtain and walked out of the exam room looking down at the wedding band on her finger. *Funny*, she thought, *it seems so natural on my finger I didn't even notice it was there*. But, the nurses in the ER had certainly noticed and word spread through the hospital like it was an infection that had broken out. Some of the nurses figured Doc McGarrity must be knocked up.

Chapter 38

AFTER THEY'D BEEN BACK in Paintsville a week or so, Dr. Hall called Docs Kitchen and McGarrity to his office. When they arrived they found Mr. B. T. Tucker sittin' with Dr. Hall chawin' on this and that, Bobby tellin' joke after joke, like bats flyin' from a cave ablaze. Dr. Hall looked at Docs Kitchen and McGarrity and said, "This is B. T. Tucker, he works one way or another, for most of the coal companies around these parts." Interruptin', B. T. Tucker said, "Everyone knows me as *Bobby*... At least my friends do and I sure am hopin' we'll be friends."

Neither Doc Kitchen or McGarrity bothered to sit down.

"What do you want?" Doc Kitchen asked.

"I thought we could spend some time together and get to know each other, bein' that we both have mutual interests, the well bein' of the miners."

"Please get to the point what you want and I believe that I can speak for Doctor McGarrity and myself when I say that we are not looking for any new friends."

Bobby was gettin' frustrated that his extension of friendship was not being reciprocated. "Seein' as how I was tryin' to be just about as friendly as a man can be, and extending you the courtesy of the *benefits* of my friendship, perhaps I *should* get to the point. We have spoken with the Doctors De La Croix, who I believe you recently became acquainted with, and they didn't have the same reaction to your so called research about the black lung that the other doctors did there in Chicago. It seems that there was a bushel bundle of mistakes in how you all went about collecting and then analyzing what you *said* was medical fact. In *fact*, Doctors De La Croix thinks some of what you presented may not have been truthful at all, given that it flew in the face of just about all the other research out there. So, I was hopin' we could all work together on this, and Doctors Gaylord and Rafferty hoped to take the lead, but from your attitude, I don't get the impression that's goin' to be possible.

"You know, Dr. Hall," Bobby continued, "the coal companies have been *very* generous with this hospital and a lot of other ones around these parts too. I'd sure hate to see some of that generosity dry up like an overworked coal seam.

"It seems like a good friend of mine here at the hospital, who just seemed to up and disappear one day, tried to tell y'all the same thing. But you weren't listenin' then any more than you are now…"

At that point Doc McGarrity spoke up and said, "What then exactly is the threat that you are making?"

"Well, y'all are still young, figurin' out your careers. It'd probably be best if you moved on, you know the church don't take a liken around these parts of folks shackin' up, even if they're doctors and all.

"If the Doctors De La Croix, who are respected radiologists, which neither of you are, at one of the world's top research institutes, says your findings are no good, then that pretty much is all that needs to be said…"

At that point, Doctor Hall, McGarrity and Kitchen began to laugh. "Well, *Bobby*," Dr. Hall said, "I've pretty much been sittin' here listenin' now to what you had to say, figurin' I'd be respectin' of that. Let me tell you a little story, if you've got just a minute, your time bein' so valuable and all. Not many know it, well outside of my lovely wife of forty-five years now, but I served at Hacksaw Ridge with Desmond *Tommy* Doss. Y'all know he was awarded the Medal of Honor for being' about the bravest man that God ever had the good sense to create.

"Well, I was servin' right alongside him as a medic too, Jap bullets flyin' every which way. There was one boy who was hangin' onto the cargo net for dear life, that'd been hung for the soldiers to reach the top of the escarpment. That boy and I were pullin' ourselves up side by side, prayin' together, askin' God to protect us. Right when we got to the top of that awful cliff, Leroy, that was the other boy's name, grabbed hold of me and used my shoulder to push himself over the top of the ridge. And then those yellow devils sprayed that poor boy so bad with machine gun fire they shot his head right off. It went on like that for eleven straight days. I saw men torn apart, I saw bravery that defies the ability of any man to be that *brave* and I saw men act like thugs to protect their own cowardice, sending good men to die in their place. I even saw one Lieutenant take a piece of shrapnel and gouge his leg with it so he could get a Purple Heart."

At that point, Bobby interrupted, "Well, it sure is a good story but..."

Dr. Hall waved his hand for Bobby to shut up. "Let me tell you what it has to do with. I've been the Chief of Staff here at this hospital now for as long as I can remember. When I came back from the war, seein' what I'd seen, I signed up for medical school, swearin' I'd become as good of a doctor as I could be, savin' lives where I could. And, Bobby, if you think you are going to waltz in here, any more than Ox did, any more than Tony Boyle did, and threaten me or two of the finest physicians I have ever known, then you can get your goddamn ass, and God forgive me for using His name in vain, not only out of my hospital, but out of Paintsville."

Bobby stood up, tossed his shoulders back in defiance and walked out the door. As he drove out of town, a pick-up truck with three miners, two holding ax handles between their legs, followed him to the edge of Johnson County.

Doc's Kitchen and McGarrity were as taken aback by Dr. Hall's profanity and rage as one can be taken aback. He was a calm, steady man and a fine physician, who they both looked up to. The coal companies were already preparing for a battle that hadn't even begun.

Chapter 39

Doctor Gaylord De La Croix and Doctor Rafferty De La Croix were disconcerted. Their assumption had been that Bobby would get an understanding between Docs Kitchen, McGarrity and the radiology program at the Institute. They liked to say that if it weren't for them that the Institute would lose its reputation for greatness. The "Radiology Department at the Institute had been *nothing* until *we* came along," Dr. Rafferty liked to say. Dr. Gaylord always finished with, "We feel that the recognition of our skills as physicians are *ripe* for the recognition we deserve." Bobby reported to him that Docs Kitchen and McGarrity were beginning to testify for miners in black lung benefit hearings. As a matter of fact, Bobby was furious when he found out that several benefit cases had been won by miners, who Bobby said, he was sure were overdoing *their* claims of breathlessness. But Dr. McGarrity had testified she was *sure*, based upon their studies, he had the black lung. These miners weren't even forty. "You're trying to tell me that this forty-year-old man, who'd been mining since he was thirteen, now is disabled because he says he can't breathe," Bobby angrily spouted to Doctors De La Croix. Dr. Rafferty spoke up and said they'd requested the x-rays from these so-called claims while Dr. Gaylord espoused that "There isn't a shred of medical evidence that this man or any of those claimants have black lung." Nodding his head in agreement, Dr. Rafferty added with indignation, "The x-rays show nothing!"

Bobby and CONSOL figured that they had to provide some kind of counter-testimony in these cases since the assignment of benefits was going to be one way or another coming out of the coal companies' pockets.

Doctors De La Croix and Bobby decided they would interview a select group of physicians, much like the coal companies had before, but this time it'd be more organized and Doctors De La Croix would *guide* them through what they needed to know as they worked in support of denying miners benefits for black lung. "These men who are making these claims better be damn near death and their lungs full of rock-solid chunks of coal before they're going to see a nickel," Dr. Gaylord said. "When we were boys, we worked hard on the farm day in and day out and we sure as hell don't make claims that we have farmer's lungs!"

Dr. Rafferty, at that point, took a deep breath, showing that their lungs we as good as the next man's. It wasn't long before another group of claims for black lung benefits was filed for a half-dozen miners from Paintsville. Bobby got hold of the claims and presented them to Doctors De La Croix, saying they said the same damn thing, "'I can't breathe!' How much longer are we going to have to put up with this, Doctor Gaylord," Bobby saying as much as asking. Dr. Rafferty figured that if they couldn't stop the awarding of benefits then they sure could slow down the process of the miners getting money they weren't deserving of. "Hell," Dr. Gaylord said to Bobby, "we can tie this up so long that most of them will be long dead before the coal companies have to pay out one cent."

Bobby thought that the Doctors De La Croix had been the men he'd been lookin' for, for about as long as he could remember. But he also thought they were the most peculiar two men he'd ever met. It was a while later that he found out that Gaylord and Rafferty even lived together, neither one ever having been married. Hell, their socks were even the same. Bobby wondered if they slept in the same bed, did they have different closets, did they bathe together, then Bobby figured that it was best if he just let things be as they may, as he wasn't for sure that he wanted to know the answers to the questions he was asking himself.

But Gaylord and Rafferty did in fact sleep in the same bed and being the exact same size wore each other's suits. Bobby as a matter of fact had never seen one without the other nor for that matter no one else at the Institute had either. They even shared the same office, their desks back-to-back.

When Institute staff saw them go by, they sniggered amongst

themselves how they seemed to waddle rather than walk.

It wasn't long after meetin' them that Bobby said to the board of directors of CONSOL, "'Y'all will like Docs De La Croix, they're workin' out just fine for us. They're up at the Inner Harbor Diagnostic Institute and they think the sun comes up just to hear them crow." For Bobby, Gaylord and Rafferty had been love at first sight.

It had been a few months after they returned from Chicago that Docs Kitchen and McGarrity had been called to testify for Teddy Latusek. He felt like he was on his last leg and there wasn't much disputin' about him havin' the black lung. His wife, the two of them bein' together since they were twelve, now had to do all the chores, the poor man could barely make it from his relaxin' chair to the toilet. Sometimes he'd get so winded on his way that he'd lose his water, embarrassing himself like a man should never have to be embarrassin' himself. Burkiie, his wife, loved her man so. Since he barely had whiskers, he'd worked the mine in one form or another. Her daddy always said that she sure could do worse for herself. Sometimes Teddy'd come home and his fingers'd be wrapped in bloody burlap, from where they'd been cut up by sharp edges of the coal, his hands were about as scarred up as his lungs. Doc Kitchen knew Teddy'd never see the other side of forty.

When they got to the hearing, the hearing officer called the proceedings to order and asked Teddy to speak for himself about why he was askin' for disability benefits and why he thought he deserved them.

"Well," Teddy said, "sir, I've worked all my life in the mines, worked hard as a man can work. When I was 'bout twenty or so, I'd a, this is embarassin' sir, I'm sorry to have to use this kind of language, when I'd go to the toilet and have to push real hard to have a bowel movement, I'd just about pass out and fall off the pot. That was just about the first time I figured that the black lung was settin' into my chest. I ain't never talked to no one but Berkiie about that, well with Doc Kitchen, and he figured too it was because I was startin' up with the black lung. But I never missed a day of work, not *one* day, mind you, no matter how hard it was for me to get my breath, then a couple of years ago, I'd just be a wheezin' to the point where I couldn't even..."

At this point Teddy began to get tears in his eyes, the droplets that ran down his cheeks laden with black specks of coal dust that had accumulated in his tear ducts. "I couldn't even have relations with Berkiie, without just about wheezin' to the point of passin' out on top of her. The black lungs taken my life from me sir. I can't even go the pot by myself now."

At that point Doc Kitchen asked the hearing officer if he could present the medical evidence to show that Mr. Latusek indeed was suffering from black lung disease. Doc Kitchen held up a series of x-rays, a chart recorder tracing of his spirometer readings and his blood gas values. He explained that, for the most part as long as Teddy didn't exert himself, his lungs could get enough oxygen from his blood to function, if you call being *inert*, he said, *functioning*. But, as Teddy's medical evidence showed, when any form of exertion was required, he could, most particularly as time goes on, be close to death.

The hearing officer had been hearing claims of being disabled now for more than twenty years. He remembered one man, whose wife led him into the hearing, who claimed he was born blind. When the hearing officer asked him for proof, he demanded that he look at his eyes, which he said were backwards in his head. "My eyeballs face the wrong way sir, when I look out I see straight into my brain…"

The hearing officer denied his claim. But in Teddy's case, he couldn't have been more convinced. It was then when a man stood up in the back of the room and identified himself as Dr. Gregory Fino.

"I am here to speak for CONSOL, who Mr. Latusek was employed by and is now seeking benefits from. We have reviewed the x-rays of Mr. Latusek's lungs and they simply do not show black lung disease. This is the opinion of Doctor Gaylord De La Croix, Doctor Rafferty De La Croix and myself. We are with the Inner Harbor Diagnostic Institute. Our opinion is based on solid medical evidence in the evaluation of Mr. Latusek's lung films. Doctors De La Croix and myself are board certified radiologists and have read *thousands* of x-rays while the opinions expressed by Dr. Kitchen or McGarrity, who are *not* radiologists, are not supported by their background or training. We respectfully request that either Mr. Latusek's claims of disability are denied with prejudice or are denied until we can more fully examine Mr. Latusek ourselves." Doc Kitchen stood up and said, "We sir, have examined Mr. Latusek and the medical findings are incontrovertible, you simply do not know what you are talking about."

Dr. Fino again stood up, when he was waved down by the hearing officer, who then said, "Since there is such a strong difference of opinion, it is necessary to table the decision until such a time where the claim can be refiled with consistent medical findings." To which he then said, "Next."

Chapter 40

BOBBY WAS ABOUT AS excited as he'd been when he shot his first rabbit, somewhere about eight or so. His daddy'd given him a Remington Nylon 66 for his birthday and said he was about as proud of a son as a daddy could be. Bobby'd never given his daddy one day of trouble. His momma had died when she'd been deliverin' him and so his daddy was raisin' him up on his own. Daddy'd been talkin' one day when Bobby overheard him say that his head had been so big that he just tore his momma in two when she was tryin' her best to bring him into this world. It was somewhere right around then when his daddy told him that learnin' how to shoot was one of the most important things that a man had to learn. More important than driving a car'd ever be, he said. "If other men know that you're a good shot, they'll be weary of messin' with you."

It was just a few days before Bobby was shootin' so many rabbits right between the eyes that his daddy had to slow down his slaughter. That was the only time Bobby had back talked to his daddy, disagreein' somethin' awful. He loved seeing the rabbit flip and roll in the air right when the .22 round bounced around in its brain. It was then that Bobby figured it'd be best if he didn't tell his daddy the number of rabbits he was shootin' and instead just kick them under the brush. He worked his way up, huntin' white tail bucks and boar, but he never lost that joy he felt when killing a rabbit. Once he'd even went out west just to learn how to tie a snare to snatch up a wolf. If they hit the snare just right, it'd catch them around the neck and "strangle the no good sonsabitches," he liked to say.

Dr. Fino had not only challenged the veracity of Latusek's disability claims, he also put it on record that Docs Kitchen and McGarrity weren't qualified to be saying what they were saying. Doctors De La Croix, Bobby thought, had come up with a brilliant way of tying these goddamn claims up for years. The coal companies were setting aside millions of dollars to pay their stockade of physicians who were willing to provide provocative contradictory testimony each and every time a claim was put forward. Plus, the Doctors De La Croix now had enough physicians who would set up in motel rooms and demand to conduct their own examinations of miners who were claiming the black lung. Dr. Fino had been the one who came up with examining miners in local motels and became a cohort of Doctors De La Croix in his dedication to thwart black lung benefits being granted to suffering miners. Putting doctors in motel rooms also created a sense of nervousness in the miners, feeling like they were being watched and that made them less likely to want to file a claim. Doctors De La Croix also let it be known every time they got the opportunity that *they* were the chiefs of radiology at *the* Inner Harbor Diagnostic Institute. Like most large research hospitals, Inner Harbor survived and was able to expand by grants and corporate contributions. The Doctors De La Croix were pulling in millions of dollars every year from the coal companies.

It wasn't long before Bobby was a regular visitor at the Institute, even having his own office there, to help generate generous donations from not only the coal companies themselves, but also from their executives.

Chapter 41

THE SDRC WAS SEEING upwards of a dozen patients a day and they could have seen twice that number if they had the staff to do the testing that needed to be done. Docs Kitchen and McGarrity were rarely working in the ER and most of their time had been allocated to the SDRC. When a miner presented symptoms of black lung, they were put through the same diagnostic protocol. And, each and every time stress was added, they barely made it through the testing. Yet, each and every time they filed for benefits they were examined by one of Institute's lackeys and found not to have black lung. The diagnosis was consistently 'emphysema due to excessive tobacco use.' Even miners who'd never smoked a day in their life were given the diagnosis because of being exposed to cigarettes and having a predisposed sensitivity to lung damage. It just went back and forth. Even with The Federal Coal Mine Health and Safety Act of 1969, there were so many caveats to the bill that the coal companies rarely had to pay benefits.

Billy Joe Buzzard was fifty-two and had been working the mines since he was ten. First as a breaker boy, then a mule driver and when his muscles got to where they could swing a pick-axe he went down into the hole. He wasn't one bit different than any other miner, coming down with the first signs of the black lung when he was in his twenties. Billy Joe was a big sonofabitch. Just about as broad as he was tall. His arms were like tree limbs and he could drill the tip of an axe so deep into a coal bed that it would take two regular size men to pull it out. His wife, Birdie, had given him six children, three now who were livin'. The other three were lost when their homeplace burned down when embers from the fireplace set their little daughter's dress ablaze. The little girl went runnin' this way and that, settin' everything in her path on fire, including her twin baby brothers. Now, Billy Joe could barely breathe. Doc McGarrity said there was no doubt that he suffered from black lung, but Dr. Fino said because of his size he had a disproportionately large lung capacity, therefore he couldn't have black lung no matter what. In most circumstances that would have been it, but Billy Joe appealed and the appeal hearing came through about six months later. For the most part that fast of an appeal was unheard of, but Billy Joe and Birdie Buzzard were seein' it as God grantin' them some reprieve from their misery. A few weeks before the hearing Docs Kitchen and McGarrity were figuring they had to do something in addition to presenting the medical evidence, since Dr. Fino would just be saying the same thing he always said.

When Doc Kitchen and McGarrity arrived at the hearing, they presented their medical evidence that Billy Joe indeed had black lung. Then Dr. Fino said, *no,* this wasn't the case. Right as the hearing officer was raising his gavel to declare a negative ruling, Doc McGarrity stood up and asked for a moment of indulgence from the hearing officer, who kindly obliged. Dr. Fino objected, immediately saying that he as the *expert* should be the last word in this matter. The hearing officer waved his hand for him to sit down and shut up. Then Doc McGarrity spoke up: "I understand there is a difference of opinion here with Dr. Fino implying that exposure to coal dust doesn't lead to black lung disease."

Then Doc Kitchen reached into a canvas bag and pulled out two WWII surplus gas masks, connected to a large silver canister which was connected to a foot pump.

"I would like to respectfully invite Dr. Fino to put on this converted gas mask." The hearing officer was demanding an answer and Dr. Fino was indignantly appalled. Doc McGarrity said, "Dr. Fino has said, at this hearing and at others, here we have a transcript of a dozen different hearings, that coal dust is not a harmful substance and will not cause any substantial damage to the lungs, in essence, it is inert. What we have in this canister is simply coal dust. In order for Dr. Fino to substantiate his assertions of the benevolence of coal dust, I would like to invite him and Your Honor to place these masks over your faces while we blow coal dust through them."

The hearing officer was appalled and Dr. Fino was enraged.

"Your Honor, we mean no disrespect to these hearings and certainly not to you. It is just that Dr. Fino has and continues to make these assertions about coal dust having no deleterious effects, and his assertions are either directly resulting in denying these miners' benefits or are tying them up for years, often until they have succumbed from black lung disease. If indeed coal dust *is* benign, and we are willing to stipulate to that, if Dr. Fino is willing to don the mask and directly substantiate his assertions to these proceedings."

The hearing officer then retorted, "I will not be a part of your demonstration, one way or another, if, however Dr. Fino wishes to demonstrate the lack of impact of coal dust by participating in your experiment, it would be beneficial to this hearing."

At that point Dr. Fino gathered his notes and said, "I have never seen such a spectacle of unprofessionalism from physicians, *never*. I have half a mind to report you to the medical board," and on that he stormed out of the hearing room.

The hearing officer waited until Dr. Fino left the room and then said, "I have never seen such a display in a benefits hearing, but… the point you were trying to make has been effective in convincing this hearing officer of the incisiveness of your diagnosis of black lung disease of Mr. Buzzard. As a matter of course and for the record, Dr. Fino's refusal to subject himself to what he had testified to as the *nonmalignant nature of coal* dust raises the specter that he may have only been representing this opinion in order to derail these proceedings and ultimately to deny Mr. Buzzard of benefits if they were appropriate to his condition. It is hereby determined that Mr. Buzzard's medical condition is, in fact, so severe as to warrant *full* and *lifetime benefits* for cause. These benefits will be awarded as will a lump sum payment, yet to be determined, going back ten years and thus calculated forward."

The hearing officer closed with, "Doctors Kitchen and McGarrity, now that you have this on the record and have in effect nullified Dr. Fino's credibility for future testimony in a proceeding of this type, *never* and I mean *never* do I want you to conduct yourselves in a similar manner, should you ever come before me again, am I clear?"

Both Doc Kitchen and Doc McGarrity replied with an affirmative, "Yes."

When Billy Joe and Birdie realized what the hearing officer had said, they both began crying. It would mean they could for the most part go off relief.

Birdie was helpin' Billy Joe up out of the chair, when he began wheezing something awful. He was spittn' up black laced phlegm and tryin' harder than he'd ever dug a pix axe into a coal bed to get air down into his lungs. But truth be told, there just wasn't any room left in the depths of his lungs for the air to go. Birdie tried with all her might to hold up Billy Joe, but he slipped out of her grip and fell to the floor. Docs Kitchen and McGarrity immediately tried to bring him back around, his eyes now rolling up into his skull and his face quickly turning blue.

The hearing officer watched in horror, never having seen a man die right before his eyes. He had always made his rulings and been on his way. For the most part every man who came before him was a case number. He was only to rule on the facts of the matter at hand. Now, Case Number 401-90-0226, Mr. Billy Joe Buzzard, lay on the ground before him, the content of his bowels now seeping out onto the floor and no matter how hard they tried, Doctors Kitchen and McGarrity couldn't catch up with the life that'd run away from his body so he could finally regain his pride at not having to feed his family goddamn government cheese. The hearing officer, not having had a tear in his eye for longer than he could remember, sat down behind his desk and wept. Since the hearing had concluded on the *affirmative*, Birdie would get Billy Joe's back benefits and about one-third of his lifetime benefits. She may still have to feed their youngins government cheese if things got bad. But now she had to figure out where the money was going to come from to bury Billy Joe.

⚭

Chapter 42

DOCTORS DE LA CROIX were fit to be tied. Dr. Fino, when he found himself under fire, had deserted his post. "Coward…" Dr. Rafferty said. Dr. Fino tried to explain what had happened, but Doctors De La Croix were accepting no excuses and on that fired Dr. Fino. Bobby was as mad as Dr. Gaylord and Dr. Rafferty, and in not too roundabout a way blamed them for another goddamn miner getting benefits for the black lung. "Why couldn't he have dropped dead before the hearing officer's decision? If Fino had carried things out, likely just a half-hour or so, Buzzard would have collapsed and that would have been it."

"Well given what happened, we will file a special appeal," Dr. Rafferty said. Whereby Dr. Gaylord filled in with, "Especially since Buzzard died in the hearing and we'll relate it to a bad heart, which was due to excessive smoking, and say that the judgment should be nullified."

Bobby thought Doctors De La Croix figuring on how to proceed was sound. Plus, just to make sure the likelihood of this happening again, the hearings should be made as long as possible. The Doctors De La Croix *hated* Doctors Kitchen and McGarrity. They were reaping the benefits of their association with Bobby. The Doctors new home in Federal Hill made other doctors jealous of their success and now they were beginning to associate with other men who could help them further along on their path of recognition. The coal companies had been very generous and grateful for their expertise and saw to it that every month or so when Bobby visited that he brought an envelope filled with confirmation of their appreciation. It was always better to have your *appreciating* come in the form of cash, that way the government didn't go sticking their nose in it at tax time.

Bobby remarked over a good sippin' whiskey to Doctors De La Croix, that this wasn't about one man, "…Hell, not even two, not even a dozen… This is about first one of these low life's gets declared disabled, then two, then it goes on and on, until the only reason the men in coal country go into mining is so they can get disability and live off the rest of their lives off the coal companies. I don't know of any job that doesn't have some kind of risk that goes with it, they know that going when they get into it. Hell, they don't have any education, they live like pigs, what the hell else are they going to do? Let me ask you this Doctors De La Croix," Bobby said. "What the hell would these poor bastards do if all of the coal just dried up, no more coal… How would they live, and all they want to do is to bite the hand that feeds them…"

Chapter 43

Docs Kitchen and McGarrity had found a way to get around the initial objections of whoever the opposing physician would be. They didn't know however that Dr. Fino would not be returning to any of the disability hearings. They also knew that what they were calling their 'experiment' would only have worked one time, but and as they had planned, they had Dr. Fino's objection and refusal on record and this could be used in future hearings. There were also rumors going around that there were going to be congressional hearings on black lung benefits and that they would be called to testify and to discuss their findings.

Epidemics are usually thought of being like the Influenza Epidemic of 1918, but the way Doc Kitchen saw it, black lung was as much of an epidemic as any other plague. Except, black lung was an occupational disease, and one that was completely preventable and was one of the few existing diseases that has a corporate lobby *for* the disease itself. It was as though everything about black lung as he and Doc McGarrity understood medicine was upside down.

What they didn't know was that Bobby and the Doctors De La Croix were working with the Institute to begin laying the groundwork for Inner Harbor to become *the* major diagnostic center that would be recognized by the Social Security Administration for the determination of black lung benefits. Private physicians and research centers could still diagnose black lung, but if the case came as an application for benefits, then Dr. Gaylord De La Croix and Dr. Rafferty De La Croix could proffer their opinions as *the* touted experts at one of the world's greatest institutions of medicine.

It was late in the afternoon when Doc McGarrity saw Bailey

Bigglesworth. He was a stout man, missing most of his teeth, with coal dust caked in just about every crevice in his face. His wife, Bea Bigglesworth, had finally gotten him to come in and see either Doc Kitchen or Doc McGarrity. He was thirty-five and like his daddy before him had been working the mines since he was just a youngin'. When Doc McGarrity asked Bea how long Bailey had been a miner, she said she couldn't rightfully say, but it'd been since she'd known him, when they were youngins together. The thing about Bailey was that he looked just odd. There was something about his eyes, the way they were darting here and there and when he stood up his gait was like he was walking in cold molasses. Bea said Bailey had been having trouble breathin' since he turned over to thirty's side. But in the past few years he'd gotten to be worried all the time that while he was underground that she was havin' untoward relations with Harley Hatfield. Bea said that was about the dumbest thing she'd ever heard in her life, Harley bein' ninety-three years old. As a matter of fact, he was just about the oldest man in Paintsville and had been a farmer all his life, and still grew and dug his own potatoes. But Bailey was havin' none of Bea's refusin' to admit her wayward ways and stormed over and accused Harley of cavortin'. Bea began frettin' somethin' awful that Bailey may up and hurt Harley so she began insistin' that he come into the clinic.

Doc McGarrity could see that his nostrils were flaring out like a horse whinnying and poor Bailey had an incomplete breathing pattern. She decided to draw a blood gas on Bailey to see what kind of oxygen saturation he had. She had Bailey open and close his palm and felt for the radial ulner artery, and then slipped a 22-gauge needle into his artery and pulled 3ml of bright red blood.

In a few hours the results came back.

Bailey only had seventy-five percent O2, he was suffering from hypoxemia. He was most certainly suffering from black lung, yet this was the first time that Doc McGarrity had seen, especially in a miner this young, what looked like brain damage from not getting enough oxygen to his brain. And in Bailey's case, it was presenting with him getting increasingly paranoid and agitated. The problem was that once brain damage occurred there wasn't anyway to treat it, much less cure him. She had him do a spirometer evaluation and a chest x-ray and her diagnosis of black lung was confirmed. But Bailey wasn't likely to be able to be cared for at home much longer. With his suspiciousness he was getting too dangerous for Bea to take care of him by herself. It would be a short time until he had to go to a rest home. When she told Moses about what she had found with Bailey, she said, "Maybe he'll have a heart attack and die. Jesus Christ," she said. "Day in and day out, this is all we see, the suffering is endless and now we're not only fighting the disease but a couple of bastards who sold their souls to the coal companies."

Chapter 44

BOBBY ONLY HAD ONE intent, that was to protect the coal companies he worked for. Folks who had to deal with him said that he made just about everybody feel like they were the most important person in his world, nodding up and down, and "um hums," galore. But if they disagreed with him then they said they had a tiger by the tail. He turned about as vicious as a man can get. Then he'd begin coughing from the four or so packs of cigarettes he smoked each and every day. The Doctors De La Croix were Bobby's men, although they'd always say that they weren't, if the idea ever came about through someone's mouth. They were just preventing men who wanted something for nothing from getting it. Bobby didn't like or dislike the Doctors De La Croix, he simply needed them and they were serving the purpose that they were intended for. Doctor Gaylord De La Croix and Doctor Rafferty De La Croix had the notion they were medical royalty at The Institute. They even had a special parking place with a drop gate for their car. The Doctors De La Croix became overtime increasingly soft-spoken. There was no reason to raise your voice, they would say. Those who worked with them said that if you disagreed with either man, then of course you were disagreeing with both and they would simply dismiss you. If reports by other physicians found positive indicators of black lung, then the Doctors De La Croix would simply *reread* the x-rays and changed the findings to the negative. It was their *right*.

They shared the Chairmanship of the Department of Radiology and were the anticipated Chief(s) of the new black lung program in development. When the medical records of Bailey Bigglesworth came to the Doctors De La Croix to review, they immediately denied that black lung was the problem. Rather, they said it was Bailey's smoking unfiltered cigarettes and an unhealthy life style, including "…drinking alcohol made in an illicit fashion. Alcohol of this type contains many toxic impurities which are the likely culprits, therefore it is our recommendation that Mr. Bigglesworth's claims of disability due to exposure to coal dust be denied. It is undeniable that Mr. Bigglesworth is disabled, however what is at question here is the cause and effect. There is virtually nothing in the medical literature to support any form of hypoxic brain injury as a secondary effect of black lung."

When Doc McGarrity heard about the findings by the De La Croix physicians she was enraged. Not only were they impeding Bailey receiving any financial support but they were also attempting to nullify her medical findings.

That night she and Moses went to Belinda's Diner. It'd been in Paintsville since the '40s. They were both weary of the constant fight. This was not what they had gone to medical school for. Yet, they knew that the work that they were doing was essential. They knew that Dr. Hall wouldn't let anyone compromise their medical judgment by being bought off by CONSOL or the other coal companies. Besides, they now had the responsibility of the SDRC. It was then that Janice looked at Moses, leaned over the table and said, "I'm pregnant."

Moses had thought that he would become a father at some point in his life, but, well, given how they rarely kept their hands off of each other… Nature had a way of moving things along, whether the timing may be right or not. His eyes began to swell as tears ran down his cheeks. "Let's go home," he said.

When they walked into the house, Moses began walking from room to room. "Okay what do you think if we make this room the nursery? It's right by our bedroom, well I guess first we'll have the baby with us…"

Janice smiled, watching Moses. It seemed that when she wanted to make her desires known, she simply dropped her dress. Moses continued to be amazed how often she had on nothing underneath. Certainly, when he turned around, this was one of those occasions.

It was around 3:00 o'clock in the morning or so when the call came. They needed Doctor Kitchen and McGarrity to come to the SDRC immediately. When they arrived Dr. Hall was already there. They found him among the debris from where someone had broken into the clinic and it looked like took sled hammers to just about anything and everything. The only thing whoever did it couldn't do was to break into the safe that Doc Kitchen had got from Freddy B. Oney, who was the president of the First National Bank of Paintsville and had opened its doors for keeping folks' money safe in 1902. Mr. Oney, when he learned of the SDRC opening its door, offered Doc Kitchen a safe made by the Old Reliable Safe and Lock Company.

"Somewhere about 1895 or so," explained Mr. Oney, "said it was that Butch Cassidy himself came upon one of these safes, looked at it, turned around and went on about his way, not even wastin' his time tryin' to break into it. It's been sittin' in the basement of the bank now for as long as anyone can remember and if you'd like it for your, well, for whatever you might need it for, it's yours."

A few days later Mr. Oney had that safe sent on over and set up for Doc Kitchen. He and Doc McGarrity without fail, each and every night, like they were practicing some kind of religion, put all of their research files in that safe.

You could see where who'd ever broke in had beat the old girl with sledge hammers, but she didn't budge an inch and all of their research files were as safe as they were when they'd put them in there, but the clinic and all of its equipment was destroyed. Aside from the anger at what had been done, Docs Kitchen and McGarrity now became more convinced than ever that their findings would not only redefine how black lung was diagnosed but also that their data was threatening to the mining companies. They felt assured that what had been done here tonight was not the action of anyone from Paintsville.

Little Jimmy Yarborough, Verka Spradlin and Mrs. Ida Savage, a few hours later, came into the emergency room, more dragging than carrying two men who weren't from around those parts. Verka's daddy had gave him a girl's name because he said it would either make a man out of him or kill him and if he became the kind of man who couldn't take care of himself, well, then he weren't no son of his daddy's. He said he had other boys he could be proud of, should the need arise. Ida was a stout woman who always carried a .38 in her bra, sayin' she didn't like to put it back down in her intimates after she fired it because the barrel was always so damn hot and it set her titties on fire. And Little Jimmy wasn't one to let no man run over top of him, drunk or sober.

The three of them had been coming back down from Turkey Knob pickin' up a shine run when they saw a couple of men, with more oil in their hair than Bud Turley had over at his gas station, carrying sledge hammers, coming out of the back door of SDRC. They figured, lookin' the way they did, they weren't from around those parts and figured it would be best to follow them to see where they were goin' to be headin' to.

When those two slick haired men were about halfway between Paintsville and Prestonsburg, Ida said they had some explainin' to do. Little Jimmy retorted that if they'd done anything to cause Doc McGarrity any sufferin', then he'd be splitin' their heads open with an axe handle.

Verka had pulled up so close behind them that the slick haired men couldn't even see their headlights. Then Verka began rammin' the back of their car. It didn't take long before the slick haired men's car began careenin' this way and that, until it went runnin' off the road, over top of a concrete culvert and landed top down in a dried out crick bed.

When Little Jimmy, Verka and Ida pulled off the road, they saw the slick haired men crawling out the busted out-front window of their car. As one of the men stood up he reached under his coat and pulled out a revolver. Just right before he was able to set the sights on Little Jimmy, Ida had her .38 out of her bra and fired two rounds, one in each leg. Her daddy had always said, "you can shoot a man in the gut and he can still shoot back before he dies on you, but if you get good, then you can shoot him in the legs and he will drop to the ground faster than a flyin' goose hit with a load of buckshot."

And sure enough he did, with his revolver droppin' from his hand as he grabbed his shot up legs. The driver of the car was tryin' to make his way out the window, when Little Jimmy tried to grab him by the hair to help him along. But his hair was slicker than owl shit on a sycamore limb. Finally Little Jimmy snatched the man by his neck and dragged him out the car window, cutting him somethin' awful with all the broken glass flickerin' in the full moonlight. Verka saw the man start to reach under his coat, like the other man had, so he figured he was reaching for a revolver too. He walked over to him and put his boot on his neck. His head got darker than a Negro's at night, while Ida went ahead herself and relieved him of his pistol.

She was sure glad she'd waited a while to put her .38 back into her bra so it didn't set her titties a blazin', Ida said.

Ida looked over and saw Little Jimmy, gruntin' somethin' awful, with an axe handle he'd gotten from the bed of the pickup truck, raised over his head, just ready to split open the head of the man with the shot up legs like a melon. Ida screamed for Little Jimmy to put down the axe handle, sayin' they needed to do some figurin' about why they been in Doc Kitchen and Doc McGarrity's place and then what to do with them. The slick haired men were in a bad way, bleedin' here and there and curled up in pain here and there too.

Ida stepped on one of the shot man's leg, causin' him to scream for God to help him, as Ida ground round her foot like she was grindin' out the butt of her cigarette. Then she stopped and then she ground again, askin' in between what they'd done and why they'd done whatever they did.

When Verka moved his foot from the man's neck, his face began in no time to look again like a white man. Neither man would say why they were in those parts and what they'd done, so Ida figured they'd been up to a real bad no good. Little Jimmy walked over to the man whose head had come back to the color he'd been born with, traced the tip of the axe handle across the top of his head and was just gettin' ready to do what he was itchin' to do in the first place, when Ida stopped him again. She then walked over to the man, took the revolver she had relieved him of, squatted down and put the barrel of the pistol right up against his private parts. "You're gonna talk now or I'm gonna blow your balls right off and then I'm goin' over and blowin' his balls off," noddin' toward to man with the two bullet holes in his legs.

"Jesus Christ," the man whimpered, "*who* are you people, we didn't do nothing to you..."

Little Jimmy looked down and said, "You came out of our friends' place, you ain't carryin' sledge hammers for no reason, the docs are about as good of people as we know, so if we ask you what you were doin' there and you don't answer, then we're gonna find out one way or another or kill you tryin."

It was then that they said Bobby had told them to drive down from Pittsburg and bust up Docs Kitchen's and McGarrity's clinic. They weren't supposed to hurt a hair on their heads, but there wasn't to be *anything* left in the clinic they could ever use again. Little Jimmy, Verka and Ida loaded the broken men in the back of the pick-up, wedged between crates of hooch, and drove them back to the hospital. When they arrived Doc Kitchen and Doc McGarrity were still at the hospital and were called down to the ER. Little Jimmy saw Doc McGarrity coming down the hallway. He went up to her and said, "We got them, they broke up your and Doc Kitchen's clinic. After what you've done for all of us, we figured they weren't up to no good, so we went after them." Ida came up and said, "Someone named Bobby told them to do it. Folks like this don't do nothin' except sittin' around eatin' flies and tellin' lies."

When they went into the examination rooms they saw the two men, one with bullet holes in his legs and one whose body was cut to shreds by broken glass and who was wheezing like a thick neck bulldog. His scruffy neck bein' bruised something awful.

After they patched up the two men, Docs Kitchen and McGarrity called D. B. Trimble, the police chief of Paintsville, who came over and promptly arrested the two scoundrels.

No matter how hard they tried the police could never link the break-in and destruction to Bobby. The man who had hired them met with them in a hotel room. He sat behind flood lights so they couldn't see his face. He just said his name was Bobby, but it could have been anybody. The two men were sent to the Castle on the Cumberland for ten years each, both were shanked in prison a few months after their sentencing.

Within three months the clinic had been repaired and reopened its doors. Docs Kitchen and McGarrity did not tell anyone that the results of their studies had been untouched.

While working to reopen the SDRC, Docs Kitchen and McGarrity reworked the results of their study and upon the reopening of the SDRC announced the publication of their newly evaluated results. They had put together a group of biostatisticians, pulmonologists and radiologists to independently evaluate their conclusions. When they responded with their report, they found based upon the information submitted to them that there could be *no disputing* of their findings. Not only had Bobby's efforts failed to destroy the results of their findings, it had backfired, giving even more credibility to Docs Kitchen and McGarrity.

It seemed like it wasn't taking long before Janice began showing. She was healthy as could be. Moses thought that with each baby pound she gained the more beautiful she was. Of course, the way it was understood to be was that Janice would quit work and stay at home with the baby. But when they discussed it Moses and Janice decided that they would take their baby with them to the clinic. Not to mention, there would be a lot of offers to help change diapers in-between patients.

Chapter 45

IT HADN'T TAKEN LONG until the Doctors De La Croix had established the Black Lung Center of the Inner Harbor Diagnostic Institute. Here they would evaluate black lung cases from all over the United States. And like all other cases coming before them as Chief Radiologists, Dr. Gaylord De La Croix and Dr. Rafferty De La Croix would have the final say. Often times, if another radiologist had read the x-rays and either of the Doctors De La Croix didn't agree with the diagnosis, the other radiologists diagnostic opinion wouldn't appear anywhere in the report.

Doctors De La Croix had developed a template for diagnosing black lung. When an x-ray came his way for review, they would put the template over the x-ray and if they didn't see a particular kind of lung shading then the person didn't have black lung disease. The Doctors De La Croix was as busy testifying for the coal companies as they were with their work at The Institute. The coal companies had a shared corporate jet which clocked most of its hours ferrying Doctors De La Croix to different disability hearings where they could directly challenge the miners claims of black lung. Initially they thought testifying was tedious but as time went on and they became masterful at challenging other physician's findings of black lung. They found great satisfaction at knowing they had impeded the outcome of the disability claim or shut it down all together. But they always demanded that they testify together, both of the Doctors De La Croix were always in the hearing room during any testimony. It was not uncommon for the hearing officer to chastise either Dr. Gaylord or Dr. Rafferty for interrupting the other and finishing what the other was about to say—not exactly sure often times which one he was really admonishing. As much as he could Bobby accompanied the Doctors De La Croix to benefit hearings. Even Bobby was "amazed" at what he called their complete dispassionate, surgical denial of claim reviews that came before them. Either they were not 'diagnosable as black lung' or 'bogus' claims based upon the miners' lifestyles. Bobby told other folks that he "…sure as hell would never want them as my doctor… But, they're one of the best damn things that's ever happened to the coal industry."

There were several radiologists that were beginning to question Doctors De La Croix's attitudes about black lung. It seemed that whenever they talked to other colleagues the conversation would drift to black lung and malingering. They seemed to have what other radiologists called a '…sophisticated hatred of miners for some reason.' The Doctors De La Croix seemingly ended most of their conversations with Dr. Rafferty saying, "Remember the great William L. Marcy's quote from 1832." To which Dr. Gaylord would then offer the quote, "To the victors belong the spoils of the enemy." For the Doctors De La Croix the coal miner had become the enemy.

Chapter 46

Doc McGarrity was always having to pee. There was no rhyme or reason, except that there was a baby using her bladder as a trampoline. For some reason, the baby knew when she was doing an examine or meeting with a patient and decided to begin bouncing. She always kept a few pairs of dry panties in her purse and by the end of the day her panty stash had been gone through. Moses always knew what was happening when he saw her uncrossing and recrossing her legs during an exam or rushing down the hallway to the restroom.

The ER seemed to be overloaded that day, there was someone behind every curtain. She had just peed and had an otoscope in little Lily Lipscomb's ear, where she saw part of a red rubber band curled up with a ball of encrusted ear wax, when she heard the whistle. At first, she didn't know what it was. But everyone else did. Suddenly the entire hospital came to life, sirens were blaring seeming from every direction and folks were running here and there, up and down every hallway. There had been a mine explosion over in Van Lear.

Dr. Hall came running, as best he could for a man of his age, and began ordering everyone ready to receive causalities for anyone who may be found alive. Doctors in their private offices knew that when they heard the wail of the siren, to close their doors and head to the hospital.

Doc Kitchen headed immediately up to the mine. Bodies were already being hauled down the hill in the back of pick-up trucks. When he got to the site, the boss man said that right as the afternoon shift was being rolled into the hole, the support beams gave way and dropped straight down on them. They were only a hundred yards or so in when the supports gave way. Seems like the beams'd been there about as long as anyone could remember and just rotted away from the inside out. Fourteen miners were in the minecart when it all came down. Other miners were already digging the men out as best they could, and "…so far there ain't been none been found alive."

Doc Kitchen put on a hard hat and worked his way back to where the other miners were pulling men out. Most of the miners Doc Kitchen saw had massive head injuries and upper torso injuries. Their heads were crushed or split apart from where the beams and decades of spikes had been what one digger said was nigger rigging to hold up the mountain they were exhuming. Body after body was dragged out from under the debris, mangled and some crushed beyond recognition. Two miners who'd been side by side happened to be right in between where two beams had fallen and escaped the devastating impact of a joist directly onto their heads. Instead, the ends of the beams had caught both miners in the back of the neck causing severe injuries to their cervical spines. But they were alive. Doc Kitchen, as he watched the men being extricated from the mine shaft, thought that the story of this mine collapse would focus on the men whose lives had been taken. But as so often happens, those who survive have devastating injuries that never get talked about except to say, 'so many dead and so many injured.' Living with these kinds of injuries would be life changing, the recovery brutal. As he tended to the two men as they were pulled from the rubble, Doc Kitchen knew that he and Doc McGarrity were in for a long haul in the ER to stabilize the miners, before they could be transferred to Lexington where they had more clinical resources. But if they didn't stabilize them, they would either die on the way or end up being quadriplegics.

There were no ambulances. There were only three for all of Johnson County and they had all been called out, in different incidences right before the mine collapse. He had the men bound to plywood boards and their heads strapped down and bricks placed up against their necks to stabilize their spines, as best he could, and then taken to the hospital by pickup trucks.

Doc Kitchen arrived back at the hospital right before the surviving miners did. "They have severe cervical spine injuries. As best as I can tell without x-rays, we will need to fully stabilize them with Halos before we transfer them to Lexington," Doc Kitchen said to Doc McGarrity. When the men were carried in, they were moved onto a gurney and wheeled into examination rooms. Their injuries were almost identical, where the ends of the beam had gone in-between them, catching their necks one right after the other. They were checked for any other internal injuries, vital signs and then x-rayed. Each miner had their opposite shoulders broken with bruising here and there but no life-threatening injuries, other than the damage to their C-spines. The x-rays showed that their cervical spines were severely crushed but miraculously they had full functionality and feeling throughout their bodies. One man was exhibiting more signs of shock than the other, so they decided to treat his shock while they worked to attach the Halo brace then the vest to the other man to stabilize him.

Doc McGarrity put a rolled-up towel under the miner's neck to as much as possible align the vertebras in his neck. Doc Kitchen then placed the Halo ring slightly down from the equator of the miner's skull and gently tightened the positioning pins to hold the brace in place. Injecting lidocaine into four positioning holes around the perimeter of the brace ring caused a slight reddening to the area. Then he began screwing the skull pins and tightening them into the man's skull, while Doc McGarrity continued to help stabilize the brace. They then fitted the Halo vest to the miner's chest and then attached the braces' stabilizing rods to the chest vest.

Doc McGarrity had never seen a Halo brace fitted and even for a physician there was something about using screws to hold the brace in place by pinning them directly into the skull that made her slightly sick to her stomach. Both of the miners had been knocked unconscious and were beginning to come around. The miner who was exhibiting more signs of shock had stabilized and was lying beside the miner who had just been placed in the Halo Brace. Suddenly seemingly to realize he was next, he began screaming, "Oh Jesus Christ, Jesus Christ!"

Doc Kitchen ordered 5mg of diazepam IV and waited a few minutes until the drug began to take effect before he and Doc McGarrity fitted him in the Halo also. There wasn't much more they could do, as the men would need a neurosurgeon to do spinal surgery and of course they were facing a *long* recovery. When he realized what the miners were going to need, he had ordered an ambulance from Lexington to come and transport them.

The ambulance arrived a few hours after the mine collapse, the attendants loading up the two Halo brace bound miners who were shortly on their way to the western side of the state. It wasn't long after the ambulance left for Lexington that the dead began to arrive. No matter how accustomed one is to seeing dead bodies, to see so many at one time seems like a violation of creation, especially with what some called the *raw* dead, not dandied-up and these poor men were *certainly* specimens of the raw dead. Each miner had massive crush injuries, their brains were coming out their ears, eyes, mouths and whatever vast injurious crevices that resulted from the weight of the mountain debris that had collapsed on them. Many of the miners' faces were so mangled that they weren't recognizable. A few of them had beam fragments imbedded into their chests, causing their hearts to rupture. Each and every man was caked in crimson-streaked coagulated coal dust. Doc Kitchen had their bodies lined up, side by side on gurneys brought in from every part of the hospital. There would have to be pronouncements done for each man with the official cause of death. The wives of the men were beginning to come to the hospital. It had happened so many times before. Sometimes just one miner was killed. Perhaps he got caught in-between two coal cars and crushed to death, or a piece of equipment had malfunctioned and killed him or maybe he slipped and a drill he was using had spun free and bored through his heart. But, my God, twelve men killed. Christ!

Doc Kitchen and Doc McGarrity went from man to man, did a quick evaluation and pronounced them. Charles Preston, the undertaker, had come on over and was walking beside Doc Kitchen and McGarrity shaking his head, saying that most of the folks he'd buried over the years had been miners. Even way back in 1921, when the Paintsville Furniture and Undertaking Company had begun because miners were "dying, left and right and there weren't anyone to give them a proper sending off, so that's how we all, in one way or another, got into the undertakin' business. How many are there, let's see, one, two, three…twelve. So I guess with this many and from the looks of the coal dust all over them we can just call them the dirty dozen."

He and his helper, Grady Graves, who was from the Little Canada area of Jackson County, which sat right above Horse Lick Crick, would be loading the bodies up, three at a time, stacking them on top of each other, making four trips back and forth to get them all. They were already crushed all up, so bein' one on top of the other weren't goin' to make no difference.

Grady wasn't all there, all the folks knew that, he'd likely been born that way, they'd say. He didn't have so much as a driblet of being bothered by much of anything. Grady used to say just about every day to Mr. Preston, or anyone who bothered to hear, "Why do they call them *wakes*, these folks are *dead* and they sure ain't gonna be *waking* up..." It never seemed like anyone could give Grady a good enough answer to ever stop him from asking the same question again and again.

The one thing that Docs Kitchen and McGarrity noticed about each miner, whose ages went from nineteen or so to about fifty or thereabouts, at least those whose chests were split wide open, was that they had lungs that looked like charred wood. "One way or another," Doc Kitchen said, "the coal companies kill the people that work for them." The funerals would be quick. Folks were so accustomed to goin' to funerals, that for some, it was just part of livin' there in Johnson County, Kentucky.

It was now late into the night and Doc McGarrity's ankles were swollen and she had to pee so bad that her back teeth were floatin, or so she'd heard one of the nurses say more than once.

It was too late to cook so they went to Ethyl's, which fed the truckers as they came through on their way to Huntington and serving up breakfast *"24 Hours a Day, 7 Days a Week, 364 Day a Year* (Closed on Christmas Day to Celebrate the Birth of Our Lord)."

It was Friday eve, as they called Thursday night, and they weren't on call through the weekend. They had decided on which room to turn into the nursery and Moses was remodeling it. This weekend it was going to get its first coat of new paint along with the rest of the house which sorely needed it.

Right after they had fitted the Halos and shipped the two miners off, Felix Flannery rolled through the ER on a little cart that a couple of the facility engineers from the hospital had fixed up for him. He lived at the hospital now, odd as it was. In its entire history there had never been a patient that had lived at the hospital. But poor Felix couldn't find a rest home that had the capabilities to take care of him. Well, half of him anyway. He had to be lifted every night into his bed and then all of the tubes draining this and that had to be moved too. As time had gone on Felix was developing a decubitus right on the coccyx and it was encircling his lower back, seemingly day by day, like a growing tree ring. Except this was a virulent bed sore, one that seemed to have a mind of its own and one that seemed intent on ingesting poor Felix. It acted like a chimera that had attached itself to him and was scheming to eat him alive. The thing stunk to high Heaven and even poor Felix would sometimes vomit from the stench. But Felix, even though he had no bottom half, had the biggest stack of girly magazines that anyone had ever seen. *Rapture, Natural Sunbathers, Mayfair,* stacks and stacks were spread everywhere in his room. Sometimes the nurses would walk into his room and he would be laying on his belly, a nudie magazine under his chin, with his eyes rolled back in his head, living in a world he could never again hope to be a part of. Felix once told a nurse that he had a dream where the top half of a man had been all shot up and Doc Kitchen had cut the unfortunate fellows bottom half off and sewed it onto him, making him whole again.

Just about every one saw Felix every day because he was always rolling through the corridors of the hospital. He'd been known to slap the nurses on their bottoms when he rolled by, but they'd say, "About the only thing we can do is not put him on his cart and just leave him in bed," but, none of the nurses had the heart to do that. So, they just tried to twist their butts out of arm's length as Felix rode by. But he only slapped Doc McGarrity's hind end one time though. Felix had been rolling by, when he swatted her on the ass, when Doc McGarrity grabbed the back of his cart, spun him around, bent down and said, "If you *ever* swat my ass again, I'll take every magazine you have and burn them, then I'll make sure that the mailman *never* delivers another girlie magazine to you again…"

After that poor Felix never so much as came near Doc McGarrity's bottom.

Chapter 47

DOCTORS DE LA CROIX and The Institute had lobbied that they should become the facility that would offer the final opinion as to whether a miner had diagnosable black lung. After all they were considered the world's number one medical institution and Doctors De La Croix were the chief consultants for the coal companies, therefore by self-declaration had evaluated more x-rays by miners who claimed they had black lung than any other radiologist. During one of the hearings where the Doctors De La Croix had challenged the findings of Doc Kitchen, Dr. Gaylord said, "We don't need the medical literature to inform our findings." With Dr. Rafferty indignantly adding, "There are *no* radiologist as competent at reading x-rays as we are. *Therefore*, there is no reason for us to waste our time with literature that is uninformative..." Then in a remarkable display of verbal synchronicity, the Doctors De La Croix together said, "We *are* what may be best referred to as *the* gold standard when it comes to diagnosis of black lung disease. And in that we will not be challenged."

Bobby was almost always close by when Dr. Gaylord and Dr. Rafferty testified or offered their opinion when they appeared in person. He was the choreographer of what and how Doctors De La Croix testified. It didn't take much to shine up the Doctors De La Croix's apple. But the power they had was staggering. Miners would go before the disability board and either be flat out turned down because of the horde of denouncing physicians or have their cases buried deeper than the mines they helped dig.

Docs Kitchen and McGarrity continued methodically to work with miners who were suffering from the effects of black lung. It wasn't long before their baby was born when they talked about leaving Paintsville to go somewhere else where their work wasn't under constant assault and ambush. But, Doc Kitchen and McGarrity had in many ways been at least somewhat responsible for stirring things up and they couldn't live with walking out now. And, most importantly, they had each other and just about another to go home to each night. The other thing they had discovered was that the miners, even the ones suffering with black lung, loved mining. As the men were sitting in front of a spirometer their wives would be saying how much their husbands loved being underground.

"I think it's in his blood, he loves seeing the coal run."

"Why he comes home as worn out as can be, but he's full of stories about this and that, all the men are."

"They know that if something happens all they got is each other, and by God their gonna do all they can to save one another, even givin' up their own lives if need be."

"That's just minin…"

"Y'all probably didn't know, but miners'l even wash each other's back, if their particularly caked up that day, they ain't queer or nothin' like that but they take care of each other, they got to, no one else does."

Chapter 48

THAT AFTERNOON DOC MCGARRITY called Doc Kitchen into the examination room to have a look at Zip Kazeey. Zippy, as his daddy and now his wife had called him, was pushing fifty. He'd been born in the hills somewhere around Bald Knob Hill and had just about finished the fifth grade of school. It wasn't too long ago that he started coughing up blood, well kind of rust covered and just about doubled over every time he began hacking. His wife, Augusta Magnolia, figured that he'd come down real bad with the black lung. But as Doc's Kitchen and McGarrity began examining Zippy they thought the diagnosis was more dire. They'd seen miners coming in who didn't have black lung but instead had squamous cell carcinoma of the lungs, kidney cancer, bladder cancer and stomach cancer. Zippy didn't have black lung, how'd he'd been able to escape it, well, Doc McGarrity said, "That's a question for God. *But,* he's going to die from lung cancer."

As they began to look back at the cancers that were more prevalent, they found that the majority of the cancers that kept showing up were impacting miners. The effect of being exposed to coal dust in all of its various forms was devastating to these men. It was as though coal dust was a virus, Doc Kitchen called it an "occupational virus."

There were legal requirements in place for using respirators and different ways of digging the coal but most of the regulations were rarely enforced. And now with longwall sheering the amount of coal dust that was being spewed in the air was so great that massive coal dust storms occurred underground, exposing the miners to an intensity of coal dust that had never been known before. The mine inspectors would come along to say what was wrong but before long many of them would be seen coming out of a trailer that the mine bosses kept parked at the back of the mine lot where whores would help the mine inspectors see things the *right* way instead of what the mine bosses called the *wrong* way.

It was then that Doc Kitchen and Doc McGarrity began anew to collect figures on the cancers that the miners were coming down with. They looked back in the hospital medical records twenty years and broke their work down by the kind of cancers, age and occupation. Now though they had strong correlations between black lung disease and an array of cancers. The longer the studies went on the more solid the correlations went on. And, equally as important, the ire of the coal companies turned to rage. Coal was now linked to not only one life-threatening illness but now Docs Kitchen and McGarrity showed it had crept into the world of cancer. The cancers had been associated with exposure to coal dust with benzene and other hydrocarbons.

Once it got inside you, it never left and then one way or another it worked its way throughout your body until it killed you.

Doc Kitchen and Doc McGarrity's mind had been awakened to how the miners were used as chattel by the coal companies since the beginning, but now they realized these men were worth less than machines. The coal companies would repair machines, and for the longwall spinner to be down meant the loss of twelve thousand dollars *per minute*, but they would spend ten times that amount to deny *one miner* benefits which amounted to about $80.00 *per month*. The question for them would become how to control their rage and continue unencumbered with their work.

When Doc McGarrity walked down the street folks would rush to help her if she was carrying groceries, saying that a woman in her condition shouldn't be lugging a bag of food around, sometimes they would even admonish Doc Kitchen, saying, "Now honey, *where* is your husband, lettin' you carryin' around a heavy bag like that?" Both she and Doc Kitchen were loved and respected by the folks around Paintsville. It wasn't uncommon for many of the people they met on the street to have been themselves related to someone or knew someone who'd been doctored by one of them. Hell, sometimes both.

One night as they were talking, Moses asked, more to himself than to Janice, how many tragic stories were necessary before something changed. Something that lasted—not the usual short-term hypocrisy. Then he looked at Janice's swollen belly and wondered what kind of world their child would come to live in.

Chapter 49

Docs Kitchen and McGarrity were combining their research on black lung with their findings on coal particulates and certain cancers. The SDRC was now a resident placement facility of University of Louisville School of Medicine for pulmonary research. But, Doctors De La Croix and The Institute challenged whatever research would come out of the SDRC. Even though the research was compelling, it was tainted by such a renowned facility being dedicated to making the findings of Docs Kitchen and McGarrity seem anemic.

Shortly after the SDRC announced their findings about cancer and coal distillates, Bobby and Doctors De La Croix met with the special advisory committee of the black lung facility at The Institute. Even though Bobby wasn't a named member of the advisory committee, he always was there. There was never a decision made without first talking over things with him. Bobby, when he was in his early years, had spent time workin' the mines. He still had scars on his knees and elbows from crawling through twenty-inch-high thin seam mines. He'd seen a lot of men injured beyond repair or just up and killed by flyin' debris but it hadn't had any effect on how he thought about miners. It had only seemed to harden him more.

Even though the SDRC was mostly independently funded by the endowment that Spencer Duty, Jr. had created, it was still in need of grants and Federal funding. For the next phase of their research Docs Kitchen and McGarrity needed a new type of x-raying equipment. Computed Axial Tomography, CAT scans, had been used for brain scans in England but now they were being used for whole body scans, including lung scans. But they were expensive. Docs Kitchen and McGarrity spent three months writing a grant for one

146

of the new CAT scans. They knew nothing about grant writing but had the folks at the University of Louisville School of Medicine look over their application and either say yea or nay. The application they said was about as tight as any they had submitted themselves. Once the proposal was sent along it got rerouted to the Doctors De La Croix for their opinions as to whether they actually needed such a complex piece of diagnostic equipment. They wrote their response to the review committee ending with, "We can see no reason why a facility of the size of the SDRC and the inadequate credentials of the sponsors (neither of the physicians are radiologists) of the proposal would qualify for the requested funding. There are many institutions which could benefit from such technology and serve a much wider population, the SDRC is not one of them. We would therefore respectfully recommend that this proposal be denied."

When the grant was submitted to the National Institute of Health, Elven Beaker, who was the head of the Submissions Program, had been told that The Institute wanted any requests for money from the SDRC to be reviewed by the Doctors De La Croix. There wasn't likely more qualified physicians to be able to assist the grant selection committee in making their decisions about who to give money to, when it came to anything radiologic.

The Doctors De La Croix reported to their Board that they had successfully thwarted Docs Kitchen and McGarrity from getting the new diagnostic equipment. Bobby also stood up and announced that CONSOL was sponsoring a special Rhine Valley River Cruise for all of the Board members and the Doctors De La Croix to show their appreciation for all they were doing to help advance energy production in the United States. One of the Board members asked if the statistics on life expectancy was right, that people in the Eastern Kentucky coalfields ranked in the lowest ten percent in the country. Doctors De La Croix assured the Board members that statistics are often presented to present the bias of the researcher. The Board could be assured that these numbers weren't any different.

Chapter 50

LABOR ALWAYS SEEMED TO come early in the morning, and Janice's labor was no different. It was 3:00 A.M. when her water broke and contractions started. Dr. Hall met them at the hospital, saying that there was no one who was going to deliver her baby except him, after all they'd had asked him to be the baby's godfather, so… It was going to be a short labor.

After about twelve hours Janice screamed, "Jesus Christ!" And upon checking one of the nurses said that the *ring of fire* had begun, the baby was crowning. In a couple of more hours, Dr. Hall caught Isabella McGarrity Kitchen at six-twenty, weighing "…six pounds, six ounces" he said. Upon seeing the world outside of the womb for the first time, Isabella began crying. A swat on the bottom wasn't even necessary. Dr. Hall laid Isabella in Janice's extended arms, and at that very moment when their eyes met for the first time, Isabella stopped crying.

Moses was pacing in the hallway outside of the delivery room. In a short while he was introduced to his daughter, wet and wrinkled, as he took Isabella into his arms.

Janice was in the hospital for three days, being tended to just about better than anyone had been tended. The nurses argued each and every time about who was going to take Isabella into Doc McGarrity for her feedings. Every time Doc Kitchen had a few minutes between patients he was seen running down the corridor to Janice's room, his white coat fanning out behind him, trying his best to be there for each feeding. He also had one of the orderlies bring another bed into her room so he could sleep there. On the third day, Janice and little Isabella were discharged to home.

The day after Isabella arrived the SDRC was notified that it had been denied the grant. Buried in the denial was the Doctors De La Croix letter, on The Institute's letterhead, signed as physician reviewers for radiological requests.

Doctors De La Croix decided they needed to know more of what Docs Kitchen and McGarrity were doing. It seemed as though, beside serving as contrarian reviewers for black lung claims, their other fulltime occupation was being obsessed with the work of Doctor's Kitchen and McGarrity. They were seemingly, day-by-day, breaking new ground in the diagnosis of black lung. But that work involved pulmonary functioning and so their research was having an impact in countless other areas of clinical medicine. Where more and more, the only thing that the Doctors De La Croix were known for was being schmucks. Docs Kitchen and McGarrity were known throughout the medical community as being physicians whose work was impeccable. And, they were also known as having integrity. Their work could be questioned and discussed, if a valid concern was found in their data, then they discussed it and reexamined how they came to their conclusions. But it was also known that discovering an error in their findings was rare.

Chapter 51

DR. RED MCINTOSH HAD graduated at the top of his class from the University of Alabama School of Medicine and was looking for a residency when he saw an announcement for an opportunity at the SDRC in internal medicine with a concentration in pulmonology. Dr. McIntosh was an affable man with a heavy southern drawl. It wasn't long after he was interviewed for the residency opportunity that he was at the top of the list and shortly after that offered the position.

He arrived with all that he owned in his car, the trunk filled with medical books and the back seat with what few clothes he owned. It wasn't long before he was the first to arrive and the last to leave the clinic. He was good with the patients but it seemed he was having trouble getting along with the other physicians and especially the nurses and orderlies, for that matter. Docs Kitchen and McGarrity had established an atmosphere of mutual respect, where folks had developed an attitude of working together. But Doc McIntosh didn't like to be questioned by anyone, including Docs Kitchen or McGarrity. It didn't take long before the nurses hated working with him and talked about him behind his back, mostly making fun of his name.

Doc Kitchen and Doc McGarrity had talked to him but it went in one ear and out the other. The longer he was there, the more of a prick he became. He even asked around if there was anything he could do to stop Doc McGarrity from bringing Isabella into the clinic. "A kid doesn't belong here," he'd say.

Doc McIntosh had been there about six months when it first began to happen. Docs Kitchen and McGarrity took their research at the end of each day and put it into the safe, spinning the dial and making sure it was as tight as a drum. The only other folks that they knew had the combination were Freddy B. Oney, Doctor Hall and Nurse Abigail Abernathy, who had worked with Doc Kitchen since just about the first day he came to town. She also loved Doc McGarrity and would just about walk in front of a charging horse for her. And God help anyone who said a cross word about little Isabella who she thought nothing of carrying around on one hip as much as Doc McGarrity'd let her.

One morning when Doc Kitchen went to get their previous day's work from the safe, he found it in a disarray. The three ring binders looked like they had been moved around on the shelf of the safe and the binder rings had a few pages caught in between where the rings came together. Doc Kitchen didn't say anything but called together Doc McGarrity, Doctor Hall and Nurse Abernathy. The first thing he did was to say that he was not accusing anyone of anything, he just thought that they may have a rat amongst them. Even though it wasn't necessary Nurse Abernathy spoke up and said she hadn't ever even had the need to open the safe. Doc Kitchen assured her that even if she did, he had no concerns about her integrity. There was something else amiss, he said. It was decided that rather than say anything they would keep his concerns to themselves, but be more vigilant as to who was going near the safe, who was near them when they opened up in the morning and if anyone was staying late.

Chapter 52

Docs Kitchen and McGarrity met with Chief D. B. Trimble and said they had some concerns that someone was getting into the safe. They had confidential medical information in there and wondered if there was anything that could be done.

"Well," he said, "it ain't money and you don't know if something is being taken, from what y'all are sayin' it may be that someone's just lookin' at things. So, I guess y'all should ask yourselves why anyone would want to look at anything in there. Hell, I'm a guessin' now, but if I looked at what you've got in there, I wouldn't even know what I was readin'. If it ain't money, then what is it that somebody wants? I can't come in an start an investigation, but what I can do on the Q.T. is have my men cruise by and keep an eye out for lights at night they might be seein' when they aren't supposed to be seein' any lights. Y'all let me know when you're leavin' and when you're commin' and I'll do the rest. If my men see anything they'll either come and get y'all or call you, whichever works out best for you."

Chief D. B. Trimble's wife, Blanche, who he'd been married to through about forty Kentucky summers, was losing her mind. She hadn't started wandering too much yet but it wouldn't be long before she did. He and his youngins did their best to keep an eye on her but sometimes his men would find her walkin' here and there, sayin' she was goin' back to Prestonsburg to see her mommy and daddy, who'd been dead now for most of the Kentucky summers that they'd been husband and wife. Blanche had been the president of the PTA on their church council and every year put on the best damn ice cream social ever seen around those parts. It seemed to come on her real fast, not rememberin' things, gettin' confused when she shouldn't be

152

and now gettin' lost and confused at the same time.

Doc McGarrity had been caring for her, but there wasn't much she could do except give her tranquilizers to try and calm her down, but sometimes the now fortuneless Blanche would get so worked up that they'd have to tie her to the bed. It wouldn't be long now before they had to put her in a rest home and do their visitin' there. But, for certain, if there was anything Chief D. B. Trimble could do to help the docs, well it'd be done.

It was always just about the hardest thing watching someone lose their minds. Doc Kitchen and McGarrity could always see the tell-tale signs that for the most part you'd never be thinkin' second thoughts about. Losin' words that shouldn't be gettin' lost and then makin' excuse after excuse as if the word was hiding on purpose. Like they was hidin' under a rock and the rock'd day by day get more covered with leaves, until finally you couldn't see it at all. And when their memories left them, they'd make up what they could remember to make up, until that disappeared too. And then one day only the shallow shell of who they once were would disappear like a puff of smoke as though they'd never been there in the first place.

One night Doc McGarrity went down to the ER to find Mr. Ephraim Badgett. He'd been brought to the hospital by his boy Enoch because, Enoch said, he'd been told that his daddy'd gone over to the neighbors and started peeing on their dog, Blue, who by all accounts didn't take kindly to being pissed on. Well, Mr. Ephraim—he was always called *Mr.* because, even though he had no education, he acted like he did and would spout this and that about this and that, making it sound like he knew what he was talkin' about even if it made no real sense at all—Ephraim'd be layin' down on the gurney, then sit straight up and then lay down and sit straight up and so it went. But he didn't have any idea in all of the world where he was. The problem was that he'd been sayin' things about this and that for so long that it took a long while to figure that Ephraim was not just losing his mind, but that it had done left and would never be found again.

Doc McGarrity got told by Enoch that his daddy'd been pissin' on his neighbor's dog and how upset the dog was, but that she had to do something to help Ephraim. No matter what though she couldn't do anything to help Enoch's daddy. He'd just have to take him home.

JOHN E. ESPY

Like Chief D. B. Trimble's wife of many years, she could only give him tranquilizers. Enoch asked what was goin' to happen to his daddy. Doc McGarrity told him that the daddy that he'd knew before was not there anymore and he'd *never* be back. There was nothing that could be done. It was then that Enoch said, "He should just be put down. I know I'm talkin' about my daddy, but he'd a never want to know he was like this, and he don't know and that ain't right…"

As Doc McGarrity pulled the curtain back and walked out of the ER, she knew she couldn't disagree with him.

Well about three o'clock in the morning or so, when the knock came at the door, Doc Kitchen walked downstairs and saw through the window Constable Everett Blevins, who folks also called Little Everett, because his daddy was Big Everett, standing on the front porch, dripping wet from up from running up the driveway from his patrol car.

"Sorry to be botherin' you, Doc, but the chief said if any of us saw anythin' out of the ordinary at your clinic to come and get y'all right away. We knew y'all weren't there, and there are lights on, looks like a flashlight, the way it's moving around and all. I'll take y'all on down if you want."

Moses told Janice what Little Everett had told him. She'd be staying with Isabella and he would go down to the clinic.

Doc Kitchen had the Constable pull behind the delivery doors. They walked quietly around to the side of the building, where they saw through Doc Kitchen's office window the light from a flashlight flitting around here and there like it was confused what it was supposed to shine on. Constable Blevins unsnapped the leather strap of his holster and had his .38 in hand before Doc Kitchen could be offering up a disagreement. But when Doc Kitchen slowly pushed his gunned hand down, Constable Blevins didn't offer any disagreement back.

Moses said, "I know who it is and I'd like to take care of it in my own way, okay?"

They made their way out of the alley and talked mostly about Little Everett's baby girl who'd just begun teethin' on the way home. He said his wife, Trinity, had been rubbin' a touch of shine, "just wet on the tip of her finger, mind you" on his baby daughter's gums. "Trinity's Mamaw was from Arkansas and she gave her an old bottle

154

of Mrs. Winslow's Soothing Syrup, it looked like it was a hundred years old, so we figured it was too old to be usin'."

Doc Kitchen told him to come around to the clinic tomorrow and he'd give him something that would work a lot better.

When Moses got back home, he told Janice what he had seen and now what he was suspecting. So, they figured it would be wise to devise a plan to let the culprit give himself away.

Chapter 53

SOMETIMES YOU BRUSH UP against something that you don't realize is fate setting something down before you that will in some way alter the course of your life. It may only happen once, or it may be something that happens that keeps calling out to you like an apparition trying to come back from the Acheron.

Later on, Doc McGarrity realized that's what had happened when she ran into Enoch and Ephraim Badgett.

She had been late in the ER sewing up Albert Chauncy, who most folks just called cockeyed because he always held his head to one side or the other, it didn't seem to matter and whatever side he was holding his head, he talked out of the cockeyed side of his mouth. So, whoever was talkin' to him didn't know if they were supposed to be lookin' at his crooked head or his crooked mouth. He had just about cut off his thumb tryin' to draw cut a board with his bandsaw. He was pushin' the 2x4 along the blade with his thumb when the cock of his head seemed to get in the way of his pointin' eye and he sliced off a wafer of that toe-thick digit right along with the hunk of wood he was cuttin'.

After she was through sewin' him up, Enoch came in again with his daddy Ephraim. But this time, Ephraim's head was as blue as a freshly hung whore. Doc McGarrity walked over and examined Ephraim and concluded that he was unequivocally dead, which she couldn't put in her physician notes, so she just wrote, "BID."

Ephraim didn't show any signs of trauma, no signs of having had a heart attack and no apparent injuries. She asked Enoch how his daddy died. "He died like he'd a wanted to. Go ahead and call the law, I know I did wrong, but I couldn't let my daddy go on like that."

Doc McGarrity took Enoch by the arm, pulled him into another room and said, "Enoch, I know you did wrong, I know, but we're going to keep this between us, just you and me. I didn't know your daddy, never met him, except when I saw him in the ER, but what you did you did because you loved your daddy and I don't want you to go to prison or even *worse*, so I want you to *never* and I mean *never* tell *anyone* about this. This is the kind of thing that you can't ever tell *anyone* at any time in your life, *ever*. As far as I can see, your daddy died of complications of dementia. That is what I am going to write on the death certificate. What you did was a very hard thing to do that I believe your daddy would have himself done if he could have. So, you were likely only carrying out the wishes of Ephraim."

Enoch was a man not prone to tears, which were welling up in his eyes. He nodded to what Doc McGarrity had said, as he walked out the door.

A few days later, Doc Kitchen came to Doc McGarrity and said Chief Trimble wanted to meet with them in private.

Chapter 54

BOBBY CONTINUED TO CONGRATULATE the Doctors De La Croix on what became *their* denial of benefits to miners. Even though miners had to apply for benefits through Social Security, Doctors De La Croix and their confederates were continually speaking against the veracity of their claims. The money they were bringing into The Institute was astronomical. Even the administrative judges who were hearing the cases were appalled by the Doctors De La Croix's medical opinions but… they said in their opinions, that even with the testimony of Doctor Kitchen or Doctor McGarrity and other physicians advocating for disability, the miners, who were "clearly disabled," were not able to provide enough clinical evidence to overcome the contradictory opinion of the mining companies' *experts*.

The Doctors De La Croix and The Institute's attorneys made certain that each and every physician who testified as part of Doctors De La Croix's group were certified as *experts* in the area of pulmonary and black lung diagnostics. In *every* opinion that the Doctors De La Croix delivered on the part of the coal companies, they ended their report with, "Large masses found in the lungs, probably tuberculosis, histoplasmosis or similar fungal disease. Black lung not indicated. Clearly many miners are getting payment for a disease that they're claiming that is in fact some other disease process, which when one examines the record carefully, the miners themselves are likely responsible, such as for example excessive smoking."

Doc Kitchen or McGarrity would challenge Doctors De La Croix's remarks indicating that histoplasmosis is a fungal disease caused by bird droppings. Dr. Gaylord or Dr. Rafferty would invariably reply, "There are a lot of Starlings in Kentucky and it is known to have a large bat population which also transmit histoplasmosis in their droppings. Obviously, as with other claims we have been retained to testified in, *these* physicians are not qualified to offer an expert opinion."

Dr. Kitchen asked whichever Doctor De La Croix was speaking at the time to clarify what recent medical literature he had reviewed on black lung disease. One or the other Doctors De La Croix retorted, "We do *not* require medical literature to render an opinion on a disease process that any first-year radiological resident should be able to discern causation."

It was in October that the annual meeting of The Coal Institute was taking place. Their slogan said that they *"Believe in the importance of preserving and promoting the worldwide coal industry, enriching coal knowledge, and inspiring coal support for the future."* Bobby was the keynote speaker and at the end of his address, he said, "I have a surprise tonight. I asked some good friends of mine and who are even better friends of the coal industry to join me tonight. But they didn't know that I was going to be talking about them. Dr. Gaylord De La Croix and Dr. Rafferty De La Croix have become one of the coal industries best friends and advocates. They put together a group of the best radiologists in the country to counter the *erroneous* claims by coal miners that they acquired black lung disease from working in coal mines. Doctors De La Croix and their associates have continually disproven claim after claim that these miners have filed. They don't deny that they are suffering from an illness but that illness has mostly been of their *own* making. The qualifications of the Doctors De La Croix are impeccable and their opinions rendered at the claims Review Board have shown themselves to be unimpeachable. The Doctors De La Croix have saved the coal industry millions of dollars. On a personal note, the Doctors De La Croix have a become good and loyal friends, not only to me personally but also to our industry. Therefore, I would like to present this Award of Appreciation to Dr. Gaylord De La Croix and Dr. Rafferty De La Croix."

It was then that Bobby called the Doctors De La Croix to the podium accompanied by thunderous applause and a standing ovation. The Doctors De La Croix said it was one of the proudest moments of their lives.

Chapter 55

Doc McGarrity told Doc Kitchen what she had done. "It was obvious that Enoch had put his daddy out of his misery and I didn't say anything. I told him to keep quiet about what he had done." Both, Doc Kitchen and Doc McGarrity were frightened that somehow Chief Trimble had found out and was beginning an investigation.

When Chief Trimble arrived at the clinic, he looked forlorn. Here was a man whose long and hard figuring on something had etched his face with deep crevices of consternation. It was a foreboding of what he had decided he was going to allow to come out of his mouth and say to another person.

When they all sat down, Chief Trimble made sure the door was closed and asked them if anyone could hear them outside of the office. When he was assured no one could, he began. Doc Kitchen and Doc McGarrity were not expecting what they were about to hear.

"Blanche is losing her mind, y'all know that. She don't have any idea who I am, doesn't know the youngins, messes herself and sits, when she can sit, and just rocks, and now can't even breathe on her own. Blanche would never want to live like this, hell she wouldn't want me to see her like this. She was a very proud woman..." Tears began to well up in his eyes. "I could shoot her, but I can't do that to her. I could hold a pillow over her face, but I can't do that either. I want to take her off of the ventilator. Will y'all help me?"

Doc Kitchen and McGarrity first said they could make her comfortable if he decided to do that, when Chief Trimble interrupted, "I don't want her to suffer any, *at all*, I want it to be fast, I know what I'm askin' without askin' and I'm guessin' you know what I'm askin', can you help her?"

Doc McGarrity asked Chief Trimble to step out of the room for a few minutes while they talked. When he left, they both thought of the irony of why he'd come. They also both knew what it could be like for a patient coming off of artificial ventilation. She was senile. Hell, since she was on a ventilator it meant she not only couldn't breathe on her own, it also likely meant she didn't *remember* how to breathe. *If* they *helped* Blanche, it would mean that they would be hastening her death, they would be directly participating in her demise. It wouldn't be just making her comfortable, there wasn't enough morphine in the world for that. Administrating the morphine would have to be at a much higher dosage than usual and intravenous.

In a short while they called Chief Trimble back into the office. "What we would like to do is to have Blanche moved here to the hospital. The sooner the better. Then we want you to say goodbye. We won't lie to you, as you know Blanche is *not* going to come back from where she is, she is gone and other than her vital functions she is *dead.* When we turn off the ventilator, she won't begin breathing on her own, but let us add, *if*—and it would be a miracle if she did—she did begin breathing we would immediately stop whatever we were doing, and we want you to understand that."

Chief Trimble said he understood.

"When we turn off the vent, she will quickly begin gasping, then we will begin administering morphine through her IV line. We will *assure* you that we will not let her suffer. You cannot be there, we will, for her dignity, have the curtain pulled and it will take about half an hour to forty-five minutes for Blanche to pass away. Do you understand what we are saying?"

Again, Chief Trimble said he did. He stood up and said he would make arrangements to have Blanche transferred to the hospital.

Blanche came into the hospital a few days later, tubes tucked here and there, and the ever present *puut... sss..., puut... sss* hissing from her Assistor vent. Doc McGarrity had her moved to a ward where there were few patients. In a short while Doc Kitchen showed up. They pulled the curtain around Blanche and looked at each other without saying a word. Doc Kitchen looked at his watch. It was three-fifteen.

Before they turned off the Assistor, Doc McGarrity gave Blanche a 10mg. of Morphine intravenous push. Within a few seconds Blanche's respiration, even on the vent, had decreased. Doc Kitchen then lifted the breaker cover and then turned off the vent. Blanche immediately began gasping for air. Doc McGarrity then pushed 20mg of Morphine; Blanche's air hunger dissipated. Then in a few minutes her air hunger began to express again. Doc McGarrity then pushed 100mg of Morphine into Blanche's IV line. Her respiration showed and slowed and slowed, until her chest rose no more. Blanche was dead. Doc Kitchen and Doc McGarrity sat in the room with Blanche for the full forty-five minutes and recorded on the medication administration sheet that they had given her 10mg every ten minutes until 130mgs had been administered. "Patient was pronounced at four o'clock."

As they had requested, Chief Trimble was not at the hospital and had said goodbye before Blanche had left the rest home. Doc Kitchen and Doc McGarrity drove over to his homeplace and told him his wife had passed away. She had died in no pain, and for all practical purposes had fallen asleep, to never wake up.

Chief Trimble said the only thing he was worried about was that he would go to Hell, having did what he'd done. Doc Kitchen said what Chief Trimble set in motion and what *they* did was merciful. It is no different then maybe taking too long with a patient whose been shot in the head, the bullet has bounced around in his skull and destroyed his ability to ever recover. He will be in a deep coma for the remainder of time that his heart keeps beating. "The heart and the brain aren't really married, it almost seems like they live separate lives inside the same body. But," Doc McGarrity spoke up and said, "once the brain decides it's over there isn't much the heart can do about it."

Chief Trimble was a six feet, six inches one time miner.

It was always said about him that he had fists of iron so "You'd better not be goin' and gettin' hit by him." In the few minutes before they left, Chief Trimble began crying, crying like neither of them had ever seen a man cry before. He also kept thanking them, "I'll *never* forget what you've done for Blanche."

Chapter 56

IT WAS LATER THAT night that Doc Kitchen moved all of the black lung research to their house. He figured the best place since a safe hadn't worked was to put them in plain sight. He took all of the files and transferred them to old photo albums that Spencer Duty, Jr. had but never used. Then he labeled them and sat them on the bookshelves. It certainly seemed like a good idea. The only other folks he told were Dr. Hall and Chief Trimble.

The next day Dr. McIntosh was doing a workup on Eurcle Skaggs, listening to his chest, moving his stethoscope here and there, asking him "to take a deep breath and hold it."

It was hard for Eurcle to hold his breath, because he didn't have much to hold. He'd become a frail man, even more frail than the men with the black lung. Now Eurcle, who was only in his fifties, had come down with lung cancer. It never was determined if he had the black lung, but it didn't matter much. He wouldn't be alive long enough to develop much more of anything, not even a cold.

Dr. McIntosh had softened up over time and wasn't being so difficult. But the past few weeks he had changed and seemed to becoming more disagreeable each and every day. Eurcle tried his best to sit up straight while Dr. McIntosh listened to his chest. He just didn't seem to have the strength to hold himself upright, and kept collapsing into himself. Dr. McIntosh, not even offering to help him hold himself up, pulled his stethoscope off Eurcle's chest, sighed and said, "Can you sit up, so I can do my job!"

Eurcle raised his head and coughed out a glob of bloody sputum into his hand.

"Jesus," Dr. McIntosh said, showing his disgust. "You people act like animals. It doesn't matter if I can't listen to your lungs, you're going to die anyway."

Then he stormed out of the examining room. Eurcle's wife, Jewell, wiped his mouth and chin, helped him to stand up as best as she could and made their way to the door. She asked the nurse on the way out if Eurcle could have some morphine, that his chest was hurtin' somethin' awful. The nurse went to Doc McGarrity, who didn't understand why Dr. McIntosh hadn't gone ahead and prescribed the morphine.

Everyone knew poor Eurcle was sufferin' about as terribly as a man can suffer. One of the nurses who had known Eurcle from when they were youngins together said it was like Eurcle would take in a breath and as soon as the air made it to his lungs the cancer would abduct it and hold it hostage. Even with the little breaths Eurcle managed to take, the lung cancer was so greedy that *it* wanted it all.

Eurcle and Jewell had sat down to take some of the burden of standin' off of them both. Doc McGarrity found Dr. McIntosh and asked him why he hadn't prescribed the morphine for Eurcle. "He wouldn't cooperate, I couldn't even listen to his chest, if he hadn't smoked so damn much, he wouldn't have got goddamn lung cancer. Jesus, don't these people *ever* take responsibility for anything they do! He didn't ask for any morphine," Dr. McIntosh said.

Doc McGarrity said that he had a standing order for morphine in his chart. There hadn't been time to review Eurcle's chart, Dr. McIntosh said, he was just too busy to read every chart. The entire time he kept rubbing his eyes.

Doc McGarrity wrote a script for morphine and gave Eurcle an injection before he left the ER. She also said to come back if the pain got worse and left word for the ER to contact her directly should Eurcle return that night. Then she told Doc Kitchen what had happened, since he was the resident supervisor.

Chapter 57

THE NEXT NIGHT AGAIN about three or so, Constable Blevins was knocking at Moses and Janice's door. When Moses made his way to answer the knocking, the Constable said he'd seen the light again in Doc Kitchen's office. He wondered what he should do. Doc Kitchen said he would take care of it in the morning, thanking Constable Blevins for taking the time to come by. The Constable apologized for gettin' the Doc up, him and the other Doc having a baby and all. "I know y'all need your sleep, when you can get it!"

The next day Doc Kitchen and Doc McGarrity called Doctor McIntosh into their office. Immediately Doctor McIntosh was prickly haughty. "I know why I'm here, that Skaggs patient didn't ask for morphine. There wasn't time to read his chart, he's dying anyway, what the hell are you going to do with a patient like that?"

As he strung together his string of excuses, Doc Kitchen looked at him and said, "I guess you'd have more time to review patients' charts if you got some sleep at night."

Immediately, Doctor McIntosh became as quiet as a church mouse. "I don't understand," he said.

"Of course, you do," said, Doc Kitchen. "The question is why have you been breaking into our offices and rifling through our research files?"

Doctor McIntosh began sputtering and stammering, like he was looking for a piece of fresh fruit on a tree where there wasn't any. Doc McGarrity then said, "The question we have is, what are we going to do with you? Chief Trimble can prosecute you for theft and breaking and entering, but we want to hear what your reason is before we press charges."

Doctor McIntosh, looking hangdog, cupped his slung forehead in his hands. "I had no choice, if I didn't do it then something about me would be used against me. I was told to copy your files and send them to an address I was given. Unless I did, something about me would be sent to the medical school and that would be it for me. I would be thrown, one way or another, out of medicine."

Doc Kitchen asked what in God's name was so terrible that could be used against him.

Doctor McIntosh replied, "I'm a homosexual."

"Christ," Doc McGarrity said.

"I would never be able to see patients again, can you imagine if my colleagues new about me, what they would do, how could I treat male patients?" Doctor McIntosh went on. "No one in medical school knew, they suspected, but that is different than somebody knowing for sure that you're queer."

"Remember Dr. John Fryer, the psychiatrist who stood up in a *rubber mask* and *wig*, and announced to the whole world that he was queer. They did *everything* to destroy him, *everything*. Being homosexual is a form of *madness*."

Doc McGarrity said, "Do you have any idea who these people were who were threatening to expose you? How did they first contact you? Someone must have said something about you to someone, otherwise they couldn't have found out."

Doc Kitchen spoke up and said, "Doctor McIntosh, we don't think any less of you, it doesn't matter to us. You're entitled to your life, whatever that is. And we can see that you were in an impossible spot. We have a pretty good idea who these people are. Did you actually send any of our research to the address they gave you?"

Doctor McIntosh said he just could not bring himself to, but that he had planned to send it soon. He still had the copies in his room, but he had not mailed them off. "We would like what you copied back. We are going to publish it; it is not a secret. We just don't want it to be misconstrued and for someone to prepare rebuttals or attempt to discredit it before it is peer reviewed and published."

"I'll go pack my bags and get the material and bring it back over," Doctor McIntosh said as he was standing up.

"It's not necessary to pack your bags," Doc McGarrity said. "I think I can speak for Doctor Kitchen when I say that we don't want you to leave. You made a *damn* big mistake but you didn't try to lie your way out of it, you came clean with us. But these people may expose you, so I think we should be prepared for that. I don't think Paintsville would be very accommodating if they found out. You would be called awful names and some folks would stop coming to see you. Let me ask you a personal question: how could these people prove you're homosexual, I know that is a terrible question, but it may have bearing..."

Doctor McIntosh again said there were a lot of rumors when he was in medical school, but he had never been arrested. Had he ever had sexual relations with anyone else in his medical school class? He said that he had, but they had been very discrete.

"How had the relationship ended?" Doc Kitchen asked.

"We decided that to continue was going to end our careers so we stopped. He got married to a pediatric resident right before he began his residency in dermatology."

"Jesus Christ, what bastards these people are," Doc McGarrity said and then added, "my God, what kind of world have we brought Isabella into? We don't want you to leave, but you may have to. You may have to go somewhere more accepting of your circumstances."

They decided that it was best to end the meeting now. If Doctor McIntosh was exposed, what would it mean for him being able to remain in medicine? Their research hadn't been sent off so the integrity of their findings was still intact.

Doctor McIntosh left and went back to the rooming house where he was staying. He got the copies he had made and then on the way back to the hospital he went by Eurcle and Jewell's homeplace. When Jewell came to the door, Doctor McIntosh said, "Hello Mrs. Skaggs, I came by to apologize for the way I treated your husband, there is no excuse for it, I am really ashamed of my attitude toward you and Eurcle. Please let me know if there is anything I can do for you."

Jewell said they were just getting ready to set down for supper, and would he like to join them? Doctor McIntosh nodded yes, opened the rickety door, swatting away flies clinging to the screen and joined Eurcle and Jewell in their prayer before they partook of their nightly meal.

Jewell bowed her head and said, *"For home and friends and daily food we give thee thanks and praise, blessed our use of food we take and guide us all our days, amen..."*

Eurcle didn't have much of an appetite and even less wind to lift his fork from his plate to his mouth. Jewell wiped his chin, which at suppertime always seemed to have slobber-coated whiskers and his tongue kept goin' this way and that lookin' for the corners of his mouth. He never failed to nod "thank you" even though most of the time chewing his meat took most of his spark.

It'd been a long time that Doctor McIntosh did not feel withdrawn or distant. Now, the circumstances of what was happening with the patient he was tending to penetrated him enough to be hurt. When Jewell said the dinner prayer, Doctor McIntosh silently asked God to forgive him for what he'd done.

Chapter 58

DR. GAYLORD AND DR. RAFFERTY assured Bobby that they would have copies of Doctors Kitchen and McGarrity's research soon. They said they had contacts at the University of Louisville School of Medicine. Doctors De La Croix had discovered something that would be very damaging to a resident working down in Paintsville. They hadn't received what they were waiting for yet, but expected it soon. "Once we get whatever they've done, and we're sure there will be errors in their methodology, we will publish a rebuttal, which we can then use in disproving claims where they make a *declaration* of themselves as experts. In other word, we will use their own research against them."

Bobby listened to Doctors De La Croix, wondering to himself what made them click. It always struck him as odd that Dr. Gaylord and Rafferty had such impeccable credentials but seemed hell bent, no matter what anyone else said, that they were always *right*. It was all that seemed to matter to them and from that they were able to extract a sense of power. But, for Bobby, the Doctors De La Croix had been God sent, or "…maybe…" as he liked to joke, "…sent straight up from Hell in a golden chariot."

Chapter 59

Doc Kitchen and McGarrity worked almost day and night, with little Isabella often attached to Janice's breast, getting their research together. It showed that black lung was clearly associated with increasing the likelihood, if the miner *lived* long enough, of developing various cancers—certainly lung cancer, but also bladder cancer because of exposure to coal dust. Like in the lungs, coal dust distillates that get broken down in the body get expelled through the bladder. But, like other chemicals folks are exposed to, those poisonous substances stay in the bladder for hours before they are peed out. And during that time, they are absorbed into the bladder wall. A few times is of no consequences, usually, but *years* of day in and day out exposure, in an underground cave where there is no ventilation, has devastating effects. The utter peril of the human body to being exposed to coal dust just couldn't be overstated.

When Doc Kitchen and Doc McGarrity laid out their research, they were taken back by the crushing effects of mining. They had seen the effects on the men and their families, as they treated each patient. But now it was as though the one picture had metamorphosed into a deadly collage. For these men, it wasn't *just* a job. When you got old enough, you went to work in the mine to help the family survive. And you never left, you worked until you were old enough to go underground. The mines swallowed up each and every miner's family like a Terrible Dogfish.

Doc Kitchen and Doc McGarrity had figured that someone associated with the mines was out to discredit their work by pilfering their research and discrediting it. There was a heinousness here, a vileness to the men who would try and use medical evidence against the very people who made them wealthy. They hoped that their work would provide a foundation to build further research.

Doctor McIntosh gave Doc Kitchen the address where he was supposed to send the files that he had taken. Doc McGarrity put together a 'packet' of information for whoever would pick it up.

In her letter she wrote,

> *To Whom It May Concern;*
>
> *Thank you, for taking an interest in our work. Obviously, you were so riveted by our findings that you exerted extreme methods to obtain them. However, we have decided that it would be best to present our findings to a wider professional audience rather than to present it to someone who appears not to have the education or clinical qualifications to correctly interpret the meaning of our research. We suggest that you find someone to help you understand the disease implications of chronic exposure to coal dust and its correlated chemical toxins. Again, we thank you for expressing an interest in our work.*
>
> *Moses Kitchen, M.D. and Janice McGarrity, M.D.*

She then bound together five-hundred black pages, a brick and her letter and sent the packet to the address Doctor McIntosh had given them.

Chapter 60

THAT MORNING DOCTORS DE La Croix stopped to check the post office box to see if the information they were expecting had yet arrived. When Dr. Gaylord swung open the postal box and saw the package, he was elated. He was also surprised how heavy it was. It was the first time Dr. Rafferty could remember seeing his brother running, carrying the package, with a smile on his face that conveyed his delight that their plan of extortion had born fruit.

After they got to their office they had their secretary call Bobby, who was in the city for a board meeting. "Come to our office, we have something to show you…" Doctors De La Croix were going to wait for Bobby to arrive before they opened the packet. In a short while Bobby arrived at The Institute, making his way through the labyrinth of floors and offices to Radiology. The Doctors De La Croix met Bobby. He had never seen them so lively, usually there was a deliberateness in their steps, but now they walked with long strides, talking endlessly about this and that, and anxious to get to their office. When they entered the office, Bobby saw the package sitting on a conference table in the middle of the room.

"There it is, we have been waiting months for this. This will change everything. It is likely that many of those damn free loaders won't even bother to bring claims because we can now refute *anything* before they even say it. We now have copies of *all* of the so-called research that those charlatans in Kentucky have done. Our people can tear it apart before they can put it to use in claim disputes."

Bobby was not just curious but continually amazed at the tenaciousness of Doctors De La Croix. In some ways he thought they were out of their minds.

Dr. Gaylord, with Dr. Rafferty peering over his shoulder, began ripping away the wrappings enshrouding the package exposing the contents of the box. The brick first came into view, then the typed letter, then the sheaf of papers. Lifting the ream out of the box, he fanned through the stack. *Nothing,* blank pages… Dr. Rafferty read the letter.

Bobby, having been astounded at the Doctors De La Croix's tenaciousness just minutes before, was now astounded at their tantrum. As Dr. Rafferty read the letter, he screamed, "*Who* in the goddamn hell does *she* think she *is*! They aren't going to get by with this!" Then he wadded up the letter, threw the stack of blank pages across the room and shoved the brick onto the floor, storming out of the room, with Dr. Gaylord close behind. This was the second time they had been made a fool of by these people, who were nothing more than farmers who also happened to be doctors, Dr. Gaylord ranted, "Goddamn farmer doctors. They think they are *somebodies*. But *they* are *nothings*!"

Chapter 61

Docs Kitchen and McGarrity decided the best way to present their findings was to establish the SDRC Memorial Medical Conference. It would occur each year in of all places Paintsville, Kentucky, and each year it would have a different subject matter that would be at the cutting edge of medicine. But it would always be research based, and subjects that required deeper research. The first SDRC Medical Conference would be on The Multiple Long-Term Effects of Exposure to Coal Dust. The response to the conference was overwhelming. Physicians and researchers came from all over the place to listen and ask questions about the effects of coal dust. Even toxicologists came to understand how coal dust tore apart the body. And politicians came to understand how they could use the research against their opponents. The Doctors De La Croix chose not to attend the conference. It was shortly after that that Doc Kitchen and Doc McGarrity were asked to testify before Congress. The SDRC Medical Conference had caused some quake in the complacency of the attitudes toward black lung disease and how it destroyed lives.

Chapter 62

LITTLE ISABELLA WAS WALKING and talking now. Nurse Abigail Abernathy was about as much as a grandmother as could be to her, always fussing with her hair and it seemed just about every day she had a new color bow. But given that she was at the clinic every day, she had more mammas and papaws as any little girl had ever had in her whole life. Sometimes she would sit on Doc Kitchen or McGarrity's knee while they would be talking to a patient. Thing was, she was a wonderful little girl. Even though she was always at her mommy's and daddy's knee, she ain't spoiled one bit, folks would say.

It wasn't well known around Paintsville, but Doc Kitchen and McGarrity, not being church goers, had never tithed. So instead, they talked with Reverend Burton about figuring how much money he needed each month for folks who had little to eat or were in need of this or that. Then he'd quietly tell Doc Kitchen or McGarrity and they'd make sure he had what he needed. They also asked Reverend Burton if he would, should they die, take Isabella and raise her as one of his own. They had no relations and so they wanted to make sure she'd be taken care of in case of their demise. What they had also done was to invest the money Spencer Duty, Jr. had left so that no one coming to the clinic was ever charged one red cent for anything, including medications. Thing was, folks showed up with offerins of bags of corn, apples and whatever else they might be growin' up that year and at Thanksgiving and Christmas time there was a bounty of food delivered up to the clinic.

Right after the two men had busted up the clinic, miners began patrolling twenty-four hours a day, all year long, even on Christmas day. Word got out that any man who'd do harm to Doc Kitchen or

McGarrity or the clinic'd have to answer to a cadre of miners, who'd say, "There's some mighty big mountains and some pretty deep holes around these parts."

Chapter 63

ONCE DOCTORS DE LA CROIX got over their perturbedness, they realized that their best course of action was to simply go on as they had. Doctors De La Croix or their people'd show up at disability hearings and simply say what they'd always said and for any of the physicians the miners had bamboozled into testifying for them, well they had to prove that the Doctors De La Croix or their associates were wrong. Delay, delay, delay…

In fact, though, it wasn't *just* delays. Unbeknownst to the Doctors De La Croix, they had not only established with other physicians to supply dubious medical opinions, they had also potentially setup the other physicians, who were supplying much of their responses through the United States Mail System, to be guilty of violating the RICO Act, as well as federal fraud enrichment claims. Bobby figured at some point this could be the case, but he never said anything to Doctors De La Croix. There was just too much to be gained. CON-SOL, who Bobby was now the President of, was saving millions of dollars in claims monies and stopping dead in its tracks any law suits brought forth by the goddamn miners. The mines *needed* mining, folks needed to stay warm and their lights on and the miners *needed* a job. There would always be coal, there would always be mines, and well, miners are a dime a dozen. You spend one dime and you replace it with another. Bobby had no love for miners, no love for the Doctors De La Croix but he *loved* the coal industry.

It was *the* economic dirt of the United States. Whatever he could do, he would do to work the mines from atop. He'd use the miners as his arms to bring up from the inside of the earth the black rocks. It wasn't that different than the Pharaohs using the Israelites. Bobby liked to secretly think of himself as a modern-day Pharaoh, reading Exodus 1:11 over and over again for inspiration, "*Therefore they set taskmasters over them to afflict them with their burdens. And they built for Pharaoh supply cities, Pithom and Raamses.*"

It was on a particularly snowy day in Baltimore when Bobby told the Doctors De La Croix that the miners *were* like the Israelites in some way. They were uneducated and always dirty, "You just can't get them clean, they are more like oxen, beasts of burden... They will always be the have nots to be had."

The Doctors De La Croix appreciated his sentiment. They saw what the other kind of "have nots," as the Doctors De La Croix began to use the phrase, looked like when they came into The Institute's ER and one or the other was called down to read an x-ray. "Christ, they shoot, stab each other, kill themselves in one way or another, why the hell do we bother saving them at all?" If they said it in front of Bobby, he'd always say, "But, what would we do without them?"

Chapter 64

CALLS WERE COMING IN right and left for Doc Kitchen and Doc McGarrity to talk to miners at the UMW Union Hall meetings. Folks were gettin' more and more riled up about being told they didn't have this or that, even though by the time a miner was in his forties he was about as broken down as a man can be and still be walkin' upright.

"We can't breathe, we can hardly walk, our bones never stop aching, we blow black snot out our noses and we're on a slow boat to hell and all y'all say is get your goddamn asses back to work…"

Almost all of the miners had had claims that had been denied. Even when they went to the company doc with their complaints, they'd just say what the company docs had been sayin' since 1920 or thereabouts. Docs Kitchen and McGarrity mostly just answered questions. They all knew who was sufferin' from what. The black lung didn't hide itself. Once it got started up inside you, it let it be known that it was comin' for you and there was no stoppin' it.

At one meeting Orey "Brownie" Poole stood up and started ramblin' on. It seemed that Brownie had been a breaker boy way back when. Well, as he got older, and in those days had received one too many beatings from the boss man for smartin' off and doin' some figurin' on his own, he told his daddy that he didn't want to work the mine. He had his sights set on workin' for the railroad, and workin' his way up to engineer for the Miller Creek Railroad that ran between Paintsville and Van Lear.

At the meeting, he explained his daddy hadn't take kindly to that notion and said he'd do what he'd been told he'd do or his daddy said he'd beat him within an inch of his life. The thing that Brownie never told anybody his whole life was the reason he didn't want to become a miner was because he was fearful of going underground—bein' closed up in a box goin' down into the hole, even if he made it, havin' no place even to stand up, havin' to shat in a shovel and flip it onto the conveyor belt hopin' it didn't come back at you. But the worse part was the dark.

"It'd be like bein' buried alive," Brownie'd think to himself. Once he got big enough his daddy said it was time and if he didn't go down in the hole, he'd better be movin' his self on because a fourteen-year-old youngin ought to be helpin' his family make ends meet. They'd brought him into this world and by God he could get his hind end to work to help give back what unselfishness had been shown to him. Early that mornin' when Brownie showed up for the whistle call he was shakin' so bad the piss was just about runnin' out of him. He crowded alongside the other miners as they were lowered down to the first leg of the hole. Then when they hit bottom, they had to crawl just about a half-mile to begin pickin' away at the coal seam. The lamp on his head was the only light there was. Brownie pissed his self twice before his got to the opening where they were to begin pickin'. After just a few swings of the pick, Brownie had all he could take and he lost his mind. He started babblin' about this and that, takin' the light off his helmet and shinin' it in his face, feelin' like he'd just been buried and then had woke up with nowhere to go.

When he stood up that night at the meeting hall, he'd not been a miner for years but the men still let him come to all the meetings and took care of him as best they could. He'd left his mind down in that hole that day, long ago, and since then he hadn't made one lick of sense. But the folks understood that happened to men sometimes underground. There was lots of things that happened underground that nobody talked about, even the Tommy Knockers comin' out of nowhere stirin' things up scared the daylights out of the miners who'd seen them. Most of the older miners though brought them a sandwich or a hunk of bread so they wouldn't be causing no trouble. It was different being down in the hole, seein' things, hearin' things that folks up top don't.

At one particular meeting that Doc Kitchen and Doc McGarrity were at there was a lot of whisperin' at the back of the union hall right underneath the bulletin board that had all the meeetins' listed for Johnson County, month by month, unless somethin' came up that needed discussin' before one meetin' or another.

Later on, Eli Sanders, who had been ordained by his congregation as the Pastor of the Holiness Pentecostal Church of God, told Doc Kitchen that the miners at the back of the union hall had been discussin' a sightin' that kept bein' seen. *They* was bein' seen by *all* the miners, when they'd blasted into another room, figurin' they'd made a room big enough for both of *them* to show themselves.

It seems that longer ago than most memories go, Mickey Hartley'd been workin' a seam here and there when he swung back his axe and its back pick caught a piece of ceilin' timber. Mickey, likely before figurin', pulled hard tryin' to loosen it, which caused the ceilin' to collapse right on top of him.

Mickey was buried under a ton of slate about as fast as a man can think a thought. His white mule'd been buried too. Well, Pastor Eli went on to say that when the other miners told Mickey's wife of not too many years that the mine had claimed him for its own, she began screamin' and runnin' wild like a ghost of gnats to a light. Irene—that was Mickey's wife—was in the #5 Company Store down in Van Lear, gettin' herself a couple of yards of cotton that she'd saved and saved for to make a new dress to up and surprise Mickey, who she loved, as she'd say, "More than a sack of taters."

Well, she was so taken over by such consuming misfortune that she jumped straight off the porch of the #5 Company Store, flailin' her arms this way and that, and unbeknownst to her woeful mind, ran straight into the side of the #1 Train that was just pullin' into Van Lear Junction. Irene was killed in such a way that folks couldn't even begin to imagine her in their rememberances.

When the miners saw the apparitions of Irene and Mickey show up down in the hole, the men working that seam went crawlin' and runnin' as fast as one can crawl and run underground, climbin' over top of each other to get topside. Georgie Hoskins said Irene and Mickey walked right out of the rock. Rufus Sergent and his youngest youngin' Yancy saw the wraiths of Irene and Mickey first, Harry Fain was working right beside them and couldn't believe his eyes. The men just stood there, leaning on their picks and shovels, watchin' Irene and Mickey move around the room like they was touchin' the walls, tryin' to find their ways back into the rock. Georgie Hoskins said, once they were up top, that he'd been told by his granddaddy that if you see the dead down in the hole, *just leave them be*, don't bother um at all.

"You may think they're tryin' to find their way out, but they ain't. Let um be! They're lookin' for somethin' but we cain't know what that is until it's our time…"

Since he'd come to Paintsville and growing up in Butte, Doc Kitchen had heard stories about miner visitants showin' up underground, scarin' the Dickins out of the miners. But, most of the time, they came to tell the men the mine wasn't safe and they needed to get up top just as fast as they could.

Sometimes for Moses there was a sense of wistfulness in hearing the tales, they in one form or another had been a part of his youth. He had spent many hours telling Janice the legends of the leprechauns causing a ruckus. Sometimes if they were too consumed by agitation, they might even up and decide to kill you.

"Best to be on their good side. You may not see them for a while, but before you're done with your last day of minin' they'll come to you. *Everyone* sees them one time or other," the old miners would pass on to the youngsters whose hands weren't all calloused up yet.

That night at the union hall, with the men talkin' at the back and all, some of the miners were gettin' nervous already about the next day's minin'. One thing for sure, Docs Kitchen and McGarrity always respected what the miners and their families said they saw.

"One person can't figure out another man's experience for him," Doc Kitchen would say. "If we try, we're sure to get it wrong, and if we're not being asked for our opinion, then we're likely to come across as being critical."

As they walked out the door, Doc Kitchen and Doc McGarrity heard a man from the front yellin', "Thank y'all…" and wave.

Then to close out the meetin' Blind Burl and the Horseless Rustlers came up front and began to play

> *"Oh Lord, Oh Lord*
> *I'm a callin' to Thee*
> *Please open the door or*
> *just let me be*
> *The Pearly Gates*
> *are a baitin' my soul*

I'm a callin' to you Lord
to come and get me
I done died once,
don't want to die twice
Eternal life
was your promise to me
Oh Lord, Oh Lord,
please come and get me"

Chapter 65

THE FACT OF THE matter was that Docs Kitchen and McGarrity had got a reputation not only for the black lung, but also as tenacious physicians. Other Docs would say, if Kitchen and McGarrity can't figure out what's wrong with you, then it doesn't yet have a name.

Funny thing was that Bobby, getting older now, was getting stiffer. Just about everywhere his body bent was buckling up. He talked to Doctors De La Croix about it who said it was just age. Bobby had even insisted that they x-ray him to see if there was anything that didn't look right. Reluctantly Doctors De La Croix did and said their initial impression was correct, "You are just getting old and are having some arthritis setting in…" was their consensus. The problem was Bobby kept getting stiffer and stiffer. But especially his jaw. Again Bobby, this time demanding Doctors De La Croix take more time and try to understand what was happening to him, got no further this time than last, except that they said likely he had a touch of TMJ and he should see a dentist. Even as a young man his jaw had always been tight and some of his muscles too, but then it just seemed to clear up and he learned to live with a bit of stiffness. But *now*, he was getting to feel like his whole body had been put in a cast and, where it hadn't been before, becoming excruciating. Bobby contacted the big medical center up in Rochester, Minnesota, who said they preferred to send for his medical records first. When they got the records from The Institute, collectively dictated by the Doctors De La Croix, there was no reason for them to question their clinical understanding of the symptoms that Bobby was presenting and referred him back to The Institute, "…for any necessary follow up…" Bobby, consumed with desperation, then took a step that he never imagined himself taking. He made a call to Paintsville, Kentucky.

When Doc Kitchen received the call, he was taken back, it was like, as he told Doc McGarrity, getting a call straight from the Devil himself. But… he listened to what Bobby was calling for and said he would see him for a consult, as long as he and Doc McGarrity saw him together. A few days later Bobby arrived at the clinic. When Docs Kitchen and McGarrity laid eyes on him, they thought, there sits a dead man. When Doc Kitchen had met him before, he seemed vibrant, a man with eyes that looked like a crook who thinks he has God in his pocket, but vibrant. But now…

As he spoke his jaws were tight and Doc Kitchen thought they looked like they were ossifying. Bobby said he had been diagnosed with TMJ and the Doctors De La Croix had said he was "Just getting on in years." The first thing Doc McGarrity wanted was a series of x-rays. Bobby spoke up and said again that Doctors De La Croix had done x-rays and they had found nothing.

Doc McGarrity said she wanted her own. They also took a complete medical history and discovered he's had a painless mass on the scapula when he was three years old. After surgical removal of this mass, he experienced stiffness and slowly progressive limitation of neck motion, but then seemed to return to normal functioning. Over the next twenty or so years, he had periodic stiffness here and there, mostly in his joints and muscles. A musculoskeletal examination showed a stiffing of the neck, jaw, spine, knees, shoulders and hips and incomplete extension of the elbow. Doc McGarrity said he looked like the Tin Man without oil. Doc Kitchen expanded the x-rays ordered by Doc McGarrity to a full body view.

When they got the films back Doc Kitchen and McGarrity were shocked at what they were seeing. The radiography of the neck, spine, head, shoulder and feet demonstrated an ossification that they surmised went back years. And clearly the ossification was increasing every day, as was demonstrated by Bobby's complaints and growing agony. The lateral neck radiograph also showed such a hardening of the trapezius muscle and that his spine wasn't far from fusing.

Doc Kitchen had only seen one case like this before and it was when he was in residency. There was no cure. The odd thing was that the disease was believed to be hereditary and typically showed up in childhood and then progressively got worse over time with no abatement. Bobby's appeared to have shown up when he was a child but then somehow went dormant and then began to reappear with an odd retributive justice as he entered his elder years. But, without a doubt, Doc Kitchen said to Doc McGarrity, Bobby was turning to stone. Especially around his neck and throat.

It was the next day when they met with Bobby.

"We know what is wrong with you. Unfortunately, we don't have good news for you. The medical term for what is afflicting you is *fibrodysplasia ossificans progressive*. It's also called Stone Man Disease. It is hereditary, and usually comes on in childhood. Yours apparently did, but then it, for some reason, at least the major symptoms, seemed to turn off. But, as you have gotten older, it has turned back on and, I am sorry to tell you, Bobby, but there is no cure.

"Typically, it is not fatal, per say. In essence the disease itself doesn't cause death, but what happens is that your muscles, connective tissues and joints are all ossifying. In other words, turning to bone.

"That's where the name comes from, *Stone Man*."

"What about surgery, to cut away the bone?" Bobby asked.

"Surgery actually makes the disease worse. Trying to cut away the excess bone growth intensifies excess bone development. Even routine surgeries that don't involve bone can create inflammation and stimulate a bone development reaction."

"So, are you telling me I am going to die?"

"In a word, yes. Giving how rapidly the ossification is developing, and especially around your throat and neck, you will probably die of what is called cardiorespiratory failure from thoracic insufficiency syndrome. In other words," Doc Kitchen said, "it will be like you are lying down and someone increasingly places large rocks on your chest, causing you not to be able to get enough air into your lungs.

"What is happening is that the intercostal muscles that are in between your ribs are ossifying, turning to bone so your ribs can no longer expand as you breathe air in. Plus, it appears that your neck is also ossifying rapidly."

"Will I be in pain?" he asked.

That was when Doc McGarrity spoke up. "The attitude of most of the medical community is not to tell the patient the truth. To try and soft peddle the severity of the condition. Doctor Kitchen and

I will not do that, if you don't want us to. If you want the truth, I will tell you."

Bobby, without any figuring, said he did.

Doc McGarrity said, "If I was in a similar position, I would not want to die the way Doctor Kitchen described. You can be made comfortable, but you are basically going to suffocate to death. You will have a breathing tube in at best, be heavily sedated because your rib cage will not be able to expand and you will suffocate, even on a ventilator, you are going to suffer. You have decisions to make. There is nothing from a medical standpoint we can do for you. We can give you some medication to dull the pain you are having but as time goes on, and I must tell you that time appears to be closing in rapidly, you will shortly have to be hospitalized."

Bobby looked up and said, "Then I should get my affairs in order and…" he didn't finish his sentence.

Docs Kitchen and McGarrity looked at each other. Doc Kitchen chose his words carefully. "If someone is not a physician and cannot acquire certain, say barbiturate medications, then the choice should be carbon monoxide, in a garage, with a full tank of gas and undiscoverable until after the car completely runs out of gas."

Bobby sat quiet. "I guess doctors don't get asked that question too often?"

"In fact, we do, but doctors deny that dying, be it suicide or by a terminal condition, happens. But we are *all* going to die of something. Some people have tragic depressions or psychotic disorders. But then there are others who are rational and don't want to die to what amounts to a horrible death. There are hospices in Great Britain but not too many here in the United States yet, hopefully there will be in the future, so people won't have to suffer so horribly as they die. We are sorry you had to come all the way down here to get an accurate diagnosis. But we're more sorry we couldn't give you better news."

As he was getting ready to leave, Bobby said, "The Bible says that the soul rises up into the throat right before death, what does that mean for me?"

"I simply don't know," Doc Kitchen replied.

Bobby left Paintsville enraged at Dr. Gaylord De La Croix and Dr. Rafferty De La Croix for the countless times asking for their help and for what was clearly negligence in reading his x-rays. Instead, Bobby had received nothing but platitudes. Docs Kitchen and McGarrity could have declined to meet with him and he may still be facing ambiguity about his pending death. If he had a choice, he preferred facing death. At least now he had some time, difficult or not, to put some things right.

The first thing he did when he got back home was to sit down at his typewriter.

> To Whom It May Concern,
>
> *I write this of sound mind but not of body. I am turning to stone. I have been told I have a rare condition called Stone Man's Disease. Where my body will literally turn to stone (bone) and I will die a horrible death. The stoniness is already beginning to consume me. Let is also be known that once I have my affairs in order, I plan on terminating my own life. No one else should be considered a participant in my decision, as it is mine and mine alone.*
>
> *I do not wish to die before I can set somethings right for which I am responsible and for the countless lives of miners that I have ruined or hastened their death in one form or another. I have always worked hard for the people that I was employed by. But, as I look back, my judgment and being too full of myself put the company over the people who worked for them.*
>
> *I have been a coal man all my life. But for me, each and every miner was expendable and replaceable. Men to be used and I find it disguising to admit, but also used up. From early in my career, I approached miners this way. For that I am truly sorry. And, for that, I have no way of making amends except to write this letter.*
>
> *Over the past years, I have employed Dr. Gaylord De La Croix and Dr. Rafferty De La Croix as physicians to counter each and every claim for black lung disability benefits from coal miners. Doctors De La Croix became the Co-Chiefs of The Diseases of the Lung Center, at the Inner Harbor Diagnostic Institute. They had and currently have the final say on each and every x-ray where there was a question of black lung being the diagnosis.*
>
> *I employed the Doctors De La Croix with full knowledge of my board. In the Doctors De La Croix I found two individuals who, for whatever their reasons, were more than willing to cast aside*

their ethics and medical judgment and declare each and every case of possible black lung disease null and void. Over the years that Doctors De La Croix have been affiliated with me they have reviewed more than 3,500 medical records, x-rays and patient interviews. Together, they have testified at an equal number of disability black lung claims hearings. During this time Doctors De La Croix had not found even one case of black lung disease. These were decisions made by the Doctors De La Croix and with my blessings, my boards blessings and with the full and complete knowledge of The Inner Harbor Diagnostic Institute. For these decisions, Dr. Gaylord De La Croix and Dr. Rafferty De La Croix have been and are extremely well compensated for falsely stating, time and again, to see any indications of black lung disease.

People in the coal industry will remember me for saving them countless millions of dollars and liability. For those miners whose lives I participated in their destruction and their families being destitute I will be remembered for being the pariah that I am. I can only pray that writing this, at the end of my life, will make my time in Hell shorter.

Accompanying this letter will be thousands of patient notes and other documentation which prove claimants' medical findings were altered to support the Doctors De La Croix's medical opinions. In each and every case, where a claimant's diagnosis of black lung was made by either Moses Kitchen, M.D. or Janice McGarrity, M.D., there can be no doubt of the accuracy of their medical opinion. Doctors De La Croix made their research into the causative factors of black lung a personal vendetta. Their personal reasons for their actions are unknown to me.

Let it also be known that Doctors De La Croix and myself hired two individuals to destroy the black lung clinic that is run by Doctor's Kitchen and McGarrity. We also threatened to black mail a Doctor Red McIntosh, who is another physician at the clinic, to steal Doctor Kitchen and McGarrity's research findings. This was done as to attempt to discredit their work before they had an opportunity to publish it and once again, undermine any claims that coal miners made for disability benefits against the mining companies. I ask first and foremost for forgiveness and secondly for someone to investigate that what I am stating is factual and truthful. The enclosed documents should be enough to substantiate my claims. I am truly sorry for what I have done. The world will be better off without me. I guess that is what God is saying also.

Signed: B.T. "Bobby" Tucker"

Bobby then pulled his will from his desk drawer and began reviewing it. He had no family, no wife, no children. He'd been a loner most of his life and had planned on leaving any money he had made to the coal industry, in some form or the other. In his final days he decided against it. Everything he had was being willed to the SDRC.

It was a month after he had gone to Paintsville that Bobby pulled his car into his barn and slid the doors closed. He had a couple of cows on his land that had been there for about as long as he'd owned the farm. For some reason or other he'd never butchered them. They had to be about ten or so. He put a rope around them and led them over to his neighbor, who Bobby said he could have if, after being around for so long, he too promised not to butcher them. His neighbor said they could spend whatever years they had left grassing here and there.

"Probably be tough anyhow," the neighbor said.

Bobby said he just didn't have time to keep an eye on them anymore, so he patted them on the head and walked away. After he closed the barn doors, he took a handful of barbiturates, slid a green garden hose deep into the tail pipe of his car and taped the end of the exhaust close. Then he ran the hose through a window, cranked it up and taped the inch or so opening where the hose came through, closed. Then Bobby started the car. He leaned back, not knowing what to expect. His body was stiff and his jaw was so tight he could barely eat. Bobby decided that he wouldn't try to breathe deep and just let himself takes breaths as best he could. In not too long of a time, Bobby began to hear barking, it was though a dog was just on the other side of a hill, running toward him. It wasn't long before the sound was cresting over the hill. There was the white lab with his caramel-colored ears that he'd had when he was but a young man, Suma the Wonder Dog, he called him. He remembered that Suma would come to him, sit by his side, snort and toss his head toward where the sweets were kept. Then Bobby would say, "Is it treat time?" and walk side by side with Suma to discover what seemed to be a surprise every time. It was also a time before Bobby became the man who was about to go to Hell.

Right before Bobby went to sleep each night, Suma would come up and lay his head against the bed for one last gentle tussle from Bobby's hand. There hadn't been much that Bobby had known love for, but Suma gave him the opportunity to know what love was. And now, as he began to drift off for the long sleep, Suma had come back to meet him. Bobby wasn't sure where they were going as Suma led him back over the crown of the hill but he hoped that God had seen his letter of apology as atonement for his sins.

In a couple of days, the farmer he had given the milk cows to had come over to tell him that those were the damn friendliest head of cattle he'd ever known. "Damn things come up and rub their heads up against you, like they're some kind of pup or something. Almost like their saying in one way or another *not* to butcher them. Well, hell, I've even started talking to them. Don't know quite what's wrong with me," was what all he was going to tell Bobby. He looked around for him but couldn't find him anywhere. The old farmer went over to the barn to check and see if his car was there, knowing he parked it there, when it'd been raining or thunder storming and the last couple of nights it'd been pretty windy and stormy. When he slid the barn doors back, he saw the back of Bobby's head through the still slightly fogged up car window. He was sitting straight up, his head slightly cocked to one side. The farmer opened the car door and abruptly stepped back from the smell of spent exhaust, excrement and death. Bobby, as best he could tell, looked like he had a bad sunburn. He figured from seeing so many dead farm animals over the years that Bobby had been dead a couple of days or so. Likely, he thought, since just about the time that Bobby gave him the milk cows.

When the police came it was determined to be a suicide. They towed Bobby's car out of the barn and sent his body along to the morgue for an autopsy. The coroner commented that even with rigor mortis, Bobby seemed stiffer than the usual dead body.

Chapter 66

A FEW DAYS AFTER Bobby killed himself, Dr. Hall called for Doc Kitchen and McGarrity to come over to his office. When they arrived, they saw an opened package with sheafs of paper stacked on Dr. Hall's desk. "I received this today and it is something that you will want to see." He handed Doctor Kitchen the letter that Bobby had written and included in the packet he had sent along to Dr. Hall. Doc Kitchen held the letter so both he and Doc McGarrity could read it. They were shocked by his revelations. He had brought everything out into the open.

"Since the two of you have come to Paintsville there has been more going on here than in the last hundred years. We used to be just a small coal mining community town. But I don't think we can say that any longer. So y'all have read the letter that Bobby wrote, he also put a small note in there to me that said he has sent another packet, just like this one, to a fellow named Gordon Welty, he's a sociologist at the Center for the Study of Labor Economics, and he's apparently done a lot of work on labor abuses and that sort of thing. So, what's going to happen now, I just don't know. But I think that Dr. Gaylord De La Croix and Dr. Rafferty De La Croix's self-declared reign as kings could be in jeopardy.

"By the way, I also just found out that Tough Tony was found guilty of murder again, after his original sentence was overturned. So, it looks like he's headed off to prison for good, well for the rest of whatever time *he* has left."

Chapter 67

PROFESSOR GORDON WELTY WAS a tall man, sandy haired, with a long neck. Well, he thought it was long, no one else did, but he was known to always wear turtlenecks and be constantly tugging them up so they hid his Adam's apple. Folks who knew him said he was just about the smartest person they ever knew. Containing his intellect was like shaking a bottle of seltzer and expecting the lid to hold tight. He was also known to be a man of integrity. He'd written a lot about how things can be twisted this way and that to *prove* what amounted to much of nothing. But those kinds of folks use the word *proof* like a whore persuades her curb-crawler that he's the greatest lover she's ever had.

Professor Welty had heard of Bobby but he'd never had the occasion to meet him. But he also knew just about everybody who knew what integrity was said that Bobby was somebody who'd never even met the word. His dedication to doing *anything* to advocate for the coal companies likely would have made Faust begrudgin'. The same day that Dr. Hall had received the packet from Bobby, Professor Welty got the same package. When he unwrapped the bundle, he thought he had been handed the cup of Christ.

Document after document showed that Dr. Gaylord De La Croix and Dr. Rafferty De La Croix had deliberately misread miners x-rays, cavorted with the coal companies, received hundreds of thousands of dollars in *inducement* money *and* even tried to undermine Bobby, by secretly writing letters to his board, saying how *they* could do more to help the coal companies *expand* their influence, if they'd just put them where Bobby was. The documents were a course in manipulation. Showing how Bobby knew *exactly* how to say what to *encourage* the

193

Doctors De La Croix to do whatever he asked and then to think it was their idea. "The desperate are easy to push this way and that, you just have to use the right lever." Dr. Welty decided that he should contact Doctors Kitchen and McGarrity.

Chapter 68

IT ALWAYS AMAZED MOSES and Janice how fast Isabella grew. Not only physically but her intellect too. But of course, unlike most little girls, she was exposed to things day in and day out that most children, probably a good thing never had the opportunity to see. At the SDRC there was a lab that her momma and daddy had set up to study the effect of coal dust on rats. One afternoon, Doc McGarrity was checking the rat room, to see if any of the rodents had died. When they did, Doc McGarrity did a necropsy on the rat, carefully removing and infusing the lungs with formalin. Well, on this particular day, Isabella was with her momma, when Doc McGarrity found a dead yearling. She asked Isabella if she wanted to go with her to cut open the rat or if she wanted to go find her daddy. Isabella, without hesitation, said she wanted to go with her momma. Then, for whatever reason, thinking it was a good idea, Doc McGarrity asked Isabella if she'd like to cut open the rat.

Doc McGarrity showed Isabella how to lay the rat on its back, pin back the feet, lift up the nap of the neck and then take a pair of iris scissors and make a cut into the flesh of the rat. Then to cut straight through the rib cage and down to the abdomen. Isabella stood on a stool and watched carefully. Then she asked her mother what she was going to do next. "I am going to blow the lungs up, like a balloon, with the fluid that is in the container, hanging right up there." She pointed to what looked like an upside-down bottle, with a tube coming from it, with a needle that had a small bulb on the end.

"Can I do it?" Isabella said.

Doc McGarrity scooted Isabella close to the necropsy table and slipped much too large latex gloves over her hands. Then she said, "This is very delicate, you have to be very careful, and you have to respect this little rat. She died so we can help figure out how certain diseases affect the lungs…" Then she showed Isabella how to carefully lift the trachea and snip it right where it attaches to the neck. Isabella delicately cut the top portion of the trachea and then lifted it gently away from the other tissue in the neck. Then Doc McGarrity reached up and pulled down the rubber hose with the bulbous needle.

"Now you are going to slip this end into the tiny hole in the piece of tissue you are holding with your forceps. That tissue is called the trachea. And when you slip this needle in, we will open the valve that controls the liquid and then it will fill up the lungs like a balloon. See these right here?" She pointed to the lungs. "When we start letting the fluid run in, they will swell up. Now we don't want too much liquid to go in, because we don't want them to pop."

Isabella slipped the infusion needle's bulbous end into the trachea. Doc McGarrity was impressed at how careful she was. There was no fooling around. Isabella behaved with more seriousness than Doc McGarrity had seen some medical students behave in anatomy class. Then Doc McGarrity said, "Okay, now we are going to put some of the fluid, it's called formalin, into the lungs. That's called infusing the lungs."

Isabella repeated back what her mother had said. Isabella held the trachea with her forceps while Doc McGarrity opened the valve that controlled the flow of formalin. Isabella watched as the lungs swelled.

"WOW!" she exclaimed.

Then Doc McGarrity tied of the trachea with a suture to prevent the formalin from leaking out. "Now, we have to cut out the rest of the lungs. I'll do one side, you watch me and then you do the other."

Doc McGarrity cut the connective tissue that held the lungs while Isabella held her gaze to what her mother was doing. Then Isabella tentatively made the same cuts, nicking the heart.

"Did I do it wrong?" she asked.

"No honey, you did it just fine. It takes a *lot* of practice and each time you get better and better at it."

They lifted the freed lungs from the chest of the rat and placed them in a jar, also filled with formalin.

"Would you like to do it again some time?" Doc McGarrity asked Isabella.

Her answer was a resounding yes. "Momma, can you get me my own gloves?" Isabella said.

Chapter 69

ONCE PROFESSOR WELTY HAD gone through all of the documents he'd received from Bobby, he began to think about how best to proceed. That afternoon he called Doc Kitchen. Hearings were going on in Congress about black lung benefits to miners and their families. And, Professor Welty said, they were like most hearings that took place in Congress.

"The hearings are a spectacle and make declaration after declaration with gavel pounding assertions that whatever the hearings are about are an outrage and this and that will be different, but alas... The folks that are the subject of the hearings send representatives, but mostly as a way of finding cracks to exploit, while admitting no wrong doing. So even if they took the material to the hearings there likely would be so many objections to presenting it that the objections would outlive the hearings and the package of material would be buried forever," Professor Welty said. "They'll probably end up passing *something* but whatever timeline they put on it for implementation will just allow for strategies to undo it or calculate the profit loss of ignoring it. My recommendation is we publish it as an expose."

And on that, when Doc Kitchen and McGarrity discussed it, they decided that Professor Welty was right. They had seen thousands of miners over the years who had suffered at the hands of the mining companies. It never ended. Even they, in dedicating their lives to treating and advocating for the care of these men and their families, grew weary at times. They also knew that when they talked about black lung to their colleagues, they would see the frowns and hear the excuses as to how they had somewhere else they had to be.

Chapter 70

PROFESSOR WELTY, SHORTLY AFTER he spoke with Doc Kitchen, came to Paintsville. He, Doc Kitchen and Doc McGarrity spent the next few weeks going through the material that Bobby had sent off. They set a room up in their house that they called the *war room*. There they laid out the countless reports, the evidence that countered the medical reports, many were their reports filed on behalf of miners from Paintsville. Others were reports from physicians who had diagnosed black lung that had been discredited by the Doctors De La Croix standing on the plinth of The Inner Harbor Diagnostic Institute. There were even reports from judges that had found Doctors De La Croix and their colleagues' judgment questionable. One judge even wrote that the Doctors De La Croix and their colleagues, "…so consistently fail to appreciate the presence of black lung on so many occasions that the credibility of their opinions has to be questioned, Administrative Law Judge Alan B. Levine."

But, like all other judges who questioned Doctors De La Croix or their cohorts, his opinion was nullified by the fact that The Inner Harbor Diagnostic Institute stood behind everything that Dr. Gaylord De La Croix or Dr. Rafferty De La Croix's brigade of radiologists opined. Doc Kitchen found documents that showed that The Inner Harbor Diagnostic Institute charged ten times the cost on a basic chest x-ray. Paid, always in full and without delay by the mining companies. All of the Doctors De La Croix's opinions regarding cases they had been retained to review closed with, "…If there are any questions regarding the diagnostic interpretations set forth in this review, it is recommended that the individual in question secure a lung biopsy."

It was simply a rubber stamp that closed out every report. But a lung biopsy was a hospital procedure, beset with the possibility of exposure to a fatal infection, especially in patients so medically compromised and vastly more expensive than the miners had money to afford. The Doctors De La Croix had told Bobby that this would allow them to build a gray area in all of their reports. It would prevent any law suit that they may be exposed to from going forward. Therefore, it would indemnify them from any and all responsibility.

As Doctors Kitchen, McGarrity and Professor Welty reviewed the documents, they were astounded at how dedicated the Doctors De La Croix and Bobby had been in their efforts to deny miners benefits. They could understand Bobby's motives, "but, the De La Croix brothers?" Professor Welty said.

They had it all at The Institute, but they had sold their soul. And for The Institute to have supported Doctors De La Croix was pathetic. It took weeks to organize the documents. The next step was to publish them.

Chapter 71

WHEN THE DOCTORS DE La Croix learned that Bobby had killed himself, they found themselves more briefly distraught than they would have thought. But at the same time, they knew that in Bobby's death, their importance to the coal companies had grown. The Doctors De La Croix would become the unified voice that would in every way represent the interests of the coal companies against the claims put forth by the miners. The coal miners would be kept in *their* place, and the *rightful* order would be maintained. The Doctors De La Croix had no idea what Bobby had done.

Chapter 72

DR. MCINTOSH MET WITH Doc Kitchen at the end of his residency. He already had some time in but now he was approaching his boards and time to move on. "You're a damn good physician, I don't know what your plans are and we got off to a rocky start, but we would like to offer you a permanent position here."

Doc McIntosh said that he'd figured that even though Doc Kitchen and McGarrity had understood why he did what he did, he never thought they would offer him a position at the SDRC. At the same time he said, "I don't know that I have ever felt so accepted anywhere I have been. I know there are people who are suspicious about me, and what I am, but they don't talk about it and no one has ever called me a derogatory name."

Doc Kitchen responded with, "From our perspective, what you are is a good man, your choice of who you love or choose to be with is your own, it has no bearing on who we know you to be. I hope you will consider our offer."

Doc McIntosh had also developed a relationship with Isabella. It seemed she was always running to him as much as she was running to her momma and daddy. Doc Kitchen and Doc McGarrity had kept quiet what Doc McIntosh had done way back when. And now he had blossomed.

One afternoon, when Doc McIntosh was at the clinic, Nurse Abigail Abernathy was helping to hold up Tennessee Percy, after he'd gotten winded going to pee and couldn't get back to his bed on his own. Tennessee was somewhere in his fifties but he looked like he was upwards of a man whose time on earth was nearin' its end. Right as Nurse Abigail Abernathy was liftin' him off the pot, he looked at her and said, "I can't even chase my hounds up into the hill no more, I guess I have to give that up along with everything else too." And then, Nurse Abernathy jerked up straight as a stick, making poor Tennessee have to grab hold of the sink. It was like Nurse Abernathy had been struck by a bolt of lightnin', falling onto the floor, jerkin' every which way one can imagine. Later on Tennessee told Doc McIntosh that he'd never in his life seen anything like it.

Doc McIntosh came running as fast as he could to keep Nurse Abernathy from hurtin' herself as much as he could. He gave her Lorazepam and Phenobarbital, makin' her seizin' begin to subside. As Nurse Abernathy began to come around, she said nothing like that had ever happened to her before. She was getting to the years of her life where most folks are thinking fondly of a white porch with a cushioned rockin' chair and reminiscin' to anyone who'd listen of days gone by. But, Nurse Abernathy, when someone'd brought up her retirin', said she was havin', "None of that," and for the question asker to be on their way.

After he got her stabilized, Doc McIntosh sent her over to x-ray. When he got the call to come down to radiology, Doc McIntosh found x-ray technologist Kay Yoakum, who was known to make just about the best spoonbread anyone had ever ate, cryin' her eyes out. She pointed at Nurse Abernathy's films that were on the viewer. When Doc McIntosh saw the x-rays, he knew there was no hope. Sitting in Nurse Abernathy's frontal cortex was a massive glioblastoma, makin' things about as bad as it could get. How had it not caused her problems before now? he wondered. It was enormous. Patients with glios' can last for months, sometimes even a year, but Doc McIntosh didn't think Nurse Abernathy would last more than a few weeks. The hardest part, aside from telling her, would be telling Isabella.

Chapter 73

PROFESSOR WELTY AND DOCS Kitchen and McGarrity now had everything laid out and ready to go. It was agreed upon that they would be mentioned as part of the expose but the author would be Professor Welty. It would be published under the masthead of The Center for the Study of Labor Economics. Copies of the article would also be sent to all of the major news organizations.

It was a Thursday morning, humid as hell, the USS Constellation was rocking against the waves rolling into the inner Baltimore Harbor. The Doctors De La Croix had just returned from a well-earned vacation, as they would say, to a desk piled with second opinions. The claims, especially since Kitchen and McGarrity acted like diagnosing black lung was some kind of goddamn religious calling, were coming more and more. Bobby's suicide had done what the Doctors De La Croix had imagined. They were flying here and there, more than they were anywhere near their office. Always "first class," they'd say, "in the air and on the ground." It was rare that a day went by when they didn't get a call from this coal company or that congratulating them and offering them this for that. Doctors De La Croix were always on the congratulatory phone calls together. It had gotten to the point where they needed another secretary just to take calls from different executives of different coal companies.

When they got to their office that morning, the CEO of The Institute met them. "We need to talk with you now, please come to the upstairs conference room." The Doctors De La Croix were about as befuddled as could be, looking back and forth at each other as though one of them was withholding the answer from the other. When they got to the conference room, the board president, two board members and in-house council were also there. Sitting on the conference table was copies of a long, detailed article, authored by Gordon Welty, Ph.D. and mast headed by The Center for the Study of Labor Economics.

The article not only cited each and every transgression of Bobby and the Doctors De La Croix, it also implicated Inner Harbor Diagnostic Institute as co-conspirators. Immediately the board members and the CEO began distancing themselves and The Institute from Doctors De La Croix. It seemed as though the corporate ardor between the Doctors De La Croix and The Institute had waned. As Dr. Gaylord De La Croix and Dr. Rafferty De La Croix read the report, they felt thunderstruck. Clearly, they knew that everything The Center for the Study of Labor Economics had published was true but where in the hell had they got their hands on such a comprehensive set of confidential documents? The report went all the way back to when the Doctors De La Croix were surgeons in Vietnam and traced their association up to when Bobby had killed himself. Plus, who the goddamn hell was Gordon Welty?

After they finished reading the report, Dr. Gaylord said, "Well, of course we are going to counter these allegations," with Dr. Rafferty nodding in agreement. "This will ruin us."

It was then that the CEO of The Institute said, "No, Doctors, that's not how this matter is going to be addressed. First off, the board knew *nothing* about how serious your involvement with the coal companies is. Secondly, this Institution has only supported you because of what you told us. We are administrators and we do not interfere with the clinical matters of our physicians. So, from this report, you have clearly misled this Institution and its concerns and therefore we are not only immediately suspending your privileges, we are also opening our own investigation into your collective work at the Center for the Disease of the Lung. We will be initially issuing the usual, we stand by you, etc., etc. But, let there be no mistake about it, when the two of you walk out of this room, you will be met by security and they will escort you off The Institute's campus. Neither of you are to return to the campus without your legal council and without a scheduled appointment."

The rest of the board and the in-house council sat quietly, acting appropriately indignant.

The Doctors De La Croix couldn't believe what was being said to *them*. A few short hours ago The Institute was, aside from the coal companies, their most ardent supporters, and now… the Doctors De La Croix's world was crumbling around them. They had thought it odd when they greeted their secretary and she cast her eyes down and nodded.

"This is an outrage! We will sue each and every *goddamn* one of you…" the Doctors De La Croix collectively screamed in one voice. "You know what *we* have done for this institution." Answering their own question, they again said together, "*We* have brought in millions of dollars and now you turn your backs on us?"

The CEO stood up and motioned for the in-house Council to open the conference room door. There stood two hospital security officers, who motioned for Doctors De La Croix to accompany them. As he walked toward the door, Dr. Gaylord said they had to pick up their personal property from their office *and* their patient records. One of the security officers told Doctor Gaylord and Doctor Rafferty that would not be possible. All of their personal effects would be collected and placed with security and their attorney could pick it up at a later date, but *none* of the patient records or any patient material would be permitted to leave the campus nor would they have any further access to any patient material, it was the property of The Inner Harbor Diagnostic Institute *not* the Doctors De La Croix.

In a short while the explosive report had reached the main stream media. And, in equally short of a while, The Institute issued a brief statement, "*Dr. Gaylord De La Croix and Dr. Rafferty De La Croix are established radiologists in good standing in their field. To our knowledge, no medical or regulatory authority has ever challenged or called into question any of their respective diagnoses, conclusions or reports.*"

Professor Welty was getting calls from all over, requesting interview after interview. He was also getting requests from different regulatory agencies to produce the actual documents that his report was based on.

It was long after the report came out that the United States Department of Labor issued an emergency bulletin to all of the district black lung claims offices. The SDRC received one of the Bulletins.

District Black Lung Directors are hereby instructed not to positively credit any of Dr. Gaylord De La Croix or Dr. Rafferty De La Croix's negative readings for black lung disease. The District Directors should accord no weight to any offered medical opinion from either Dr. Gaylord De La Croix or Dr. Rafferty De La Croix. Those claimants who have had black lung benefits denied based upon the medical opinion of either Dr. Gaylord De La Croix or Dr. Rafferty De La Croix should be contacted within the next ten days and encouraged to refile their disability claims. For those individuals who have died since their claims submissions, their immediate next of kin should be contacted for resubmission.

There was also an emergency announcement from The Institute. "After a *long* and *arduous* internal review, The Inner Harbor Diagnostic Institute is immediately terminating its Disease of the Lung Center. There is no further information available at this time."

Senators and governors from the coal producing states collectively issued statements about the tragedy that was revealed by the report. The Doctors De La Croix tried with all their might to get in touch with the *friends* they had made in the coal industry. But, try as they might, no one wanted to talk to them. They even showed up at CONSOL headquarters but weren't able to make it past the main doors, where they were met by building security and told to leave.

Dr. Gaylord and Dr. Rafferty figured it was time they gave an interview. They were *the* top radiologists in the country. Other radiologists had clamored to have an audience with them, to obtain their view and opinion on difficult cases.

"I don't understand," Dr. Gaylord said in the interview. "This Welty fellow isn't a doctor, he isn't a radiologist and he has no medical training what so ever. We don't even know who the hell he is. Do you understand how many x-rays we have read? We can determine whether someone has black lung *instantly*." Dr. Rafferty filled in, "Some people have said we are doctors for the coal companies, but we are not, *we* are physicians for *many* companies. Companies are exploited constantly by people who simply don't deserve the money they illicitly reap. This kind of clinical misrepresentation by *these* people hurts everyone and takes advantage of the goodness of companies. In the case of black lung, coal companies ask us for our opinions which we give them *and* we are *entitled* to our opinions, whatever those opinions may be. We have yet to find anyone who can challenge our medical opinion with any veracity or convince either of us that we are wrong."

The interview didn't last very long. When asked if they were terminated from The Institute, Dr. Gaylord responded, "We *fully* expect to be reinstated any day now. The Institute is *fully* aware of the exceptional nature of *our* qualifications. We are simply more intellectually honest than other physicians."

"We have always taken the high ground as doctors," Dr. Rafferty concluded.

Chapter 74

Docs Kitchen, McGarrity, and McIntosh and Isabella sat with Nurse Abernathy in her final hours. Her respiration had slowed to being barely visible, but she didn't appear to be in any discomfort. She had no family and shortly before she drifted off into her final coma, she told Doc McIntosh, who told her he was planning to make Paintsville his home, that she had left him her homeplace.

"You need a place to settle down," she said.

Moses and Janice had told Isabella that 'Auntie,' as Nurse Abernathy called herself to Isabella, was dying. There was nothing that could be done. She said that she wanted to be there when Auntie died. Truth be told Doc McGarrity gave Nurse Abernathy a little extra morphine to make sure that there was no possibility of her suffering. Her last breath came right before the sounding of the three o'clock mine whistle.

For this brief moment Nurse Abernathy's dying had taken precedent over what the release of the report had caused. Professor Welty was testifying at the emergency hearings that resulted from the report. Doctors De La Croix, in spite of being subpoenaed, simply refused to participate. The Institute sent what seemed like an entire law firm to the hearings. They fielded questions from the hearing representatives with questions of their own, and "how *dare* the implications," they would retort. "To subject an institution with the international reputation that The Institute has is an *outrage*…" frequently slamming their portfolios together for effect. The word 'outrage' seemed to be worn thin throughout the course of the hearings.

Chapter 75

THE PHONE CALLS FROM the local Disability Services Offices to the denied miners was settin' off conniption fit after conniption fit. Black lunged miners who were still alive were hearin' that they should reapply for benefits, because the doctors that'd testified against them were no longer considered credible. That meant they'd have to get more money together, which they didn't have, and then go through all the rigmarole all over again. Plus, since those doctors had been gotten rid of, who knew the mining companies'd put up against them now?

Phone calls were coming from twenty-five mining state disability offices, where Dr. Gaylord or Dr. Rafferty and their brigade of deceivin' doctors had blocked miners from getting benefits. The Doctors De La Croix even hired themselves a bodyguard because they were afraid someone was going to come up behind them and kill them with a pick-axe. Folks who knew the Doctors De La Croix said that they walked around sweatin' like a sinner in church. Sometimes even dabbing the sweat off of one another. One miner who was interviewed about threats of the Doctors De La Croix bein' done in said that, "…it wudn't bother me none too much, they're a couple of cusses whose corn bread ain't done in the middle, it'd be best for all concerned if someone just put um down like you would a rabid dog…"

It wasn't long after The Institute had done what they called their Internal Review that a U.S. Senator himself demanded a copy of the report. The Inner Harbor Diagnostic Institute CEO called the Senator and said it wasn't none of his business and since it was done by an *outside party*, he didn't have no right to it. He too was pretty damn mad, as he'd say. But his damnation didn't do him one bit of good. Pretty much The Institute just said *no* and that was the end of it. Indignant damnation has the lifespan of a mayfly.

Chapter 76

Doc Kitchen and Doc McGarrity were gettin' calls from miners' wives they'd seen years before wantin' their help in tryin' again to get their deservin' benefits. As time had gone on, the men they'd seen early on had been smothered to death by the black lung. The only thing that was left were their families. Hell, a lot of their boys were now men and miners themselves. And now like a stagnant lake, they had been afflicted by the black lung.

With so many cases of black lung, Docs Kitchen and McGarrity had pretty much established that coal dust was one of the most dangerous things that a man could ever be exposed to. They had already figured out that coal dust was contributing to stomach cancer but they hadn't figured out why.

Then Therlo Bailey walked in, huffin' and puffin'. In his late forties, he was now a man who ran his damndest to catch up with the breath that always seemed to be out runnin' him. When he came into the ER that day though he said he was in about as much pain as a man can endure. He'd be mighty obligin' if Doc Kitchen could be of help to him. Therlo was a Negro and had been in the mines since he was a boy, doin' what boys do when they ain't got nothin' else to do and had to be helpin' their momma and daddies. His momma and daddy had been one of the few Negro families there in Paintsville. The family had been over in Van Lear but folks there a long time ago said it'd be better if they moved on to Paintsville, if they were goin' to stay around at all, where they maybe'd run into some others of their own kind, because they sure weren't gonna run into any of them over in Van Lear. Therlo could never say how his momma and daddy had got to Van Lear in the first place, it seemed like he just

211

woke up one day and they was there.

Well, that day, he had tears running down his cheeks and told Doc Kitchen he'd been shattin' blood real bad, vomitin' everything he tried his best to keep down and he'd lost so much weight that he wondered if folks could see him when he turned sideways. He also said his belly, which was blown up like a dead muskrat that 'd been layin' out in the sun, was doublin' him over with pain. When he looked at Doc Kitchen, the white of his eyes was a cowardly yellow. It didn't take Doc Kitchen long to figure out that poor Therlo was dying of stomach cancer. He had the black lung too but the stomach cancer was going to take his life before he had to suffer with being strangled to death from the inside out. The thing was Therlo was *still* goin' down in the mines. Doc Kitchen told Doc McGarrity that he'd never in his life seen anything like the steadfastness that miners have for taking care of their families. "They work until they can barely move and then the other miners, when they see that they're sick, pick up their work load, so they won't lose a day's pay if they can help it."

Doc Kitchen told Therlo what he had and that there wasn't a whole lot of anything that he could do, but Therlo had to stop working or he was going to get so bad that he'd die in the hole. Therlo disagreed about as much as a man can disagree and said he had to feed his wife and two youngins being that his wife was on the slow side and couldn't do much, so he had to make sure she was taken care of, especially since she couldn't read or write. Doc Kitchen, even when he got older, never in his life, figured out why he said what he said, but then he said to Therlo, "I want to see what you do underground, I want to go down with you."

When he told Doc McGarrity what he wanted to do she was about as mad as a hornet. Mostly though she was worried. After he got Therlo some pain medicine, and something to help with the bloody diarrhea, he made arrangements with a bossman he knew at the mine to go down with Therlo in a few days.

When the morning came for Doc Kitchen to go underground with Therlo, he had no idea what to expect. He was given a hard hat with a light, a heavy coat and for the most part told to keep his head down and stay out of the way.

Ten men crowded into a cage and lowered down. As they descended, it got darker and colder. Doc Kitchen never thought of himself as being afraid of small spaces but the deeper he went underground, the more he felt like he was being entombed. The air was dank and foggy. The cable holding the car kept slipping, dropping a few feet every time it did. The other men seemed unbothered by it, having lived with it day in and day out for years. Doc Kitchen felt nauseous every time it slipped and then caught itself. When they got to the bottom, they unloaded. The other miners helped Therlo out of the elevator cage. Then they loaded themselves into a hopper and began a horizontal roll. One of the miners tapped Doc Kitchen on the shoulder, right before the wheels began rolling and said, "Duck."

"Jesus!" Doc Kitchen said to himself. The hopper seemed to pick up speed as they moved forward and the sound of the metal wheels against the track was deafening. Therlo was barely able to hold himself upright. And it was pitch dark. When they finally came to a stop, one of the men switched on his headlamp, climbed out of the hopper, made his way to the wall and threw an arm switch, which turned on a light. The hole stank of wet excrement from where the men had found a spot and used it for a toilet. But the dank fog in the air was filled with black specks of coal. It was impossible to see clear anything. The rock surfaces all looked out of focus, and the floor was wet with filthy water drippin' from the ceiling.

Doc Kitchen thought he was going to die.

Therlo made his way over to him. "First time downs like this for everybody. Don't make no difference, we all have to go through our first time in the hole. I've seen men as big as trees, not a one you'd want to tangle with, thinkin' they'd just ride on down and it'd all be okay. But once the cage loses it light, they go real quiet like. I've seen some of those men get to the bottom and start cryin' like babies. So, you know, you're doin' real good. Just find you a spot where you ain't near a pickaxe and you'll be fine. Just yell out if you need me Doc."

The crew boss told the men what needed to be done and they went and did it. He didn't follow them around and dog on them. Most of the men took turns, swappin' on and off helpin' Therlo. It struck Doc Kitchen that it didn't seem to matter to the other miners that Therlo was Negro. It just seemed like down here the *only* color was black. After a few hours, the crew boss called time for lunch. The men clustered together and opened their lunch pails. They all pulled out a slice of thick bread and some of the fortunate miners had a slice of ham that they folded their bread around. There wasn't a one that wasn't drinking tea. Therlo had insisted on his wife packing another slice of bread and some tea for Doc Kitchen. Most of the men ate their bread slowly, some started by drinking their tea. Those men opened their lunch cans and left their slice of bread sitting on top of the lid, then they unscrewed the top of their tin bottle and drank their tea. They would go back and forth between their bread and their tea. Always deliberate and slowly. At lunch they seemed too exhausted to talk much. But—and then it struck Doc Kitchen so hard that the thought seemed to light up the hole—as the men left their bread atop their lunch cans, it began increasingly to get peppered with the coal dust that was floating in the mine air. The slower a miner ate, the more peppered his bread became. It struck Doc Kitchen as odd that each man would put the lid back on his tin bottle and yet leave his bread uncovered.

"Jesus Christ," he thought, "these men aren't just breathing coal dust, they're *eating* it!"

When he got to their homeplace, the first thing Moses did was bathe. In a short while Janice started to get in with him, as they were alone because Doc McIntosh had taken Isabella fishing, but he was so distraught about being covered in coal dust that he wouldn't let her be near him.

"I know it is only anecdotal but I think I know why these men get gastric cancers. The common thinking is because of the coal dust in the air, which I think is true, but…"

He then explained how not only were the miners breathing coal dust, they were also eating it. "The dust accumulates, like we've seen on autopsies, in the lining of the stomachs and overtime induces malignancy." Janice looked at Moses, standing naked in front of her, waving his hands excitedly about what he had unearthed. She dropped her robe to the floor that she had put on after Moses had waved her away. Then she and Moses took each other into each other's arms and hoped that Doc McIntosh and Isabella were catching a lot of fish.

It was the following Monday that Doc Kitchen saw Michael S. Day, known for just about all his life as Stevie. It started when he was a youngin' and worked his way up from a mule driver to a crew boss. The men who worked with him said they'd go through 'hell and high water' for him and if there was ever a man who deserved to hold his head up, then it was Stevie. He'd been luckier than most, it seemed like he just dared the black lung to come after him. He'd seen other miners coughin' and wheezin' some in their twenties and some in their fifties, but he threw his chest out and said, "Come on ya sonofabitch, you ain't gonna get me you bastard."

Stevie's wife, Rosie, them bein' husband and wife now forty years, had brought him into the SDRC that afternoon. Poor man was breathin' about as hard as a man can breathe and his belly was swollen up somethin' awful. Rosie said he'd been doin' the best a man can do but he was reachin' the end of his rope now. He couldn't even make it up on the cot so Doc Kitchen could examine him, so he had to get down to listen to his chest and what was left of his lungs.

Doc Kitchen wrote in his doctor's notes, "Lungs sounds – Rales, bubbling and gurgling… Extreme difficulty oxygenating…" Requires immediate O2… Patient presented to ER in critical condition, extensive black lung symptoms, has applied for and been denied disability many times. He is at a point where he is incapable of functioning. Admitting patient to hospital for pain control and appropriate measures…"

Stevie and Rosie had heard about Docs Kitchen and McGarrity and drove over from West Virginia, right around Glen Fork and across Laurel Crick. They figured there wasn't much that could be done but they doubly figured that at least they'd be taken seriously. Doc Kitchen called Doc McGarrity and told her he had just admitted a man from West Virginia who likely wouldn't make it out of the hospital. Come to find out the last expert from the coal companies to testify against Stevie had been the Doctors De La Croix. They'd said he had some shadowing on his lungs, but he more likely had tuberculosis and emphysema—tuberculosis from living an unhealthy lifestyle and from smoking. Doctors De La Croix wrote in their case rebuttal, "These people just don't seem to understand that they don't deserve a lifetime of benefits for medical conditions that they have brought on themselves. It is highly recommended that benefits be placed on hold until such a time that a pulmonary biopsy can be done."

Doc Kitchen did his best to keep Stevie comfortable during his last days. They brought a cot in for Rosie and the nurses brought her in food so she wouldn't have to leave Stevie, just in case he died while she was out. Somewhere in the middle of the night, Stevie started gasping and vomiting up blood. Rosie screamed at the top of her lungs for the nurse to come in and help poor Stevie, but there just wasn't enough left of Stevie to save. Most folks when they die don't stiffin' up right when they die, but Stevie, when he drowned in his own fluids, threw his arms outward, movin' them back and forth like he was, with all his might, like he was tryin' his best to stay afloat. Stevie told Rosie he didn't want to die. He said he had some life to live but even if he did stay alive, Stevie said, he didn't know how he was goin' to do what he said he wanted to, not bein' able to breathe and all. Rosie sat beside Stevie, his chest now flat, his face beginning to turn blue like his lips had been for so long now. She felt relieved on one side of the room for an end to his sufferin' and, on the other side, her heart was broken. Stevie'd always been a good man. The only pride he ever knew was his means to provide. That was all he wanted. He never seemed to want much for himself. There were times in those early years when he'd suddenly not be interested in eating supper with Rosie and their youngins. He'd sit down to supper, and together they'd pray, "*In the fellowship of the Lord, we give thee thanks and praise, for this food we are about to partake.*" Then Stevie would look around, see how much was in the stew pot in the middle of the table and whether Rosie'd had enough flour to make bread that day. If he saw that the pot was only half full, he'd lean back in his chair and say, "Y'all, my belly's a grumblin' for some reason or other, so y'all go on ahead, and help yourselves. I'm just not feelin' up to fillin' my belly all the way up."

He never thought that Rosie and the youngins did any figurin' about what he was doin'. But they all knew. They also knew that it wouldn't do a lick of good to say a word, Stevie'd just say for them to go on their way and to leave him be.

"If I was a hungry, I'da say so," he'd say. Stevie was just as proud when he came down with the black lung. Never wantin' anyone to help him stand up, never wantin' anyone to help him to the outhouse. But he sure would laugh, sometimes until he'd be chokin' because he used so much of his air laughing, when someone, usually from up North,'d say, "What do you mean *outhouse*? You folks don't *still* use an outhouse?"

There was something about watching Rosie softly stroking Stevie's arm. It was as though she expected him to come back from where he'd gone, anytime now.

Chapter 77

IT HAD BEEN A fairly long time now since Stevie had passed on when Doc Kitchen got a call from Michael S. Day, Jr., Stevie's son. He said that his mother had been sayin' how his daddy had been treated with respect that he hadn't been treated with before he came to the SDRC. He just wanted Doc Kitchen to know that he'd been talkin' to miners just about everywhere there was coal minin' and if there was coal minin' there was the black lung. Mr. Michael S. Day, Jr., since it'd come out about Doctors De La Croix and The Institute was himself organizing miners into a class action law suit. The attorney was Abraham Cassin, ESQ. out of the Nation's Capital. It was going to be a nasty fight, he said.

Doc Kitchen and McGarrity, at least for a short while, felt a sense of relief. For so many years now, they had been working not only with the men and their families who suffered with black lung, but had also testified in hundreds of cases and in just as many cases their work had been turned upside down because of the stature that the Doctors De La Croix's had established through their association with The Inner Harbor Diagnostic Institute. Their clinical evidence and presentations at the hearings for their patients were, as they liked to say, *incontrovertible*. But, time after time the miners had walked out of the hearings with *nothing*.

Cassin brought in hundreds of miners who'd been denied claims by Dr. Gaylord and Dr. Rafferty. As he looked at the case, he found out some of the shenanigans that they'd pulled with Bobby and The Institute. It wasn't just that the Doctors De La Croix's disagreed with the claims of the miners, but they were the hub that figured out how to organize their denials and to designate coal miners as a prejudicial group. As Cassin began to research the case, he also discovered what the law referred to as a *misappropriation of funds for the purpose of enriching a person of power or influence, who uses the power or influence to make a different individual, organization, or company more fiscally prosperous.* He sat behind his desk and realized that he had a RICO case on his hands. My God, he thought, coal miners were almost a *race* of people who had been bred for the sole purpose of exploitation. These men and their families were thrown out like squandered time. Replaced by the coal companies like time was infinite. They were kept like slaves. The addition of filing a RICO action as a co-inciding litigation would allow the litigants of the class to add what were essentially criminal violations. He also added claims of fraud, tortious interference with occupational economic interests, negligent misrepresentation, and unjust enrichment. Cassin finished the complaint with, "*The litigants engaged and enjoined in a pattern and practice with the obvious intent to defraud at least hundreds of toxically injured coal miners of Federally earned and due benefits.*"

Cassin called Doc Kitchen and McGarrity to help him understand more of the material questions about the medical implications of black lung. Their medical testimony had been contested more than any other physicians. Plus, what they had to say and their research into black lung disease had altered the way physicians worldwide understood and diagnosed the disease. Recently Doctor Kitchen had even published an article, "Risk of Gastric Cancer in Coal Miners with Black Lung Disease," which expanded the understanding of exposure to the deadly effects of coal dust. Cassin had also called upon Professor Welty to testify about how he received the packet of material from Bobby, which, as carefully as he kept everything from his time with the Doctors De La Croix and The Institute. It was almost as though he was preparing for a defense should anything ever come up.

Chapter 78

Doc McIntosh had been going to Lexington for years to meet men. It wasn't something he could do in Paintsville, but Lexington was an hour or so from Cincinnati and so there were a lot of homosexual men who came to some of the discreet clubs. On one of his last visits, he had met a flight attendant from Québec. He was a young, blond man who traveled the world. On this trip he had a nice layover and decided to visit one of the local clubs. Gaëtan was very popular that night and it so happened had an immediate attraction to Doc McIntosh. Their dancing went long into the night. He didn't have an early departure and so he invited Doc McIntosh to spend the night with him. It was an exciting evening. Gaëtan was fascinating, well-educated and handsome. When they said goodbye, Gaëtan said he would be coming back soon and took Doc McIntosh's phone number.

He never heard from him again though. It was about two months after they had met when Doc McIntosh got to feeling about as sick as he'd ever felt. When he went to Doc Kitchen, he said that he felt like he'd been kicked by a horse. The muscle aches and night sweats were the worst. He'd wake up in the morning and his sheets were sopping. Plus, he could barely move, he was so exhausted. Doc McIntosh's ailment went on for a few more months on and off and then just as suddenly cleared up. His work with black lung patients from the SDRC also got pulled into the class action suit.

Chapter 79

DOCTORS DE LA CROIX and The Institute, as well as the other physicians who were their co-connivers, knew service of the suit was coming. But the afternoon that the servers served each *entity* named in the suit was one filled with talks of revenge and ways of undermining the arguments made against them. They had been expecting the basis of the law suit but most certainly not the RICO allegations. The Doctors De La Croix said they were *not* crooks. They were the most *respected* radiologists in the world and "…let them be *damned*, that they accuse *us!*" And added, "…it wasn't enough that these goddam miners were too lazy to work, *now* they don't want disability, which they don't deserve, *now* they want *millions* so they can live like people who *are* educated and gave them the only job they were even remotely qualified to do!"

Cassin conducted deposition after deposition, flying all over the country, deposing physicians that were part of the Doctors De La Croix's duplicity. They all said the same thing in one way or another. "Our medical opinion is based upon the scientific interpretation of the clinical facts and x-ray images, that were given to us to evaluate, based upon the patient's history and current levels of functioning."

"We as *experts* are entitled to our opinions and do not have to secondarily *litigate* that opinion."

"All that we have to say regarding our opinion is expressed within the context of the report generated."

This was the response by the physicians in each and every deposition. There was no reason to respond, to answer questions, just use the same strategy as they used in a claimant's hearings, bury the case in distraction and motions.

Chapter 80

Doc Kitchen and Doc McGarrity continued seeing patients at the SDRC. There was little change, but their dedication to their work never wavered. The coal companies said that miners had to wear respirators now but the coal dust was so fine it would seep behind the mask and cause a concentrated buildup of coal dust particulate that was even more dense than going without a mask. The heat from working so hard in the hole never gave you a good seal against your face. Those men who wore beards would go home with coal dust caked in their whiskers. Some of the mines provided showers for the men, but they only put out cold water.

Doc McIntosh had seemed to be better, but he was noticing that he was having diarrhea every other day or so. He also got a coughing fit anytime he got riled up about something. Everything just felt off, sometimes nothing specific, but it was like he had something inside him that moved from here to there, causing him not to feel like himself along the way. Isabella was saying to Moses and Janice how tired Doc McIntosh always was. Some of the nurses even found him sleeping here and there when he wasn't seeing patients. He'd asked a couple of folks that he knew over in Lexington if they'd seen Gaëtan and they said they heard from someone else that he'd died a while ago now.

It was shortly after Isabella said she was worried that Doc Kitchen saw Doc McIntosh walking a bit off kilter through the clinic. He asked him what was wrong. Doc McIntosh said he had a bump on his foot, it didn't hurt, just caused him to walk a little crooked. He said he'd probably picked up a plantar wart somewhere. Given all that Doc McIntosh had been through lately he said he'd better have a look. They went into Doc Kitchen's office and Doc McIntosh took off his shoe and sock. Right beneath his middle toe, and hard to see unless you could get a close look, was a small, purple, inflamed bump. For a moment Doc Kitchen leaned back but said nothing. Then he said, "I want to do a biopsy. It's probably nothing but I just want to make sure." Doc Kitchen also noticed something else: Doc McIntosh seemed, as he later told Doc McGarrity, *foggy*.

Later that night, Moses was himself off kilter. When Janice asked him what was wrong, he said he wanted to go out on the screened porch and talk. Through all of their years together, Moses had been steady, rarely had she seen him distraught like this. And she was concerned that there may be something wrong between them that she was not aware of. When they sat down, he began telling her about examining Doc McIntosh's foot.

"He said he couldn't get his leg up enough to be able to see what the bump was, he could feel something raised, but he couldn't see it. When I lifted back his middle toe, there was a small purplish lump."

Then Janice said, "Oh my God, is it *Kaposi's?*"

"I'm having it biopsied, but I am sure it is, Pedal Kaposi's."

Janice got tears in her eyes and said, "Jesus, he's got HIV!"

Not only would it be hard telling Doc McIntosh, it would also be hard telling Isabella. It was Doc McIntosh who had become her *father in absentia*.

Chapter 81

THE CLASS ACTION SUIT was continuing. Depositions here and there by Cassin. Doctors De La Croix's attorneys *et al* were surprisingly quiet. They had done a few depositions but they portrayed themselves as almost being befuddled. Not aggressively challenging what was a multimillion-dollar class action suit with national implications. They had answered the suit *but* only saying what needed to be said.

Then notification was received that their attorneys had filed for dismissal with prejudice of the class action lawsuit brought against all concerned parties. In the demand for dismissal there wasn't even a denial of Doctors De La Croix's actions or participation or that The Institute had participated. Rather, the dismissal was based on *one* fact and *one* fact only. The motion for dismissal said that all of the concerned parties had *complete* immunity from liability, either civilly or criminally based on the *witness litigation privilege*. If the case was dismissed with prejudice, as the dismissal was demanding, it would mean that the miners or their families would get nothing. There would be no recourse. It would be over. The argument was that Dr. Gaylord De La Croix, Dr. Rafferty De La Croix and those other physicians that they incorporated into their scheme were nothing more than hired experts and The Institute was the agent of association, so they were nothing but a contractual conduit. Even the RICO aspects of the case could not be enforced as everyone was enjoined as an expert, and therefore with immunity. Judge Harvey Mudd was the judge who heard the case and said the witness litigation privilege is well known under English Law. Judge Mudd said, as he opined what his ruling may be, that "...a witness who is asked to testify without *absolute* protection may decline to do so, fearful of retribution. Moreover, even those who agree to testify may be inclined to *shade* their testimony in favor of the potential plaintiff."

It was nine P.M. when the ruling from Judge Mudd came down. "…The Gaylord De La Croix, M.D., Rafferty De La Croix, M.D., *et al*, and The Inner Harbor Diagnostic Institute., *et al.*, vs. The Collective Coal Miners Class Action is summarily dismissed with prejudice." The next morning, Cassin filed an appeal. Noting in his appeal that:

1. Gaylord De La Croix, M.D. and Rafferty De La Croix, M.D. (herein referred to as 'Doctors De La Croix') led The Inner Harbor Diagnostic Institute's Disease of the Lung Section.

2. The Doctors De La Croix and their fellow physicians understood their legal and ethical obligation, when interpreting radiographs for purposes of assessing miners "Black Lung" claims.

3. Despite that legal obligation, they intentionally disregarded coal miners' radiographs, so as to falsely attribute positive readings to causes other than Black Lung Disease.

4. The Doctors De La Croix ultimately admitted that they did not "care about the law," nor think coal miners deserved benefits just "because of masses and nodules, that have nothing to do with Black Lung."

5. In exchange for rendering knowingly *false* so-called expert opinions, the Doctors De La Croix and their associates received fees from their coal company clients that "significantly" exceeded "standard x-ray review fees."

6. The Doctors De La Croix and their associates repeatedly committed mail fraud by using the mails to receive radiographs and to transmit their false readings to coal companies, the companies' lawyers, and administrative adjudicators.

7. In roughly 3,500 radiograph interpretations, the Doctors De La Croix and their compatriots never identified black lung disease for any claimant, even though other expert physicians showed the presence of such a condition.

The *Court of Appeals* didn't take long responding. They had considered the facts of the case and issued their opinion:

> *In the United States Supreme Court decisions as well as es-*
> *tablished case law precedent, the Circuit holds that the Witness*
> *Litigation Privilege is foundational to any system of adversary*
> *justice, and is therefore vital to both federal law and the law of*
> *the sovereign states. The Court opines that if a witness were not*
> *able to testify with immunity, they would be less inclined to offer*
> *their testimony, for fear of retribution, or may purposely alter their*
> *testimony and distort the evidence. Any erosion of the common*
> *law immunity for witnesses would undermine the truth-seeking*
> *function of the initial proceeding, invite new claims by disgruntled*
> *litigants, and deter participation by those in a position to offer*
> *valuable testimony and opinion. The privilege has been around so*
> *long and recognized so widely for a reason: it allows the judicial*
> *system to work. Court designated and declared Experts clearly fall*
> *within the scope of the privilege and are thereby barred from any*
> *and all civil claims related to their testimony as experts."*

The suit was over. The miners would get *nothing*. There was nowhere to go. It was for the most part like it had always been for coal miners, a gaveling of the rights of the mining corporations to use these men as they saw fit. When Doc Kitchen heard about the Court of Appeals final ruling, he looked at Doc McGarrity and said, "Just like the Goddamn slave owners, I'm surprised the coal companies don't send the miners in here for us to sew their ears back on."

Doc Kitchen and McGarrity also got a call from Professor Welty who told them that he heard that the Doctors De La Croix were for the most part retiring. They had joined a private radiology group, but they wouldn't be taking any part in clinical consultations.

It had been a long road.

Doc Kitchen and Doc McGarrity hoped that with all that had gone on, that miners, when applying for benefits, may have a chance now. Professor Welty also humbly said he was being given a Pulitzer Prize for his work. He generously offered to share the Prize with Doc Kitchen and Doc McGarrity. Obviously without their work the revelations about Doctors De La Croix and The Institute would have never come about. Doc Kitchen said they were not surprised by his generosity but refused.

Chapter 82

WHEN DOCTORS KITCHEN AND McGarrity met with Doc McIntosh and told him the results of the biopsy, he said in broken thoughts, "When you decided to take the biopsy, I knew it was not good, and you wouldn't answer me directly and that's not like you.

"I didn't think it was a melanoma, not with the way I have been feeling. I think we need to figure out where I am in the disease. I have been treating myself for thrush so I know my immune system is getting increasingly compromised. I won't wait until the end, you know.

"Does Isabella know?"

Doc's Kitchen and McGarrity told him they had not discussed it with anyone. Doc McIntosh asked them if he could tell her. She was beginning to think about her future, and it would surprise just about everyone if she didn't go into medicine.

The next day, after she got out of school, Doc McIntosh took Isabella into his office. "There is something I have to tell you." Isabella thought he was going to say that he was going to be moving on, after all this time. "Isabella, I have AIDS. I can't pretend that it is not serious, because it is, and I don't ever want to lie to you. You know if I had ever had a daughter, it would be you."

Isabella wasn't prepared for what he had said. There was nothing to say that would mean anything, so she sobbed while Doc McIntosh held her. She said, "I don't want you to die," having seen countless deaths by growing up in the SDRC, she had seen people she had known all of her life smothered to death by the black lung, killed in tragic accidents and die of diseases, which at the time she couldn't even pronounce. But now, death had come to her in a way that she had never imagined. It also made her realize that her mother and father were getting older. Moses and Janice had been older parents when she came along and she would likely have to confront their deaths at a younger age than most children do.

Isabella surprised Doc McIntosh when she looked up and through her tear-streaked face said, "I won't let you kill yourself. I won't, I can't accept you doing that. I am selfish, I want you with me until you take your last breath. Promise me."

And in that moment, and somewhat regrettably, he nodded his head yes.

"Sweetheart, this is not going to be pretty." He then asked her if she would take his cat. A black cat, with brown stripes, one that ran right down the front of her face, Java, named for the coffee. Doc McIntosh said he couldn't have her anymore because of her litter box. "Litter boxes have a parasite from cat poop called toxoplasmosis. If I breathe it in it could go to my brain and cause a lot of problems." Java sat on his lap at night when he wrote up patient notes that he hadn't had time to finish that day. She would circle around, until she found just the right wrinkle in his pants where she would curl up.

That night Isabella, her mother and father talked and cried. She told them what she had asked Doc McIntosh to promise. They both looked at each other. Isabella also said to them, "Do *you* understand *what* I am asking him or you not to do?"

Both Moses and Janice nodded.

Isabella said, "I don't want you to nod, I want to hear you say you understand, *please*."

They did. Not long after Isabella went to bed. When she left the room, Moses and Janice turned to each other and said, "Jesus!"

Chapter 83

Doc Kitchen and McGarrity got to the hospital about six that morning. About six-thirty an ambulance pulled up and rolled Dr. Hall through the door. One of the ambulance crew was sitting astride his chest, pumping his chest with all her might. She was yelling in between compressions, "You ain't gonna die on me, Dr. Hall, you brought me and my momma into this world and I am *not* gonna let you leave it."

Dr. Hall had just been about to get into his car, when he grabbed his chest then collapsed onto his driveway. Little Jedidiah Smoker had been delivering papers when he saw Dr. Hall go down. He rode his bicycle about as fast as a boy can peddle to the little store right up the street and told them to call for an ambulance, that Dr. Hall needed help. The fire house wasn't that far from his house and when the call came in, Jewel Doiladee, who'd just got there for her shift that day, took off runnin' sayin' she could get there faster and for the ambulance to follow her. In no time flat, Jewel was sitting on top of Dr. Hall's chest and pumping for all she was worth. His head had already turned blue and he wasn't breathin' even a bit.

When Doc Kitchen met them as they came through the door, he saw that Dr. Hall's head was about blue as the jeans. They took him into a room where Doc Kitchen shocked him and ordered chest compressions longer than he thought would do any good. Then in a desperate attempt to save Dr. Hall, Doc Kitchen opened his chest, took his heart in his hand and began to pump it. But, no matter what he did, no good was to be had. Dr. Hall had passed on.

It seemed like everyone in all of Johnson County came to Dr. Hall's funeral. He'd delivered so many of the folks and their families in Johnson County that so many mommas and daddies stood up with their "I remembers…" As a matter of fact, Goldie Abner stood up and said when she was about as much of a youngin' as a youngin' can be called a youngin' that Dr. Hall rode up to her momma and daddies homeplace in his buggy to tend to her bad fever. Her momma had said she didn't think Goldie'd lasted overnight if Dr. Hall hadn't come that day. "Momma said there was snow blowin' everywhere and she didn't know how Dr. Hall ever got his buggy up the road to our homeplace. But he did, as old as I am now is sure proof of that. I found out later that the medicine Dr. Hall gave me was Penicillin and that I was the first person in Eastern Kentucky to ever get it. He for sure saved my life that day."

Later on, someone said that Dr. Hall administered the first blood transfusion in Eastern Kentucky too. Rev. Burton praised Dr. Hall saying that he wouldn't be surprised if Jesus *Himself* came to meet him at the pearly gates for all the good he had done in his life.

The service took all day and lasted into the early evening, lettin' anyone who wanted to to say whatever about the good Dr. Hall. After Dr. Hall was interred Mr. John Columbus, who'd been the president of the hospital board about as long as Malissa Osborne's husband, Earle, had been winnin' the longest beard contest down in Van Lear, came up to Doc Kitchen and Doc McGarrity, tipping his hat in politeness to Doc McGarrity of course and leanin' forward on his walking stick. "It's a sad day Doctor Kitchen…"

Doc Kitchen indeed nodded and said not only had Paintsville lost a great physician, he and Doc McGarrity had lost a dear friend.

"Well," John Columbus said, "the board met last night and we discussed a replacement for Dr. Hall. Well, a man like Dr. Hall you never *replace* but… well, we'd like you, Doctor Kitchen, to take over as Chief of Staff. You worked closest with Dr. Hall and have been a leader here at the hospital too, so we'd appreciate it if you'd consider it. It'd sure mean a lot to us all…"

Doc Kitchen had thought that he may be asked to assume the Chief position, and he and Doc McGarrity had discussed it. So, Doc Kitchen looked at John Columbus and answered in the affirmative. The announcement would be made immediately.

Of late, it had been one thing right behind the other. You get one damn thing cleared up and another is sittin' in the mail box sure as can be. After Doc McIntosh had told Isabella, she decided right then and there that she was going into medicine. She didn't think she'd go the way her mother and father had. Even though she was still young, Isabella had been reading about rare diseases for as long as she could remember. It would be but a short time before she graduated from high school and then onto college. But she wouldn't leave Paintsville until Doc McIntosh passed away. Isabella said she would be there to help take care of him.

Chapter 84

EVERY DAY THE DOCTORS De La Croix arrived at the group practice at eight. They silently acknowledged the receptionist at the desk and walked down the hallway to their office, where they were surrounded by x-ray viewing boxes. There were no films on the boxes, though. They were all glowing at about 5,000 Kelvins. When Dr. Gaylord and Dr. Rafferty opened their office door and walked in, they always dropped their heads because it was like they had walked into a waiting interrogation. They sat down in their respective chairs, sighed and waited. By the end of the day there were no knocks, no "May I interrupt you?" No "Could you give me your opinion of this film?" The De La Croix twins were always dressed impeccably, looking the part of successful physicians. But their positions at the practice was a purchased one. They paid for office space, their calls came in through the main switch board, *but* there were never any calls for consultations, only calls from someone wanting to know what the Devil had said to them at the Crossroads.

The Doctors De La Croix were dismayed when, after the Appeals Court had dismissed the Class, the Federal Claims Office issued a new mandate. Each miner who had been denied benefits based upon a clinical opinion offered by either of the Doctors De La Croix or any physician associated therein would be given at no charge to the miner a chest x-ray, arterial blood gas study and pulmonary function study—the *exact* sequence of tests recommended for years by Doctor Moses Kitchen and Doctor Janice McGarrity. The FCO had issued a similar order previously but with this one, they had claims officers hand deliver *each* and *every* letter to ensure that each claimant or his widows received them.

Chapter 85

DOCTOR KITCHEN ASSUMED THE position of Chief of Staff. The hours of sitting in meetings about this and that was one of the most deadening things he had ever done. He mostly consulted on cases now. And had even been known to wander into the ER and ask if anyone needed any help. Mostly though he bothered Doc McGarrity about patients she was seeing. It took a while but he finally convinced the board that he could best be of service elsewhere and that it would be best if they hired him an assistant. Someone who could dedicate their time exclusively to those things which weren't medical in nature. When he talked to other physicians elsewhere, they always asked him if he was still practicing where he was and if they'd got running water yet, having a hard time believing that Paintsville was still, for better or worse, a mining town. He did finally find an assistant though, Amelia Earhart, named right after the other Amelia Earhart.

Her daddy was Orville Earhart and they were from Beehive Holler. He'd married Berthie a long time ago, and it was said that from the moment they said "I do" that Berthie never let the man alone, naggin' him somethin' *awful.* "Do this, why didn't you do that, ain't you gonna do this?" Until one day he'd had just about enough. Amelia was older now and was ready to leave the homeplace too. So just abouts as she was ready to leave, her daddy, Orville, when he was gettin' a tongue lashin' from Berthie, hauled off and smacked her up the side of the head with the only skillet they owned.

But poor Orville had got his boot caught in a lose floorboard that Berthie had hounded him for *years* to pound back down, and he never would, so when he hit Berthie with the skillet, he spun around, with his foot catchin' under that damn board, lost his balance and fell right into the cook stove, puttin' a gash so deep into his skull that his brains started oozin' right out of his head. Well, Amelia did what she could do, but there weren't really nothin' to do. So, once they buried Orville and Berthie, Amelia made her way out of Beehive Holler, comin' on up to Paintsville. She was a bright girl and she told Doc Kitchen that there weren't no one who could keep things organized like her. So, he gave Amelia a chance to prove herself and by God she turned out to be the best damn assistant he could have ever asked for. Why even Doc McGarrity was known to call on Amelia to lend a hand over at the SDRC. The miners who showed up with the black lung continued, seemingly never to stop. One right after the other.

Chapter 86

As the disease progressed, Doc McIntosh regressed. Taking the antivirals, he said, was like pissing in the river. The purple splotches were thicker now, his nose completely taken over by them, even up his nose on one side, his belly was covered and one was coming for his penis too. Doc Kitchen had put him on Alpha-Interferon trying to control the KS. It took a just a week or so until the side effects of the Interferon began to destroy Doc McIntosh's desire to live. He could barely raise his arms above his head and he crawled to the toilet, sometime pissing himself before he could reach the bowl. Isabella cried each time she saw him and each time she saw him she didn't try to hide her tears. She said, "You look like hell. Like you never lied to me, I am not going to lie to you."

Right before he found out he was sick, he had been working on a clay piece. He sculpted in his spare time.

Doc McIntosh knew he was different from early on. Being never attracted to girls made it hard when he was in school. He never had many friends, but the few he had felt as odd as he did. It was when he was in his early teen years when he realized that his feelings for other boys were more than what everyone figured they should be. Somewhere along the way someone called him queer. He figured he was, it fit about as good as anything else. And as he entered his early vicenarian years he understood that being queer meant that he would most likely end up alone and without having known long lasting love. When he was in college, he met a young man who like him was bright and *different*. They were lovers for most of their time in college and then as their senior year was about to come to an end and medical school was looming, young McIntosh's lover was tied to a fence and beaten to death by a group of boys, who were more sure than they should have been that they weren't different. The boys were never found, so their difference or otherwise was never known.

In medical school he was taken aside by a fatherly physician who himself had been different for a long time. "You must never let it be known what you are. As a physician, you could never examine children and men will not come to you."

So, he didn't. When he came to Paintsville and was forced into a confession, he figured his career was over. But Doc Kitchen and Doc McGarrity, as time went on, became his family and Isabella was like the daughter they shared.

Docs Kitchen and McGarrity had enough life hanging on them that Doc McIntosh being different had no meaning for them, *except* how lonely he was at times. They knew his time over in Lexington was, as he liked to say, "My quiddity" and then laugh.

Doc McIntosh had also become a *damn* good physician. He was known to sit for hours with patients who were making their final transition. "Well, who knows really, who the hell knows," he was known to say. Men who had been able-bodied oaks all their lives, and then the black lung or the cancer would turn them into a brittle ash, their long boring roots coming to ground to breathe. He was as beloved as Doc Kitchen and Doc McGarrity.

For some reason the bug was coming after Doc McIntosh with a vengeance. It was one goddamn thing after another. And with each new infection, his immune system became more and more compromised.

With each passing day he worked on his sculpture, hoping to finish it before he died. He hadn't shown it to anyone, until one afternoon, when he asked Isabella to come into a small back room. He said he wanted to show her something.

Hanging on one wall was a sculpture. It was an island that resembled Australia. When he had been a young boy, different and lost in his room, imagining a place of welcoming, he imagined *WEPDIN*. He said he never knew why he called it what he did, it just came to him. But, over the years he began to sketch it out. To draw where he wanted it to be. Then as time went on, he would sculpt this piece and that piece, and write WEPDINs history. He even figured its geothermal history. "There was no reason not to," he told Isabella. It had grand rain forests, rich wildlife of animals that no one had ever heard of and that wouldn't be slaughtered and inhabitants that embraced those who were *different*, whatever their difference may be. Isabella walked up to the sculpture hanging on the wall and traced the many rivers with her fingertips and then did the same along the red rim of the volcano that sat at the north end of the island. She didn't say anything, instead Isabella turned and put her arms around a now frail Doc McIntosh, who said, "I want you to do something for me. When I die, I want to be cremated. I want you to spread my ashes where we always used to fish in Paint Creek, but I also want you to take some of my ashes and *paint* them into WEPDIN, right here," Doc McIntosh pointed to an area of WEPDINs great rain forest. "Maybe, my ashes will be like giving birth. I am sounding insane, I know… Then please hang WEPDIN at the SDRC."

Isabella, crying, told Doc McIntosh she would.

A few weeks after Doc McIntosh showed Isabella WEPDIN, he began coughing something awful and his chest hurt like a sonofabitch. Doc Kitchen hospitalized him and said he had pneumocystic carinii pneumonia. And on that there was no more hiding. Within a short time, everyone knew Doc McIntosh had AIDS. He was given IV antifungal medication but it was like fighting off a pissed off bear that had already gotten into your cave. It took a week to stabilize him. When he went home, he was so damn weak that he had trouble walking from one room to the other. Then to his surprise, folks started showing up. They didn't knock on the door, most of the time, they just called his name through the door. Usually, they had a big bowl of fresh chicken broth or chocolate cream pie, something soft that he could swallow easily because of the thrush that had taken his mouth hostage. The Kaposi was now everywhere on his face, his back, chest and abdomen—huge purple lesions parasitically growing, seeking to forge a bridge to other lesions. Inside, hidden, the Kaposi had also invaded every organ in his body, advancing like a conquering convoy along the miles and miles of lymph glands. When Doc Kitchen went to see Doc McIntosh, he pulled down his pants and said "look at my balls." His testicles were huge, swollen three-times what they should be, filled with lymph fluid. The skin on his legs were so dry and taut that they were cracking and had a bluish cast.

"It won't be much longer, will it?" Doc McIntosh said and asked at the same time.

Doc Kitchen said, "No, I'm sorry I can't help you."

"I know," Doc McIntosh said. "I promised Isabella, I won't forsake that promise."

That night the ER called that Doc McIntosh was coming into the ER. Docs Kitchen, McGarrity and Isabella went down to the hospital. When the ambulance crew brought him in, he was lolling his head from side to side and panting like an exhausted dog on a sweltering day. Doc Kitchen looked at him and quickly ordered oxygen. He was in congestive heart failure. Doc McIntosh didn't stay long in the ER. He was taken to a room, where Doc Kitchen, McGarrity and Isabella sat with him for the next twelve hours, when his heart simply stopped.

Word had gotten out around Paintsville and down into Van Lear too that Doc McIntosh was dying. He was a homosexual who had come to a mining town, was blackmailed by some low life sonsabitches to betray his oath, had been offered friendship and as time went on to become a beloved member of Paintsville. When folks heard it was his time, they began to gather around the hospital and sing,

> *Amazing Grace, how sweet the sound*
> *That saved a wretch like me...*
> *I once was lost, but now am found*
> *Was blind but now I see...*

Even those folks who hadn't heard about Doc McIntosh stopped by to join the crowd. One old miner, when asked what the goin' on was, said, "One of our docs is dying. He was a good man, he wasn't like the rest of us, *but* he was a good man. These docs, they got their hands full, we've just about all got the black lung and they keep us breathin' just as long as we can before we pass on ourselves. Doc McIntosh was a good man."

Jones and Preston came and got Doc McIntosh and cremated him the next day. They gave the ash filled urn to Isabella, who took a small amount out and put them into a locket. She took the rest to Paint Crick, where she found the small eddy where Doc McIntosh used to take her when she was a little girl. Isabella held up the urn, took off the lid and poured Doc McIntosh's ashes in the swirling water, saying goodbye. Then she went to Doc McIntosh's house, went into the small room where WEPDIN was hanging, dipped a brush into an emulsion of paint and ashes, and gently stroked the bristles along the small river that disappeared into the rain forest. Then she put a dab of paint and ash onto the open gold locket, forever closed the cover and fastened it around her neck.

Later that month, WEPDIN was moved to the SDRC, where it still hangs with a brass plaque that simply reads,

"WEPDIN
by Doctor Red McIntosh."

It was on the same day that Isabella got a registered letter from Porter, Banks, Baldwin & Shaw. Contained in the letter was a copy of Doc McIntosh's Last Will and Testament. Everything he had went to Isabella. She would be leaving soon for college and then onto medical school. After her experiences, particularly of the last few years, she had all but decided to specialize in rare and infectious diseases. Moses and Janice couldn't have been more proud of their daughter. Janice would tell her, "It's hard for women physicians, don't let *anyone* walk over you..." As they watched her through Doc McIntosh's illness and death, they knew they had raised a young woman who could endure anything as she went forward in her life. Isabella also treated the miners and their families with respect and understood the devastation that black lung created in their lives. She remembered when she was but a little girl, after spending months running here and there at the clinic, dreaming that it was raining black dust. But in her dream, she had everything upside down. The rain was coming up from Hell.

Chapter 87

DOC KITCHEN AND MCGARRITY had been surrounded by suffering and dying for countless years. It was one after another. Like most Docs, when they first start practice, they got introduced to death. He knocked at their door early on. And, as time goes by, the scythe swinging bastard never is far away, always letting them know it's just a matter of time before they meet up again. Then, once they settle down where they are going to be, Docs and death linger in an embattled and unrelenting fight. But the longer the Doc stays put, the more personal the fight becomes. The anonymous is replaced by the familiar. For every baby that they brought into the world, they knew that for a good number of them, they would also make the declaration that would pronounce them ready for the next world.

Most folks don't understand how close death *always* is and how *short* being alive *really* is. An undertaker's patients are already dead, so with them death has already had its way, there's no argument. Doc Kitchen remembered when he was in medical school, visiting a funeral home. The funeral director, Irv Hetrick, had been putting dead folks back together and looking nice for their families for about as long as he could remember at the time. Broken this, burned that, and sometimes just having to scoop whatever was remaining up with a shovel, dropping it in a bag, tying it shut, putting the remains in a box that locked and closing it for eternity.

When Moses asked Mr. Hetrick what it was like constantly being surrounded by death, he twisted the question a bit and said, "One thing that I have never heard talked about is that when we put that box in the grave, that's it, it stays there *forever*. Think about that, *forever*, until this whole thing comes to an end. That body will stay right there..."

When Moses asked him about cremation, Mr. Hetrick waved his hand and said, "I don't do that to a body, nope, I won't have any part of that, nope won't do it." When he was asked why he said what he did, Mr. Hetrick bowed his head and said, "When I was in mortuary school, we had to put a child, a little girl, in the oven, and Jesus, the sound of her burning up, it sounded like chicken frying and I, nope, won't have any part of it." Then Mr. Hetrick said he didn't have any more time for questions and got up and left.

Doc McGarrity told Doc Kitchen that when she was in medical school, her attendings told her the way to get along in medicine was to "remember, these are *patients* only to *themselves and their families.* But they are body *parts* to us, the *liver* in room ___, the *heart* in room ___, the *kid* who lost the eye in the ER… You always disassociate the *part* from the *patient.* It will give you a distance, and with that distance, you can come and go, just like the man who works on an assembly line."

It never made any sense to Doc McGarrity any more than it did to Doc Kitchen. They figured that the best way to make it was to talk to each other about their day's work. To know that there would be those folks who they would fret over and would bore deep into their guts and those folks who would not. The miners with the black lung and their families. Their lives were often filled with misery and longing. And, when they spoke of their struggles with Rev. Burton, he never failed to bring up Exodus and the agony of the Israelites trying to break free from slavery. Doc Kitchen and McGarrity figured the Israelites had a better chance breaking their bounds of slavery than the miners did from the coal companies.

Felix was also one of those who they would fret over. The older he got the more of what little he had left began to fail. The decubitus on his back side had gotten huge over the years. Doc Kitchen and McGarrity had taken care of him for so long. And, in an odd way, Felix was how Moses and Janice had met. It was shortly after Isabella left home that Felix began to falter.

There wasn't anything anyone could do. Doc Kitchen had gone to Felix and told him that he was breaking down. It wouldn't be long before what was working wasn't. Felix said he'd had it pretty good. Well, given the alternative and all. He whispered to Doc Kitchen that he could have his girly magazines if he'd like. But for Doc Kitchen to be sure and *wait* until he was "two cricks and a cuss fight up the road" before he took his prize possessions for himself. Doc Kitchen said he'd be sure Felix had crossed over into the other world before he accepted his offer. Felix's death came quickly. Everything finally just turned off and Felix simply went to sleep and never woke up. Doc Kitchen and McGarrity paid for him to be made up and buried proper. The undertaker even rolled up some sheets to make it look like poor Felix had some legs. Nobody came to see Felix except Doc Kitchen and Doc McGarrity. But they said he looked real good, with what the undertaker had done. "Felix would have liked getting his legs back," Doc McGarrity said, right before the box lid was closed.

Doc Kitchen and McGarrity were getting on in years. It had been day in and day out patching people up or pronouncing them dead. The years had takin' its toll. Being in such a rural area it seemed like there was always something happening where folks were killed or there was an accident, that for the most part unless you'd seen the accident happen most folks wouldn't even have believed it. There was another thing too that most folks didn't think about. In a big city hospital, patients are for the most part folks you don't know. But Paintsville is a burg in the middle of just about nowhere. Once you're around the area for a while, patients coming in all broken-up or dead are your neighbors in one way or another.

Someone once asked Doc Kitchen and Doc McGarrity if they'd thought about quittin' and puttin' their feet up and relaxin'. They had talked about it and decided that as long as they could get around and they had all their faculties that they would never stop doing what they did. There weren't that many physicians in Paintsville and especially there weren't many who knew much about the black lung, so as long as they could they would.

They often thought back about their lives together. They're coming together, both being drawn here for completely different reasons and yet both finding in each other the person they would choose to spend the rest of their lives with. Moses often remembered the first drive with Janice. Her yelling for him to pull over because she saw a sign that said *Paperweights*. What an odd obsession, he had thought. Reminiscing over cases of long ago and the struggle, even now, to try and help get the miners afflicted with the black lung, what they *rightfully* deserved. Not to mention the horrendous other diseases caused by mining. Doc Kitchen and McGarrity's greatest struggle was sometimes feeling it had been all for naught. There wasn't one case where a miner applied for benefits that wasn't still challenged. It wasn't as well organized as with Doctors De La Croix's dedicated provocation, but nevertheless, each application was pummeled in its own way. But then an old miner, tethered to an oxygen tank that he was rollin' behind him, would make his way up to Docs Kitchen and McGarrity, carrin' as best he could a pot of still steamin' chicken and dumplins. Sayin' he didn't have no money to pay them for takin' care of him, but his wife had just made a fresh pot of "chicken and slicks" and thought he'd bring some on up, them havin' worked all day and all. It always slanted their outlook back to the way it should be.

But that which they kept completely quiet about was sometimes having helped someone be on their way. Chief Trimble long ago had been good to his word that he would never say anything about their helping Blanche. And now so many years later, there had been many that they had helped. For Doc Kitchen and McGarrity, they were merciful acts. Isabella knew, and her only comment had concerned Doc McIntosh, otherwise it was never spoken of. Most of the folks they had helped had the black lung. Doc McGarrity would say to Doc Kitchen that if they walked into a room and saw someone choking to death, wouldn't they try and help?

"It's the same thing," she would say. "The only difference is to ease their suffering, because when it reaches that point there is *nothing*, absolutely *nothing* anyone can do."

Doc Kitchen responded, "We are murderers. That's what the law says."

Even when they talked at home between themselves, they did so in hushed tones, as though they were afraid the walls had ears.

Chapter 88

ISABELLA WAS FINISHING UP in molecular biology and then going on into medical school. She also studied English literature. There were several medical schools that were courting her, but Stanford was certainly being considered. Her interest in rare diseases and infectious diseases had grown even stronger, now including *where* some of the most dangerous diseases are found. She imagined some of these diseases like coiled snakes, lying in wait, until the unsuspecting come by and they strike.

Where Moses and Janice had spent much of their early lives together watching Isabella, Isabella, from as long as she could remember, had spent time watching her mother and father. As she entered adulthood, she thought back and remembered the one thing that Moses and Janice always, in one way or another, showed for each other, and that one thing was respect. Never did she remember either of them calling the other a name. They also treated *her* with respect. They raised her to be independent of them, to have her own thoughts, *not* to be an ornament for her parents to dress up and present.

When she finished her medical studies and residency, Isabella came back to Paintsville, mostly to say goodbye to old friends and for what was likely to be a long separation from her parents.

Paintsville hadn't changed much in the last few years or in many ways in the last fifty years, she thought. Some had come and some had gone and some had died. She hadn't seen her mother and father in a while now and she was surprised to see them for the first time as getting older. Neither moved with the same litheness. Their hair was now not *streaked* with gray but was grey, or maybe silver. The folks at the clinic were as welcoming as could be when she came to say hello, but… Isabella had changed also, she had grown up.

Many of the miners that she knew had died of the black lung, lung cancer, stomach cancer, "*Goddamn*" she would say, when she heard. But, when someone was brought into the ER and Docs Kitchen and McGarrity were attending, it was as though they turned inside out. They moved like dancers that had been saving everything for one more performance.

Isabella had gone to the clinic to meet Moses and Janice when the ER called and said they were needed. She watched Doc Kitchen and Doc McGarrity begin running down the hallway and through the swinging doors to the ER. There Emma Lou Riddle had been brought in along with Wayno. They'd been havin' one of their disagreements when Emma Lou stabbed him in the throat with her best bonin' knife that she'd just used to butcher that night's dinner. Here tell, Wayno came in criticizin' Emma Lou sayin' that they'd just had chicken the night before and the night before that and he wanted "somethin' other than chicken!" Emma Lou said he otta stop criticizin' her and if he wanted somethin' other than chicken then he should be makin' more money to buy somethin' other than goddamn chicken. Wayno hauled off and slapped poor Emma Lou right across the mouth, sending her reelin' back over a step stool. Well, Emma Lou hit the floor with a powerful thump and Wayno jumped right on top of her, pulled back his fist and right when he did, Emma Lou plunged that bonin' knife straight through Wayno's throat and right out the back of his neck. Then poor ol' Wayno fell right on top of Emma Lou, breakin' her nose with his head.

When Doc Kitchen saw the bonin' knife stickin' out of Wayno's throat lookin' like it was holdin' on his blue head, he figured he'd been dead just too long for there to be anything that could be done. Emma Lou didn't take much tendin' by Doc McGarrity to cool down her broken nose.

After the constable came and heard the story he figured, after havin' hauled in Wayno time after time for beatin' Emma Lou that he likely deserved to have that bonin' knife run right through his throat.

Isabella watched the goings on in the ER. The one thing that she had learned about the ER was that you *never* knew what was coming through the door. She remembered Moses and Janice coming in late one night, talking about what had just happened right as they were getting ready to leave.

Opal Wickers had gone out to her outhouse to relieve herself, when she felt a sting to the back of her head. She went onto relieving what was needed relieving and then went on back into her homeplace. The itch at the back of her head just kept getting worse so she thought she should go to the hospital in case she got bad lockjaw or something. Doc McGarrity happened to be in the ER when Opal came in. Opal said, "I got a real bad sting, Doc, the itch won't go away." When Doc McGarrity began looking at the sting, she saw a hole in the back of Opal's head. They never found out where the .22 round came from, but poor Opal had been shot. Maybe someone somewhere was shootin' squirrels and the bullet had bounced from tree to tree, ending up in Opal's head. Doc Kitchen and Doc McGarrity took her right to surgery and extracted the round. It wasn't very deep and didn't appear to do much damage. In a few days, Opal was on her way home, mostly disconcerted about who had been tendin' to her pigs.

After they left the hospital, Moses, Janice and Isabella went to Ethyl's for supper. They hadn't been seen together around Paintsville now for a long time. So, folks at Ethyl's were sure glad to see them come on over. Isabella hadn't had a pork tenderloin hot shot with extra gravy now for as long as she could remember, so on this night, that was what she ordered.

She said that this may be the last hot shot she'd ever eat, it bein' about as unhealthy as unhealthy can be. Folks came up right and left sayin' how glad they were to see her, "Lookin' just as beautiful as your momma. Not to leave out your handsomeness, Doc Kitchen" then they'd laugh and be on their way. Just before they were about to leave, Amelia Earhart came in. Doc Kitchen waved and told Isabella, "That's Amelia Earhart. She's my assistant." When Isabella heard what her name was, she said, "*You're kidding!*"

"The truth is," Doc Kitchen said, "she pretty much runs everything."

After they were home and settled in, Isabella said she wanted to tell her mother and father something. "Mom and Dad, I've never said this, I've said thank you for certain things that you've given me but I want to thank you for *everything* you have done for me. I don't know when we will see each other again after I leave. And I am going to miss you *so* much."

Janice looked at Isabella and said, "Sweetheart, the love your dad and I have for you is something that whatever we could say would not really convey it. It goes to the very core of who we are. And we couldn't be prouder of you."

Then Moses spoke up and said, "Isabella, you go live your life, milk every drop out of life's teat! We are getting older, so the truth is, when people start getting to our age, things happen. If something happens to us, you think of *you* first. If we are gone, then it won't matter. Everything is already arranged, you inherit everything, of course. There will be nothing for you to do."

"So," Janice said, "when that time comes, your dad and I want you to think of what *you* need first. We won't need anything."

Isabella wasn't surprised by what Moses and Janice said. They had always been this way. But the one thing Moses and Janice did not tell Isabella was that if and when the time came when they were both on the edge of completely failing that they would help themselves as they had helped others. They would not be a burden to her, nor would they, if they could predict it, not become disabled to where they couldn't take care of what would need to be done. It was the way *they* had lived their lives, and if possible, it would be the way *they* ended their lives. Moses and Janice since the early years of their relationship had decided that life without each other simply wasn't something they wanted to know, now that they knew life together. The trials of their life were also the joys of their life, to be *with* each other was like breathing. They had spent a lifetime watching men suffocate, they had also spent a lifetime sharing each other's breath. Moses and Janice would suffocate without the other.

It was later on when more came out about the Doctors De La Croix's dirty dealing. They had devised a plan with Bobby to try and rupture Doc Kitchen and McGarrity's relationship, both personal and professional. They had figured that the research they were doing would have less of an impact if they could get them to take up arms against each other. The Doctors De La Croix were going to put out that Doc Kitchen was having an illicit relationship. They were never going to say who the woman was, she was going to remain an enigma. Dr. Gaylord said "…it's better to keep the charade a puff of smoke, if no one can find her then no one can ever get a straight answer…" Dr. Rafferty told Bobby when they had concocted the plan. But when Doc Kitchen and McGarrity were told of the scheme, they broke out in laughter. They valued who they were *together* more than they valued who they were alone. The very idea of Doctors De La Croix's blueprint to break them apart was utterly senseless. Doc McGarrity said, the Doctors De La Croix reminded her of two jealous school boys plotting to steal the teacher's apple that her prize pupil had given her.

Chapter 89

THE SDRC WAS NOW a place where occupational and pulmonary residents sought to come. Doc Kitchen and McGarrity were considered the foremost experts in occupational pulmonary diseases. But, as they lamented, the coal companies would likely, no matter what, continue to contradict just about every piece of research they published. Miners still lined the hallways of the SDRC day in and day out, to be evaluated or treated for the black lung. There were other names for the pulmonary plague that afflicted coal miners, but they knew it for what it was, the *black lung*. The rats that carried it were the coal companies. In those areas like Paintsville and West Van Lear, there was no way to get away from it. For the most part if you were born down there, you were going to be enslaved to the mines one way or another. And you were going to get the black lung.

As you came into the SDRC there was a plaque from the Renaissance poet Petrarch that hung on the wall.

"O' happy posterity, who will not experience such abysmal woe and will look upon our testimony as a fable."

Doc Kitchen had it hung there early on. He figured there were plagues of one type or another that were mostly caused by man himself.

Doc Kitchen and Doc McGarrity didn't get called over to the ER much anymore. Their work at the SDRC took up most of their time and the demands from the residents seemed never to end. They were always wanting this or that. But—and there were more *buts* now—Moses and Janice had begun to decline. "Age is a *sonofabitch*," Moses used to say as age came to stiffen him up more and more. Janice was slipping too, saying she wasn't as sharp as she used to be. They had both talked about stopping, to travel, to do this or that, but... what they had done had been how they had lived their lives. To do something else, well, there just wasn't enough time to learn how to live differently. It may satisfy someone else, but it would be terribly unsatisfying to them. There would only be a smile here or there, but with no laughter behind it.

Moses and Janice spent hours of late walking around Paintsville, even late into the night. The police on their patrol would see them hand in hand, walking around town. And they would always stop and say hello and ask if they were okay.

One of the officers remembered being called to Florence LeMaster's homeplace, when he was just a couple of days of being called 'officer.' Her husband, Walter, had been crushed in-between two train cars at the railyard the day she gave birth to her youngin' Eunice. Well, a few months after the funeral for poor Walter, Florence called the police and said little Eunice, poor Walter's baby, was gasping for breath and startin' to turn an awful shade of blue. Officer Ephraim Pelphrey, no relations to Ernie or Emily Pelphrey, just another Pelphrey, heard the call and drove his patrol car about as fast as a man can drive to see if he could be of help. When he walked in the door, little Eunice, right at that very moment, stopped breathin'. Officer Pelphrey grabbed that baby right up, screamed for Florence to get in the patrol car and told her to hold that baby as close as she could to her breasts. Then he drove like a bat out of hell to the hospital. It just so happened that Doc McGarrity was there. He had called in that he was bringing a little baby in that wasn't breathin'.

Doc McGarrity didn't even wait for them to come on in. She went running out the swingin' doors right when Officer Pelphrey screeched his patrol car to a stop. She jerked open the door, took little Eunice from her momma and didn't even bother runnin' back inside, puttin' that tiny baby down on the hood of the patrol car and began resusitatin' her. Doc McGarrity blew her air into little Eunice's lungs, fillin' up her thorax. Then she started pumping her little chest with her finger tips. When little Eunice started gettin' her color back a bit, Doc McGarrity scooped her up and ran back into the ER.

Doc Kitchen was there now too and between the two of them, pumpin' and breathen, pumpin' and breathin' and *refusin'* above all else to give up on that little girl, Eunice suddenly began to cry. She pinked up so much that she looked like a freshly bloomed pink rose. After they brought her back, Doc Kitchen figured out she had an obstructive left heart malformation.

He took her right into surgery and did an emergency resection, saving little Eunice's life.

After a while of waitin' after Walter had passed on, Officer Pelphrey started courtin' Florence, and after another while, they became united under God. And as Eunice grew up she was told how Doc McGarrity and Doc Kitchen had saved her life when she was just youngin'. Later on, Eunice became a nurse and worked in the emergency room. She was also known after her time of sufferin' as a little baby girl as Rose.

Officer Pelphrey one night in particular remembered that it had begun snowin' about as hard as it could snow. He came upon Doc Kitchen and McGarrity holdin' their chins to their chest and tryin' to duck into doorways to get away from the blowin' snow. He stopped his patrol car and said for them to come on and get in, he'd go ahead and take them on home. Officer Pelphrey even said for them not to worry one bit, he'd get their car on home and he'd pick them up and take them to the SDRC the next day. That way they wouldn't have to drive on the icy roads. Officer Pelphrey also thought that Doc Kitchen and McGarrity looked tired and weaker than he had remembered. They also looked thinner.

Chapter 90

MOSES AND JANICE *WERE* getting tired. Not of being doctors but of being in the accompaniment of something always out of tune. It was as though 'always having something' had become 'something always having them.' They were starting to feel like two dried out reeds.

They got a hold of Isabella and said they were tired. "Just tired," they said. She was about to undertake investigative work in Liberia. A new virus was killing people and she had been called in to help figure out what it was. Isabella was hesitant for a moment, she knew what was being said to her but she also knew that this was the time that her mother and father wanted to be alone together. Isabella figured that the time had come.

Since her residency she had come to know the intimacy of death. When it comes, it can call you now or it can let you know it will be coming back later for a final visit. Most people don't get to call forth death. It's almost always the other way around. Most, if they do, rarely think it out. And then when death does come, they're not even sure what they *have* called forth. It wouldn't be long before Isabella left. She would be abroad for a while. She also knew that when she returned, she would be an orphan.

Chapter 91

IT WAS A FRIDAY. Doc Kitchen and Doc McGarrity had not gone into the SDRC. The week before they made sure their estate was in order, leaving everything to Isabella and some money to the SDRC. They had arranged for their home to be closed up until Isabella could come and open it up and do with it as she chose.

On Saturday morning, Moses and Janice lay naked in bed together. Through all these years they had never lost their desire to feel each other's bodies together. It would be something about being alive that they would miss the most. After a while they got up, bathed and dressed. Moses put on a blue pin stripe suit, white shirt and blue tie. Janice dressed in a purple dress that had lovely lace at the bottom. They made sure that all of their doors were locked and that everything had been placed as they wished. They also put a letter for Isabella in a flower covered envelope resting against a stained glass lamp Spencer Duty, Jr. had had when it was his homeplace.

Then they sat up in bed, leaning back against the headboard. "Everyone seems to die laying down," Janice said. Moses and Janice than drank a cocktail of Pentobarbital and Curare. Holding hands, they talked of the time they first met, Janice demanding to know who the hell had cut Felix in half. "My God," she said, "*you cut him in half.*" Then she laughed. Moses said he would take with him to eternity the first time he laid eyes on Janice, recalling how her hair looked like spun honey. The only reason he even considered that there may be an eternity was because of Janice.

Then Moses and Janice's heads began to bow. Had someone been watching they would have seen it was in unison, just about like everything else in their lives together. They tightened their hands together as best they could as their breathing slowed and slow… and slo… Until it was no more.

꩜

Chapter 92

On Monday afternoon James Andrew Preston got a letter in the mail.

Dear Jim,

We would like for you to come and get our bodies. Janice and I have decided it was time to move on. We were both getting to the point where life would not be meaningful for us and so we ended it on our terms. This was our decision and ours alone. Please contact Porter, Banks, Baldwin & Shaw. They will arrange for payment for your services and for our last wishes. Thank you, Jim, for your friendship and for the services you have provided all these many years.

The letter was signed "Doc Kitchen and Doc McGarrity." There was a key to their homeplace and a small note that said they'd be in the bedroom.

When Mr. Preston got there, he found them slumped over in bed, dressed immaculately and looking like they had just drifted off to sleep. They were still holding hands.

News of their deaths spread like a drought dried field afire. Folks said they imagined that Doc Kitchen and Doc McGarrity'd been around forever and a day. But folks also said, "it weren't surprisin' they did what they did and all, because it was what they'd a wanted to do. They wouldn't be wantin' to linger and all." Folks also wondered about Isabella and when she'd be coming back.

In their will Moses and Janice said they wanted to be buried right beside each other in the Paintsville Cemetery. They already had their plots. A funeral wasn't necessary, folks already knew what they looked like and that wasn't likely to change.

A bronze plaque was hung outside of the SDRC saying that it had been founded by:

Moses Kitchen, M.D. and Janice McGarrity, M.D. with funds donated by Mr. Spencer Duty, Jr. for the purpose of bringing comfort and care to the coal miners of Eastern Kentucky.

The older miners remembered them like it was yesterday and would tell the upstarts stories about them that they should not forget. "Folks like this don't come along too often, specially down around these parts," they'd say.

Chapter 93

IT WAS A WHILE before Isabella came back to Paintsville. In the instructions to Porter, Banks, Baldwin & Shaw, Isabella was notified that her mother and father had passed away. She was, as she would later say, "Knee deep in blood, in a Liberian tent hospital, trying to figure out what the goddamn hell was killing these people."

Isabella flew into Lexington and drove over to Paintsville. She didn't tell anyone she was coming. When she let herself into her family homeplace, she saw that all of the furniture was covered with sheets. It had a musty smell.

When Officer Pelphrey was on patrol that night, he saw the lights on in Docs Kitchen and McGarrity's old homeplace. When he knocked at the door, Isabella answered. "My golly, Miss Isabella, have you come back home?"

She said she hadn't, just to close things up and pick up a few things.

Officer Pelphrey inquired to know if she would be coming around and saying hello to folks. Isabella said she wasn't sure, but she would for sure try. If she needed anything, anything at all, all she had to do was to call dispatch, they'd get her whatever help she needed. "You be sure and call if we can help y'all out now," Officer Pelphrey said.

Isabella walked through the house, making her way to her mother and father's bedroom. Isabella could still see the depressions on the bed where Moses and Janice had last laid. She thought it was odd that the impressions had not gone away. There was a gouge on the doorframe where the undertaker had likely dug into it when he was taking out their bodies.

Sitting against a light was a rose-colored envelope, that simply said, "Isabella."

Dear Isabella,

Our Dear Isabella, there is really nothing more to say. We were getting on and it was time to be on our way. Your mom and I figured it wouldn't be long before we wouldn't be able to make this decision for ourselves and we didn't want to put you in that position. Everything had been taken care of and you should have already received your inheritance. We don't know if you are so inclined but the homeplace could be deeded over to the SDRC and turned into resident housing. These poor residents are always looking for someplace and it would give them a comfortable place to stay while they are here. Just a thought.

Our Isabella, we pray, odd that we would say that we know, but we pray that you, our darling daughter, lead the life that you want to live. That you remain who you are and that you continue to grow into yourself as you grow older. There was never a moment when we were not proud of you. Be well and be safe in all that life brings you. Your mother and I are off on a new adventure.

We love you,
Dad and Mom

The next morning Isabella stopped by Moses and Janice's graves. The granite headstone shaded by an overhanging willow was engraved with, *"Moses and Janice, Forever and Always Together."* Isabella kissed her fingertips and touched them to the granite. Then she drove back to Lexington and caught connecting flights back to Accra to make her way back to Liberia. Her work there had just begun.

Acknowledgements

THE *DEVIL IN THE DUST* is written about coal miners. Coal Miners from Eastern Kentucky. It takes place in Paintsville, Kentucky proper but it could take place anywhere in Appalachian coal country. Coal miners for more than a century have been for the most part held in captivity in one form or another. First with the coal companies paying them a miniscule amount in coal scrip and forcing miners and their families to buy goods at the company store to now devolving even further into formalized medical enslavement with black lung and its related conditions. Once a miner or a member of their family have *the black lung*, there is not much to be done medically. Steroids, oxygen, and bronchodilators can ease breathing in the early stages but their effectiveness wanes as the condition progresses until the miner suffocates to death.

In our literature we tend to like self-assuaging, sanitary subjects. Medical stories or tales with happy endings. To keep the gasping, palpable grief of watching a loved one suffocate to death, the smells, "watching daddy crawl to the pot..." is not necessarily something we like to read about.

In many respects media representations of suffering and dying are as the sociologist Geoffrey Gorer (1955) concluded a *pornography of death*. A way of desensitizing ourselves to the horrors that prevail. Yet of course when a hanging for example is shown in the film media they don't show the dropping of the body through the trap door, or the kicking and thrashing of the condemned or the sometimes decapitation or the loss of the bowels that accompanies a hanging. Rather, when it is presented, it goes directly from *A* to *Z*. The marching of the condemned up the gallows and then... time goes by... and an anonymous body is seen dangling from the end of a rope. The *B* through *Y* of the execution, where the horrors lie, are cleansed to preserve the fantasies of our diehard sensibilities.

The same can be said of dying from black lung. It is more difficult to read about dying from suffocation, from being *immersed* in a story, it penetrating you, like in the case of *The Devil in the Dust*, than it is from viewing a video of an emaciated miner, enslaved to an oxygen tank for what are his remaining days, gasping in-between words trying to express the terribleness of having coal dust forever imbedded in his lungs. What amounts to a thirty-second 'how horrible it is' PSA.

To this day, coal companies congest the process of securing benefits for black lung victims with agonizing delays and challenges. In 2017 there were 52,537 applications for black lung benefits. The Department of Labor of the United States Government found only 14% or 7,252 eligible. The coal industry and their cadre of physicians then challenged 70% of those 7,252 claims. Out of a total of 52,537 claim originally filed, only 2,176 went unchallenged. Or 4.14%.

Courage is being able to have the moral strength to stand firm in the face of a constant barrage of attacks from those who so often have sold their soul at the crossroads. The physicians depicted in *The Devil in the Dust* live day in and day out, not only with the true, inexhaustible suffering that black lung brings, but also with the relentless fervorous onslaught of those who chose to denigrate the *Hippocratic Oath* rather than live by it.

My express thank you to Mr. Richard Plank, a careful and thoughtful reader, but most importantly a *good man*, who read many iterations of *The Devil in the Dust* and offered many helpful suggestions. And to my wife, Treasa Glinnwater. Were it not for her being who she is life would be hollow and empty.

www.ingramcontent.com/pod-product-compliance
Lightning Source LLC
Chambersburg PA
CBHW061522050726
47503CB00015B/2530